SECOND CHANCES

WHAT HIS HEART WANTS

A WITH ALL the HEART and SOUL NOVEL

B. E. STALTER

ISBN: 978-1-7371340-2-2

Cover design by: DDDesigns

Dedication

To my biggest, most loyal fan and youngest son, Kyle. He always offers his support and the most thought-provoking criticism. Do I always listen? Don't ask Kyle that question, because it will only instigate laughter.

Love you a bunch, Kyle!

TABLE OF CONTENTS

Dedication

To my biggest, most loyal fan and youngest son, Kyle. He always offers his support and the most thought-provoking criticism. Do I always listen? Don't ask Kyle that question, because it will only instigate laughter.

Love you a bunch, Kyle!

TABLE OF CONTENTS

SECOND CHANCES

WHAT HIS HEART WANTS

CHAPTER 1

GLANCING heavenward, Emilia noticed a single, line-shaped, contrail cloud marring the otherwise pristine perfection of the vibrant blue sky. If only she could have flown away on the jet whose engine exhaust had caused that lonely vapor trail. Emilia sighed at the thought. It wouldn't have mattered what the final destination was. She wanted to be anywhere but where she was currently standing.

Emilia tried very hard to prevent a display of her raw emotions in front of the other mourners. Eyes glazed with unshed tears she swallowed hard to block a sob from escaping. Then, ignoring the minister's eulogy, she turned her focus to the beauty of the day instead.

The slight breeze that rustled her waist-length, dark brown hair and hem of her black crepe sheath dress also stirred the dappled leaves on the trees crowding the western side of the family plot. Emilia listened as various birds hidden amongst the intertwining branches trilled songs and calls to each other. Emilia wondered if their language was as complex as any spoken by human beings. It was a subject she would enjoy researching, now that she had more time on her hands for such things.

Just then, a slight gust of wind brought the scent of the freshly mown lawn around the headstones and the sweet grass of the meadow. Turning, Emilia watched while barn swallows swooped to capture unwary insects hovering nearby.

As Emilia shifted slightly to ease the ache in her back as well as her heart, she took in the sight of the colorful flowers. She'd planted them on several of the older graves a few weeks before the funeral. Emilia noticed that the flowers were attracting the bees and butterflies flitting around them. Curious, she pondered if the insects were attracted by the same desirable floral characteristics as people, such as the bright colors and alluring fragrances. Hmmm. Something else to research to take her mind off the failure that was her life. She could add that to her love of books about famous individuals who lived during the late nineteenth century. The graves from that period were the ones Emilia had honored with radiant blooms because she was fascinated by the history, clothing, lifestyle, and customs of that era.

Frowning, she glanced toward the two things that upset the beauty that surrounded her. The first was the pile of dirt off to one side that was covered by a tarp. The other was the coffin poised above the hole that she was standing beside. Once the mourners quit the cemetery, the casket lowered into the ground would be covered by that dirt to entomb her husband. The remaining soil would fill in the rest of the cavity. If only it could fill in the hole in Emilia's heart as well.

There were approximately forty people in attendance and only one who Emilia knew personally. That individual was her brother-in-law, Bain. His twin brother, Iain Duncan Andersen, was Emilia's late husband. Iain had been diagnosed with an inoperable brain tumor two years earlier when he started having trouble with his vision and violent headaches. During those two years, the disease progressed to the point where Emilia became Iain's home health care nurse in addition to being his wife. Cancer spread until three days ago when Iain lost his battle with the terrible disease.

Emilia noticed that a few of the female mourners were staring at her skeptically. They probably thought her cold-hearted since she was standing there dry-eyed. If they knew the circumstances of her marriage, they might be more understanding. Either way, it was of little consequence to Emilia. She would never see any of them again. So, their harsh opinion of her mattered not.

Emilia met Iain Andersen quite by accident in the local grocery store. She ran into the concrete wall of his chest while distracted by thoughts of the nasty confrontation she'd had with her mother barely thirty minutes beforehand. Not paying attention, she was walking with her head bent down to avoid the other shoppers' curious glances. Emilia didn't want them to see her red-rimmed, puffy eyes.

The few items in the small basket she carried by the handles spewed onto the tile floor as Emilia and Iain collided. A shiny gala apple and one blood-red orange rolled away under shelving and another customer's shopping cart. As her carton of plain, low-fat yogurt hit Iain's left work boot with a splat and burst open, the overwhelming drama in Emilia's life won out. Her false calm façade crumbled, and she promptly burst into tears. Iain took her gently by the hand, pulled a clean, cotton men's handkerchief out of his back pocket, and dabbed the tears from Emilia's eyes. Then he handed it to her and said, "Blow."

Emilia took a good look at the mess on Iain's shoe after doing as she was told. She proceeded to giggle nervously until she got uncontrollable hiccups. Talk about involving a perfect stranger in her embarrassing meltdown.

Iain seemed to take it all in stride, however. Removing the handkerchief from her hand, he proceeded to wipe the muck from his boot. Cleaned to his satisfaction, he stuffed the rag back in his pocket. It was no longer in its former pristine condition.

Then Iain grabbed Emilia's hand and said, "Let's get out of here. You need something to drink to get rid of those hiccups."

Going with Iain was the biggest mistake of Emilia's life.

Emilia had just finished years of schooling to get her bachelor's degree in nursing. Still, she was most interested in becoming a certified home health care nurse. The fight with her mother concerned her living arrangements. Her mom had a new boyfriend. So, the woman didn't appreciate Emilia's continued presence in her apartment. Her mother felt threatened because the man leered at Emilia whenever he picked her mom up for a date. Plus, Emilia was probably cramping her mother's love life. It would be difficult to get laid when your twenty-three-year-old daughter was sleeping on your sofa. Emilia couldn't really fault her mother for kicking her out. Still, without funds or a full-time job, Emilia's options were nonexistent.

Iain took Emilia to a barroom on the opposite side of the street from the grocery. Going directly to the long mahogany bar, he lifted Emilia as if she weighed nothing and deposited her on one of the tall stools. Stunned by his gallant behavior, Emilia tried to hide her blush by looking anywhere but at him. She'd never been inside a bar before since she didn't drink. So, she was very curious about the bar's interior, anyway.

When the bartender made his way to them, Iain said, "Hey, Mark. Can I get a glass of water for my lady friend?"

If Emilia had been paying attention, she would have noticed the lascivious look on the bartender's face as he gave her body a once-over. Then as he winked at Iain and Iain's smug look in return.

After placing the glass of water on the bar, the bartender took one more look at Emilia's breasts, then moved off to wait on another customer. Iain handed the glass to Emilia and told her to gulp the water. Doing as she was told, Emilia looked at Iain in amazement when her hiccups abruptly ceased. Iain winked at her then ordered himself a beer and a coke for Emilia when she declined anything alcoholic. Iain also ordered a plate of nachos for them to share. Emilia was thankful for the food. Her apple, orange, and yogurt dinner still graced the floor of the grocery store.

Iain and Emilia talked for a while about inconsequential things and exchanged small personal information. She learned that Iain was also twenty-three and owned a dairy farm with his older brother, Bain. Iain chuckled at the older part. Being Iain's fraternal twin, Bain was only twenty-four minutes older. The brothers had recently come into their inheritance when their father was gored by one of their bulls. The Andersen farm had been in the family for generations. So, the brothers had lived there all of their lives.

When Emilia offered her condolences for the loss of his father, Iain told her not to worry her pretty little head about that. "The old man was an ornery, abusive cuss. At least I don't have to worry about him losing his temper anymore."

Unbeknownst to Emilia, Iain had deliberately placed himself in her path in the grocery store. He'd noticed her when she first entered the premises. Taken with her ethereal beauty, Iain had been surreptitiously following her about the store while waiting for the perfect opportunity to introduce himself. Though tiny, Emilia had curves in all the right places, shapely legs that Iain felt belonged wrapped around his waist, and breasts that he ached to expose. Iain had big hands but knew those glorious globes were just the right size to fill them. When he'd placed her on the barstool, he'd grazed his thumbs along the undersides on purpose.

To ease the ache in his groin, Iain concentrated on asking Emilia questions. When he asked her where she lived, Emilia got choked up and almost started to cry again. Iain reached out in mock sympathy to run his hand along the curve of her jaw so he could touch her.

With glassy doe-like eyes, Emilia told him, "I don't know."

The silky softness of Emilia's skin made Iain itch to touch her more private places and to fist her glorious fall of hair as he drove himself into her. He knew she would be sweet.

And so began Emilia's colossal mistake. Iain took control of Emilia's life, and she allowed it to happen.

Iain wasn't a truly handsome man. His were what one might consider rugged good looks. He had brown hair and hazel eyes. At 6'2" tall, he towered over Emilia's diminutive 5'4". He had large callused hands, that broad well-muscled wall of a chest that Emilia had run into, and brawny arms supporting a farmer's tan. He was wearing a black t-shirt, low-slung jeans, and work boots, one of which Emilia had mucked up with her yogurt.

Since she didn't have anywhere to spend the night, Iain insisted that Emilia stay in his spare bedroom until she could figure out what to do about her living arrangements. Emilia asked him what his wife would think about that. Iain laughed and said, "No wife and no girlfriend. My brother Bain's not married, either."

Iain never really gave Emilia a chance to say no to his offer. While Emilia was using the restroom, Iain paid the bar tab. The bartender quirked his eyebrow and said, "Looks like you got lucky tonight, Iain. She's a beauty and classier than your normal hook-ups. I've never seen her in here before. Let me know when you're done with her. I'd like a go at that body."

Iain spotted Emilia returning from the lady's room, so he just winked at the bartender in response. Then he took Emilia by the hand and led her to his pickup truck. Opening the door, Iain lifted Emilia once again so that he could graze her breasts. Emilia noticed this time and stared at him with shocked, rounded eyes, the color of cerulean blue. Seizing the opportunity, Iain leaned in and gently slid his lips over hers. Emilia didn't slap him, so he took it as a good sign, fastened her seat belt, and placed another kiss on those silky lips. Then, Iain took Emilia home with him like she was a lost dog found wandering alongside the road. One he wanted to keep and train to do his bidding.

Emilia met Bain that evening. Being Iain's fraternal twin, not identical, Bain was two inches taller and even more muscular. Bain seemed a brute of a man, and Emilia was very intimidated. He grunted when Iain told him she would be staying, eyed Emilia speculatively, and turned back to the ball game he was watching on the television.

Iain put on the full-court press in the next few weeks. He seemed so sweet and attentive. The next thing Emilia knew, they were being married by the Justice of the Peace.

The honeymoon phase of their marriage lasted only long enough for Iain to bed her. Then Emilia discovered the man she had chained herself to was hiding a Jekyll and Hyde personality. Sex was about meeting Iain's needs. The only other man Emilia had been with had been loving, gentle, and concerned with her pleasure as well as his own. Iain always used protection. He told Emilia he didn't intend to saddle himself with noisy, messy, expensive brats. Those would have been good things to know before Emilia said, "I do." Too late, she'd made her bed, and now she'd have to sleep in it with her overbearing husband. Emilia did not feel that Iain was entirely at fault, however. She was grateful that he had given her a home when she had none. Still, Emilia could not provide him with the two things she was confident a genuinely loving wife would offer, unconstrainedly. Emilia loved Iain. She did, but not with her whole heart and soul. They were no longer Emilia's to give.

Iain made snide remarks about everything Emilia said, did, and even about her appearance. She was forbidden to make friends or invite anyone into his home. He didn't intend to share her attention, either. Iain felt that Emilia's focus should be on his needs and cooking, cleaning, and grocery shopping when she wasn't working.

After Emilia got her first position as a home health care nurse, her salary went into an account that only Iain and Bain could access. Iain gave Emilia a small amount of cash to keep in her wallet in case of emergencies. He also bought her an inexpensive compact car to drive to work for her nursing assignments. Emilia was confident that Iain checked her wallet to see if she spent part of that small stash. Emilia liked to keep the contents of her purse a certain way. Finding them altered on numerous occasions, Emilia never touched the money, and she was careful that there wasn't anything in the bag she didn't want Iain to see. Any personal items that Emilia needed to purchase went onto a credit card from the brothers' joint account. Iain kept a close eye on every penny that she spent. Other than rare visits to a salon for a trim, nurse's attire, a limited supply of personal clothing, shoes, and undergarments, Emilia refrained from buying anything for herself.

Thus, began years of mental and verbal abuse by her husband. During that time, Emilia did everything possible to avoid being alone with her brother-in-law, Bain, and his speculative looks. Those looks made her feel as if there was an army of ants beneath the surface of her skin, marching off to do battle with the opposing ant colony.

Unbeknownst to Iain, Emilia did assert her independence in one tiny way. She managed to circumvent Iain's confiscation of all of the money she earned. Emilia asked the agency who arranged her assignments to divert half of her salary into a bank account opened by her in a neighboring town. The other half was in check form. Emilia signed that over to her husband. Since, for tax purposes, Iain didn't want Emilia's income added to that of the farm, she filed her own separately. So, Iain never knew the total amount Emilia was earning. During the twenty-five years of their marriage, Emilia had never touched any of the money squirreled away in her secret account. It had grown to a considerable sum.

When a giant hand clamped onto Emilia's shoulder, she was startled out of her musings. The minister continued to drone on about her dead husband's virtues and good standing in their rural

13

agricultural community. Confused, she realized that her brother-in-law had moved from her side to stand directly behind her. Bain was uncomfortably close. Never having touched Emilia before, she didn't understand what he was doing. Why did he feel the need to touch her now? As he pulled Emilia tight against his body, he placed his other hand at her waist. Bringing his mouth close to her ear, he whispered, "Relax. I'm not going to bite. Do you know how sexy you look in that dress? I bet you wore it just to tease me." Pressing his erection into her back, he ribbed, "Feel what you've done to my cock?"

To those standing around them, it probably appeared that Bain was lending Emilia emotional support. Emilia hadn't picked the dress off the clearance rack because it was sexy. None of the clothing in her wardrobe was appropriate for the funeral. The black dress was the only one she'd found that was available in her size 2. When she'd tried it on, she'd paid little attention to its V-neck that showed some cleavage or to the way the streamlined design hugged her curves. She was only looking for something that fit.

To quill the nausea that was roiling in her stomach, she swallowed convulsively and inched forward to try to put some space between them. Bain chuckled softly so that only Emilia could hear.

Whispering again, he said, "You can run, but you can't hide from me. I've waited for you for a long time."

Closing her eyes tight, Emilia let her thoughts drift to the only time in her life when she was truly happy before everything turned to shit.

She'd snuck her boyfriend into the kitchen through the back door so that the neighbors wouldn't see. There was a stockade fence surrounding the property of the tiny two-story house that Emilia's mother was renting. The houses on either side of theirs were single-story dwellings. So, the wall obstructed the neighbors' view of their yard. Bordering an alley behind the house, a gate in the fence allowed undetected access to the yard from that direction.

Emilia was sixteen years old and in tenth grade. Michael was a junior. Since the beginning of the school year, they had been secretly hanging out because Emilia was forbidden to date or have friends.

Emilia was in the library the day they met. Trying to replace a book on a shelf above her head, she managed to drop everything else that her left arm kept pressed tightly against her petite body. Exasperated and embarrassed, she bent over to retrieve the offending items and cracked heads with someone else. Rubbing her forehead, Emilia straightened up and fell instantly in love with the most beautiful blue eyes attached to a very handsome face. The boy she'd cracked heads with was also rubbing his forehead. Neither of them said a single word. They just stood there mesmerized with each other.

Finally, Emilia managed to squeak out an apology, but the boy was having none of that. He said it was all his fault. As compensation, the boy invited her for a milkshake after school. Then he gently moved her to the side and told her to stay put. Bending down, he retrieved everything she'd dropped, all the while trying not to stare at her shapely legs. Smiling, he took the book Emilia had been trying to shelve and returned it to its rightful place in the stack.

They met at a small corner store after school that day and bonded over a shared chocolate milkshake. His name was Roger Michael Willis, but he said everyone called him Mike. Emilia asked him if he would permit her to call him Michael. He seemed to give her request careful consideration. As a crooked smile lit up his face, Mike said, "I think I'd like that very much."

Emilia may have fallen in love with Michael's brilliant blue eyes and handsome face with the crooked smile, but there was one feature that she found particularly endearing. Michael had dark brown shaggy hair that he ran his fingers through whenever he was concentrating hard. At the age of seventeen, he was six feet tall with broad shoulders, well-muscled arms and chest, a lean waist, and long legs. His family lived on a dairy farm on the outskirts of town, where his father was the manager. The farm also kept a herd of beef cattle for family and friends' meat supply. Michael helped with the farm chores, so that accounted for his muscles.

When she told Michael that her full name was Emilia Addison Mackenzie, he informed her that he would be calling her Emi.

Each day after that, Michael met Emilia in front of the high school after the final bell rang, took her books, and proceeded to walk her home. She told him about her mother's strictly enforced rules concerning no friends and no one invited into their home. When Emilia told him what the penalty would be for breaking the commandments her mother had laid down, Mike's posture became rigid, and he clenched his fists until his knuckles turned white. The color of Mike's eyes turned from brilliant blue to the inky black of storm clouds, threatening to dump the rain they'd held too long.

Mike hated that Emilia's mother had been beating her since she was a little girl. Then locking her in her room as punishment if she did anything to displease the woman. After Emilia was grown, a doctor would diagnose her mother with bipolar disease and give her prescription medication to combat the illness. It helped her mother's mood swings, but it never altered her feelings towards her daughter.

After letting Michael into the house through the kitchen door, Emilia removed her books from his hands. After placing them on the kitchen counter, Emilia turned back to find that Michael had stepped close. Cupping Emilia's chin with his left hand, he tilted her head. Leaning down, he swiped his tongue over her bottom lip and tentatively began to kiss her. Emilia got lost in the glide of his lips over hers. Mike took her acquiescence as a sign that she was okay with the kiss. Sliding his hand along the side of her jaw to the back of her head, he pulled Emilia in tight and deepened the kiss. If he hadn't been holding her up, she was sure she would have melted into a puddle of goo at his feet.

So, began a slow courtship until neither of them could restrain themselves anymore. For Emi's and Michael's first time together, Mike was very sensitive to Emilia's needs, kissing each inch of her skin that he uncovered. He paid careful attention to Emilia's breasts, laving them with his tongue and nipping with his teeth. As Michael pulled one nipple into his mouth, his deft fingers pinched and squeezed the other. Then he began a kissing and licking path down Emilia's stomach, pausing to dip his tongue into her navel. When he reached the juncture of her thighs, he spread her legs wide and ran his fingers through her swollen folds. Overwhelmed, Emilia bucked her hips. Placing one of his legs over hers to hold her still, Michael kissed Emilia gently, then stared into her eyes.

"Are you okay with this, Emi? We can stop, now, if that's what you want. We don't have to go any further. This first time is going to hurt, but I promise to be as gentle as I can be if you want to continue."

Pressing her lips to his, Emilia said, "I want you, now, Michael. Please don't stop."

Mike nodded. After sheathing himself with a condom, he kissed Emilia again, then returned his attention to her breasts. After sliding his fingers between her folds, Michael slipped one finger inside and began to move it in and out. Abandoning her breasts, he parted her legs, blew warm air across her clit, and licked the bundle of nerves with his tongue. Emilia could feel a gush of moisture between her legs as he slid another finger inside her and sucked on her engorged clit.

When Mike realized that Emi was getting close, he covered her body with his and slid his cock near her entrance. Looking deeply into her eyes, he entered her slowly, allowing Emilia time to adjust to his invasion. When he reached her barrier, he paused and said, "Okay, so far?"

Nodding her head, yes, Emilia admitted her feelings, "I love you, Michael."

With that, he said, "I'll always love you, Emi. For the rest of my life." Then he pushed past the obstruction, and they were truly mated.

Emilia gasped at the pain and the feeling of being stretched too wide. At the sound, Michael stopped again to give her time to adjust.

"Relax, sweetheart. The worst is over. From now on, there will be nothing but pleasure. I intend to give you a lot of that," he promised her.

They were together every school day from then on. Being separated during vacations was torture. Michael had farm chores to attend to, but they got together as often as they could.

Two days after the end of the school year, Michael showed up at Emi's house on a Saturday evening. Her mother was on a date, so Emilia was able to let Michael in.

"Why did you take a chance in coming here, Michael?" she questioned him. "You know what will happen if my mother catches us."

At that, Mike gulped and turned his head away. When he had his emotions under control enough to be able to speak, he turned back and destroyed Emilia's whole world with what he had to tell her.

"Emi, my parents are moving the family to Montana. My father got a job offer he can't pass up. He has to be there next week. We're leaving first thing Monday morning."

Stunned, Emilia started to sob, "No, I can't lose you. I love you, Michael."

Tearing at each other's clothing, they made frantic, passionate love. Michael wasn't prepared but didn't care that he didn't have a condom to use as protection. His need for Emilia was too great.

Emilia still remembered the feel of Michael's cock as it brought them to a shattering, world-shaking orgasm together.

After, they snuggled while making promises to each other. Michael would come back for Emi as soon as he graduated, and they would be married. He couldn't write to Emilia since they knew her mother would intercept the letters at her post office box.

Michael didn't know the address where he was moving, so Emilia wouldn't be able to write to him, either.

"Don't worry, Emi. I promise. I'll be back for you. We belong to each other. We'll be together for the rest of our lives. We'll have children and make a family together." Then, they made love one last time, and Michael left her.

Emilia hadn't seen him since and had no idea if he ever tried to find her. When her mother discovered that Emilia was pregnant, she quit her job. They moved to a small town in western Pennsylvania just north of Pittsburgh. The town was in Butler County and was surrounded by farming communities. After taking a position at a law firm, her mother rented a tiny house on a dead-end street on the town's outskirts. She gave Emilia the master bedroom with an attached bath and locked her inside. For the next eight months of Emilia's life, the four walls of that room were the boundaries of her prison cell, and her mother was her warden.

Just before Emilia reached full term, her mother brought a midwife to see her. The midwife would be delivering the baby. Emilia was told about the visit in advance and admonished to keep her mouth shut. She was only allowed to ask any questions about the baby's birth.

Emilia was terrified when she went into labor in the middle of February. It started as a pain in her lower back that was excruciating. As her labor progressed, the pains came closer and closer together until it seemed like one prolonged pain that would never end. Finally, the woman told Emilia to push, and her baby slid out into the world. Emilia heard the baby cry before her mother wrapped it in a towel and took it away. The midwife delivered the afterbirth, then helped Emilia to clean up and don a fresh nightgown. The woman left soon after.

Emilia never got to see her child and didn't even know if she'd given birth to a boy or a girl. When she asked her mother to let her see her baby, her mother told Emilia that she should forget all about it. The baby had been given to a deserving couple to raise.

She remonstrated, "Emilia, I'm allowing you to get your life back on track. You'll be entering your junior year of high school this fall. No one will know about your transgressions. You should thank me for saving you from the humiliation of being an unwed mother."

Emilia cried herself to sleep each night for almost a year. She prayed for her child, wherever he or she might be, and that the people caring for the baby were kind and loving. She asked God for forgiveness for losing the gift Michael had given her. Emilia was so very sorry that Michael would never have the chance to call that child son or daughter. Brokenhearted, she stumbled through the days as if wading through molasses. Nothing in her life held any meaning, so Emilia poured herself into her studies. Graduating a year late, Emilia was nineteen when she received her diploma. Having straight A's, Emilia received a scholarship to a local college.

Being able to live at home, Emilia worked small jobs while getting her degree to help pay for essentials, school books, and labs.

Her relationship with her mother became even more strained after she gave Emilia's child away. They'd never had a good relationship, anyway. So, it came as no surprise when her mother told Emilia she needed to get out and independently make her way in the world.

Once again, jolted from her musings, Emilia realized that Bain was yanking on her arm to get her attention. The service was over, and they needed to go back to the house for the repast. Bain grabbed Emilia's hand and pulled her along behind him. Since he was so much taller than her, his long legs ate up the ground. After she stumbled several times on the uneven path, Bain stopped and gave Emilia a furious look.

"Keep up, or I'll embarrass you by throwing you over my shoulder and smacking your ass," he told her.

When they finally reached the house, Emilia placed the serving dishes of food that she'd prepared the day before on the kitchen counter and table. Everyone who had attended the graveside memorial stayed to avail themselves of the free food. Most were members of the same agricultural organizations that Iain and Bain belonged to or from whom they purchased farm supplies. Several of the men were good friends of the two brothers. Friends who had been invited to the house over the years to assist Iain or Bain with farm repairs or just to watch television on game night. During those visits, Emilia was required to make food or run and fetch snacks and beer for them. Emilia avoided those men because she didn't like the looks some of them gave her.

While everyone availed themselves of the food, one of Iain's friends ran his hand along Emilia's backside as he tried to squeeze past her. There was enough room for him to get by, so she knew it was on purpose. Bain noticed and took the guy aside. Emilia couldn't hear what they were saying, but she could tell that their conversation was heated. Their expressions and posture were tense. When they finished talking, Bain glared at the man. After winking at Emilia, the man slammed his plate down on the corner of the countertop. Then he stormed out the kitchen door.

By the time the last person took his leave, Emilia was exhausted and frightened. She was alone in the house with her brother-in-law, and she was very wary of him. After Bain changed his suit and went out to do the milking, she breathed a sigh of relief.

Having slipped on an apron to protect her dress, Emilia busied herself putting the leftovers in the refrigerator. Then she washed and dried the dishes. Just as she was finishing the last sink full of cutlery, Bain came in through the kitchen door.

Grabbing Emilia from behind, he untied her apron strings and pulled her in tight against him. "Finally, you belong to me. My brother was a selfish bastard. He was fine with sharing all the other women we picked up at bars, but he wouldn't share you."

Emilia gasped and winced at Bain's remark. Had Iain cheated on her? Was she that gullible that she had no idea she meant so little to him? Now she understood why those women were glaring at her at the graveside. They were probably some of Iain's conquests. Shaking her head, tears formed in Emilia's eyes, then ran silently down her cheeks. Could her life get any worse?

Bain proved that it could with his subsequent remarks, "Before he died, Iain and I had a good conversation. He gave you to me to do with as I please. Iain said, 'Marry her or don't. That's up to you, but if you intend to make any of those little Andersens you want so badly, you'd better knock her up quick. She still bleeds every month, but she

27

might not be good for breeding purposes much longer. She's getting old.'"

Shocked, Emilia stood there too frightened to breathe as Bain ran his hands over her breasts, pausing to pinch her nipples. Then he slid his hands down the length of her torso while licking the side of her neck. Reaching the hem of Emilia's dress, Bain lifted it slowly to rub his hands up her bare thighs. He made his way to her center, then pushed her panties to the side. Dipping a finger roughly inside her, Bain pumped it in and out. Bringing that finger to his nose, he sniffed then proceeded to lick the finger clean.

"I knew you'd be sweet," he said as he pulled Emilia in tighter so that she could feel his erection pressed against her back. Emilia winced again and squeezed her eyes closed. Bain's shaft seemed far more immense than Iain's.

"It's too bad my buddy will be back in a few minutes to help me load up the prize bull I sold to a farm in Indiana. I'll be leaving for a few days to deliver it, then pick up a replacement in Ohio on the way home. While I'm gone, get rid of my brother's clothes. I'll be moving into the master bedroom with you. I'll be back sometime Friday. When I get here, you'd better be in that bed, naked and wet, waiting for the fucking I intend to give you. I've waited a long time, so get some rest and be prepared. It's going to be a long night and weekend. I've saved up a lot of fantasies about you, and I intend to act them all out. I'm not a selfish prick like my brother, however. I know he only concerned himself with his own needs. I intend to pleasure you until you're screaming my name so loud, the chickens will probably stop laying. You'll be begging me to fuck you every which way after that. You'd better not be on any birth control because I intend to get you pregnant right away. My brother was right. I want sons who can take over the farm for future generations of Andersens. You be a good, obedient girl, just like you were for Iain, and I might even consider making our arrangement legal. Then you'll have a home for the rest of your life. Misbehave, and you'll still give me the children I want, but there won't be a ring on your finger, and I'll share you with my buddies. There are several chomping at the bit to get you underneath them. Now, get out of my sight before I take you fast and hard right here against the kitchen sink and fuck up my fantasy of taking you slowly the first time."

When Bain released his hold on Emilia, her legs were shaking so badly she almost collapsed. He lifted her dress and slapped her on the ass to get her moving. Scrambling, Emilia raced from the room, up the stairs, and through the bedroom door. She could hear Bain's laughter at her hasty retreat. She locked the door behind her, threw herself on the bed, and sobbed herself to sleep.

CHAPTER 2

THE bedroom was very dark when Emilia woke up. At some point, the house must have lost power because the alarm clock's numbers were blinking at her. Lying there shaking, she was too afraid to leave the bed to find her watch. What if Bain was waiting silently, ready to grab her when she swung her legs over the side to stand? When Emilia needed to pee so badly, she couldn't wait another minute, she jumped from the bed and raced into the master bath. Then Emilia hurriedly closed and locked the door. She was never so relieved to be able to empty her bladder.

Emilia tiptoed to the bedroom door, turned the lock, and slowly inched the door open when she was finished. There weren't any lights turned on in the house, but there were muted shadows caused by the moonlight peeking through the curtains. It was just enough light to allow her to see, so she wouldn't stub any toes. Inching cautiously along the hall, Emilia paused at the door to Bain's room. She was desperate to be sure that he wasn't in there, but she stood frozen, unable to move. Finally, Emilia pressed her ear against the door. Bain's snores were usually loud enough to wake the dead, but she couldn't hear anything. Slowly, Emilia turned the knob then swung the door inward. There was no one in the bed. The counterpane was undisturbed.

Going to the window, Emilia pressed her face against the glass. The moon cast a glow over the barnyard, and she could see that Bain's truck and the cattle trailer were no longer parked beside the holding pen where he loaded animals. Bain must have left on his trip to Indiana.

Running back to her room, Emilia quickly turned on the light. Frantically, she yanked her things out of the dresser and closet in her panic to escape. When everything lay in a heap on the bed, Emilia remembered that Bain had said he wouldn't be back until Friday. However, she still needed to develop a plan. Shaking her head sadly at the waste of time and her own stupidity, Emilia sank down onto the corner of the mattress. Bringing her trembling hands to her face, Emilia balled them into fists and scrubbed at her eyes to push the bleariness away. Giving her head a shake, she knew she needed to relax and take the time to think.

Feeling dirty from having been mauled by Bain, she made her way to the bathroom. Turning on the tap, Emilia ran a hot bath, as hot as she could stand. Disrobing, she gingerly slipped beneath the water and reclined against the back of the tub. As the heat of the water began to work its magic, her muscles unwound, her frozen brain finally thawed, and thoughts started to flow.

Emilia needed to leave Bain's home before his return on Friday. She couldn't take the car that she usually drove. It was registered in Bain's name. Iain legally signed everything over to Bain when he was diagnosed with the inoperable tumor. So, her first course of action should be to determine where she was going. Then she would decide whether to rent or purchase a vehicle of her own. Emilia thought the idea of a rental was the wisest choice. She would turn it in when she arrived at her destination and decide about buying her own vehicle then.

Having saved over a million dollars in the last twenty-five years of her marriage, Emilia needn't be concerned about money for a while. Iain would have shown more than verbal displeasure if he had discovered her deception. Emilia also placed the cash that was hidden in her mother's apartment in a safety deposit box, along with the information she'd found about the baby she'd given birth to.

Emilia's mother, Eloise, had died in a car accident almost three years prior. She and her brand-new husband were celebrating their nuptials by getting drunk at a barroom. On the drive back to her apartment, they ran off the road and hit a tree. It didn't help that neither of them was wearing their seat belt. The policeman who came to notify Emilia of her mother's and step-father's deaths told her that the vehicle was going eighty-five miles an hour when they hit.

Eloise had changed jobs and moved again after Emilia's marriage to Iain. Her new apartment was some two hundred miles away. Iain couldn't be bothered comforting Emilia. He refused to take time away from his chores to assist Emilia while dealing with her mother's cremation arrangements and disposal of her belongings. However, he insisted that Emilia transfer any money her mom had in checking and savings accounts into his bank account. That only amounted to a few thousand dollars, but Iain happily took it. Not being present, he never learned about the cash. Emilia's mother was never fond of banks. Paranoid, she preferred to keep as much money available as possible.

When Emilia went through her mother's things, she discovered bundles of one-hundred-dollar bills hidden everywhere. They were placed behind pieces of furniture, under and behind dresser drawers and kitchen cabinet drawers, and stuffed in the sofa and chairs. Emilia was amazed when she found even more in numerous locations throughout the kitchen and closets in resealed food containers, jars, and cans. There was even a sealed baggie hidden in the water tank to the toilet in the bathroom. In all, the sum totaled over two hundred thousand dollars. Her mother must be insane if she believed that the money was safe from thieves.

The most startling discoveries of all were the documents and diary from Eloise's safety deposit box. There were so many revelations in that box, it would take hours to digest the implications. Placing everything in a tote to examine later, Emilia returned the key to the bank manager and drove back to the apartment.

Calling Iain, she let him know that it would be a few more days before she would be able to return home. Emilia told him she needed to make arrangements for all the furniture, clothing, and household items to be picked up. She planned to donate everything.

Iain was displeased. "Get your ass home, Emilia," he swore. "I intend to fuck you good. You know I need sex every night. I've given you enough time to take care of your mother's things. Two days, then you'd better be here."

"I'll be back as soon as the apartment is empty," Emilia responded, then winced. When Iain was forced to go without sex, she paid for it dearly. He would be especially rough when they resumed relations. She didn't make a habit of lying, but she needed that extra time to sort things out. Those few days of freedom were the only chance she would get.

Emilia had already packed and made arrangements for the apartment's contents. She intended to spend the additional time examining the documents from the safety deposit box and then doing some research.

From Eloise's diary, Emilia learned that her mother had taken a position as a paralegal in a law office near Philadelphia when she was thirty-seven years old. Eloise had never spoken of her youth, so Emilia had no knowledge of her mother's life before what was revealed in her diary. Emilia also discovered that her real father's last name was not Mackenzie.

When Eloise discovered she was pregnant by the firm's very married senior partner, she seduced a junior partner. She pretended he was the father of her baby. Taking responsibility, Philip Mackenzie married Eloise, thus giving Emilia legitimacy.

When Emilia was born six months later, Philip knew he had been duped. He was an honorable man, though, and stuck it out for over a year. Then Philip discovered that the senior partner, Bryan McDonnell, was paying Eloise every month to keep her mouth shut about the baby and their affair. An illegitimate child would have blown up the man's perfect marriage to his rich socialite wife. McDonnell's standing in the community would be tarnished, possibly beyond repair.

With this discovery, Emilia could no longer blame Philip for leaving and never coming back to see his daughter. She wasn't really his daughter after all. He did, however, use the knowledge of Eloise's deception as leverage. Eloise never received any alimony or child support, and she had to sign the divorce documents immediately.

Otherwise, Philip threatened to go public about Emilia's parentage and Eloise's involvement with Bryan McDonnell. Emilia's mother signed the divorce papers, shoved them in the envelope, and mailed them back right away. Emilia bore Philip no hard feelings for abandoning her or for the beating she received from Eloise in her mother's anger at being rejected and the loss of additional income.

Emilia's second discovery was an album that contained a birth certificate, letter, a small accounting sheet, and pictures of a girl.

Removing the letter from its envelope, Emilia slid her eyes to the signature first. It was simply signed, "*James*," but the name in the envelope's return address was "*James Roberts*." Not knowing who that was, Emilia began to read.

"*Dearest Mother, as agreed, enclosed is a copy of the birth certificate for my half-sister's baby. My attorney was able to file it to make it look like my wife and I are the child's parents. The attorney used the terrible blizzard Fair Lawn was experiencing at the time of the child's birth as an excuse for saying my wife gave birth at home without medical assistance. I understand that you will be sending a check each month for the child's upkeep and that her true mother will never learn of her whereabouts. As agreed, we have named the child*

38

after you and used my wife's mother's name as her middle name. So,

the baby has been named Eloise Lianne Roberts. My wife wants to call

her Elli for short. I will send a photo each year so that you can see

what your grandchild looks like as she ages."

There was one photo per year from birth to twelfth-grade

graduation in the album. Emilia cried so much while examining those

photographs that she made herself sick. After throwing up the food

she had eaten that day, she sat down and reexamined them.

That's how Emilia learned that she'd given birth to a beautiful

baby girl with blonde hair and blue eyes, the color of cerulean just like

hers. She liked the name Elli so much more than having to think of

her daughter bearing her deceitful mother's name. So, whenever she

thought about her daughter, she thought of her as Elli.

One of the photos was of a cute little house with a gabled roof

and white stucco siding. Emilia studied it intently. The home was

adorned with the most striking cobalt blue shutters and doors. The plot

of ground along the front was graced by brightly colored rose bushes

and green shrubbery, and beds of zinnias edged the neat brick

sidewalk leading to the street. The property had a postage-stamp-sized lot surrounded by a little white picket fence. A matching cobalt blue gate bestowed the honor of entrance to the property.

In the photo, the woman held Emilia's baby girl tight in her arms. That sight made Emilia sick with jealousy and longing. The child looked to be about two years old at the time. She straddled one of the woman's hips. The woman was short, maybe only 5'2" tall, and looked to be in her late thirties. She had dirty blond hair styled in a bob and light blue eyes. She had an attractive heart-shaped face, with a slim nose, full lips, and pencil-thin eyebrows. She was wearing a blue dress, and Emilia could see that she was smiling. The man had a very stern expression on his face. He looked to be about 5'9" tall with light brown hair peppered with gray that he wore in a wave to the side. He looked to be in his late thirties, as well. His eyes looked like they might be hazel in color. He had harsh features, and frown lines creased his forehead and bracketed his mouth. He was wearing a button-down shirt, pleated slacks, and loafers.

Emilia's daughter looked like a happy toddler in the photo. Her hair had darkened a little and was a mass of loose spiral curls that reached her shoulders. Written on the back of the picture were the names James, Lilianne, and Elli. So, Emilia realized that this was a photo of her brother, sister-in-law, and daughter.

Another photograph showed Elli with an older man and woman. The woman was plump, had a sweet face with laughing brown eyes, and short gray hair worn in a bun. She wore a cute pink dress covered with white polka-dots and a frilly apron.

The man looked lean and well-muscled. He had light blue eyes, dimples, and a square jaw. His hair was cropped short in a crew cut that was salt and pepper gray. He looked like he was wearing a Henley shirt and overalls. On the back of the photo was written *Eloise at the age of four, taken with Lianne and Jacob Williams, Lilianne's parents.*

As Elli progressed one year in age from the first photo to the last, her hair darkened until it was the same color as Emilia's. By the time Elli graduated from high school, she could have been Emilia's twin if it weren't for the age difference. She had Emilia's long dark brown hair, cerulean blue eyes, a slim body with rounded breasts, and long shapely legs.

Emilia sobbed as she realized her daughter had grown into a beautiful young woman.

What became of Elli? Emilia needed to know.

The accounting ledger showed that a sum of one thousand dollars was sent each month to James and included the date and check number. So, Eloise had kept her promise to provide for Elli's care.

The envelope for the letter written to Emilia's mother by her half-brother James showed an address in Fair Lawn, New Jersey.

That was a start. Hopefully, the Roberts still lived there.

Emilia placed all of the items into a manila envelope, then sealed it.

The next day, she drove to the local library and used their computer to do an internet search for James and Lilianne Roberts of Fair Lawn, New Jersey. When nothing came up, Emilia tried various searches for them and her daughter Eloise Lianne Roberts. Emilia also looked for Roger Michael Willis in Montana using variations of his name. The photos uncovered in her search of men named Roger Willis and Mike or Michael Willis didn't match what she believed her Michael would look like. Emilia decided against searching for any family connections concerning her real father, Bryan McDonnell. The man hadn't wanted her. Any relatives would probably feel the same.

Bereft, Emilia went back to the apartment to wait for the people to claim her mother's belongings. Lying on the sofa, she cried herself to sleep.

When the rooms were empty, Emilia cleaned the apartment thoroughly, then returned the landlord's keys. Despondent, she slowly drove the two hundred miles to the town where she kept her secret savings account. Renting a safety deposit box, Emilia inserted her mother's diary, cash, and the envelope. At least Emilia had learned that she and Michael had made a beautiful baby girl together.

Then Emilia went home and resumed her life of verbal abuse and lackluster sex with Iain.

Emilia was shaken from her abstraction when the house creaked and settled. Realizing her bath water had grown cold, she pulled the plug and stepped out onto the mat. Emilia took a pair of slacks and a top from the pile on the bed after toweling dry. With what was left of the night, she planned to separate what she needed for the next several days and pack everything else. That would be one less thing Emilia would be required to worry about. After resetting the time on the alarm clock, she placed her watch on her left wrist out of habit. That's where she'd always worn it. It showed that it was now 4:07 a.m. It was Tuesday morning.

Making her way downstairs, Emilia paused in the kitchen to make herself a cup of tea. Lying on the kitchen counter was a note weighted down by a small pile of money. The message was from Bain because Emilia recognized his handwriting.

"Sweet thing, I've changed my mind about you being naked. Buy a really sexy nightie, preferably something sheer and lacy, so I can see all those beautiful curves and those ripe nipples. I can't wait to rip it off you. Think about my cock while I'm gone, so you're good and horny for me. Remember I want you nice and wet. Wax, because I like my pussy well-groomed so I can lick you until you moan. When I ram my nine-inch shaft into you, you'll think you've died and gone to heaven. You'll feel like a virgin because I'm a lot bigger than my brother was. I'll break you in soon enough, though. Behave yourself and do what you're told. You belong to me now, and I'm not letting you go. I plan on taking good care of your physical needs, and I expect

you to take care of mine. I'm tired of one-night-stands. See you Friday."

Bain didn't even bother to sign his name, the arrogant bastard. Emilia had to stop herself from shredding the note and setting fire to it in the sink. She had no intention of fulfilling Bain's fantasies or of bearing his children. Emilia cared about Bain but was afraid he'd treat her just like Iain had. Laying the message back on the counter, she placed the money back on top.

When her hands had stopped shaking, Emilia made herself the cup of tea she'd come downstairs for and went in search of some boxes to pack her belongings. Thankfully, she didn't own much. It's as if she'd always known she would be fleeing this house someday and would need to travel light.

With all of her things boxed up, Emilia went through the dresser, nightstands, and closet one last time. The only things left belonged to Iain. If Bain wanted to get rid of Iain's clothes, he could do it himself. Grabbing a small box, Emilia went into the bathroom to remove her feminine products and toiletries. She planned to use the bathroom on the main floor for the rest of the week. The sofa could serve as her bed. Emilia never wanted to step foot in the bedroom again.

After setting everything out into the hall, Emilia took one last look around. She'd made the bed and tidied the room. There was nothing on the dresser that caught her eye except Iain's jewelry box. The sight of that box spurred Emilia into action. Iain had never purchased any gifts for Emilia except the watch. Her wedding band had been Iain's grandmother's ring and then his mother's, both of whom had died in childbirth at a relatively young age. Crossing to the dresser, she removed the watch and wedding band and placed them there. Emilia didn't want anything physical to remind her of her life with Iain. She possessed enough emotional baggage as a remembrance. The wedding band was a family heirloom and should stay in the Andersen family.

Closing the bedroom door behind her, Emilia picked up several boxes. She began the process of transferring her life to the living room. By the time Emilia had placed the box of feminine products in the downstairs bathroom, the upstairs hall was empty. Nothing left on the second floor belonged to her, and she was halfway to putting her plan into motion.

CHAPTER 3

THE sun was shining by the time Emilia finished moving her boxes. She should have kept the watch a tiny bit longer, however. Emilia forgot to reset the clocks in the rest of the house due to the power outage and had no idea what time it was. Emilia hated the thought of entering that room again, but she didn't have a choice.

Making her way up the stairs, Emilia had just stepped onto the landing when she heard a knock at the kitchen door. Making her way to the window in Bain's bedroom, she hid behind the drape and peeked out into the yard.

Damnation! She hadn't given any thought to who would be doing Bain's chores while he was away. Emilia recognized the truck parked beside the barn. So, there was no way she would be answering

47

that knock on the door. The truck belonged to one of Iain's friends, Shawn Jameson, the man who had run his hand over Emilia's backside in the kitchen during the repast. Why would Bain allow Shawn to come here when he knew Emilia would be alone in the house? Most importantly, Emilia didn't dare let Shawn inside, where he would see her belongings, all boxed up in the living room.

Shawn continued to knock on the door. When Emilia didn't answer, she could see him making his way around the side of the house to the living room door. Shit! If he placed his face against the window to peer inside, he would be able to see her stuff.

Shawn knocked again when he reached the door, then he began to pound and call Emilia's name. She could hear, "I know you're in there, Emilia. I have all day. I can wait you out. I won't hurt you, I promise."

When Emilia still didn't respond, Shawn yelled, "Get your ass to the door and unlock it. Don't make me break it down. If I do, I won't be so gentle when I take you for the first time."

As Shawn continued to pound and yell, Emilia watched as a fancy car pulled into the yard. Shawn ceased pounding on the door, and Emilia could see him shake his head as he made his way to his truck. Climbing in, Shawn started the vehicle and gunned the engine as he pulled away. Emilia watched as he drove down the lane and pulled out onto the main road, headed towards town. Relieved, she let out the breath she didn't realize she'd been holding.

Emilia didn't recognize the gentleman who exited the car, but he was well-dressed in a suit, so she knew it wasn't one of Bain's or Iain's friends who'd come calling to rape her. She could see the man making his way to the front door, so she ran into the master bedroom to grab the watch, then raced down the stairs to answer the door.

Just as the man raised his hand to knock on the door for the second time, Emilia turned the latch and opened it.

"May I help you?" Emilia asked.

"Mrs. Emilia Andersen?" the man responded.

"Yes, I'm sorry. You have me at a disadvantage. I don't recognize you."

"Oh, I am so sorry. Let me introduce myself. My name is Samuel Goldstein. I've come on behalf of a client who resides in Montana. I believe you applied at your place of employment seeking a home health care nursing position that would include lodging for an extended period. My employer chose you amongst the many applicants. If you are agreeable to the terms of employment, he requests that you make haste. Your services are needed immediately."

"Please, come in, Mr. Goldstein, and I'll make us some coffee. I didn't know that anyone seeking my services would be from another state. I'm afraid I'm not licensed to practice in the state of Montana. I would need to register. If I'm needed immediately, your employer will probably want to choose someone else," Emilia told him.

"Thank you for your hospitality, Mrs. Andersen. I take my coffee black if you don't mind. As to the necessity of obtaining a license in Montana, my employer is well aware. That won't be a problem. You can apply once you've settled in," Mr. Goldstein said.

"Well, then can you give me the particulars? This may be an answer to my prayers as my husband passed away four days ago. This house belongs to my brother-in-law, and he is not married. I've already packed to leave. I just need to take care of a few personal matters and find a vehicle to drive. I don't own one of my own."

After offering his condolences on the loss of Emilia's husband, Mr. Goldstein said, "This is most fortuitous that you are ready to move on. I have all of the information you need in this folder, plus authorization to give you the vehicle parked in your driveway for use in your journey. If you decide to accept the position, the vehicle will be transferred into your name as a bonus."

After placing their coffee on the kitchen table, Emilia sat and accepted the folder from Mr. Goldstein's hand. As she perused the contents, she asked several questions. Liking the answers that she was given, Emilia shook Mr. Goldstein's hand and thanked him for the opportunity.

"I accept the position. I can leave as soon as I load up the car and lock up the house. I'll need to retrieve some items from the bank before I start my journey. Do you need me to drop you somewhere before I take possession of the car?" Emilia asked.

"No, that won't be necessary. My employer was hoping that you would accept the position, so I've come prepared. I have someone waiting at the entrance to the drive. We'll assist in loading your belongings into the vehicle, and then we'll be on our way. I'll telephone my employer when I return to the office to let him know that you will be driving to Montana shortly. I've also been authorized to give you this money. It's to be used to pay for any lodging, meals, and gas during your journey."

After placing an envelope into Emilia's hand, Mr. Goldstein went out into the driveway to signal his assistant.

Once the boxes were transferred to the car, Mr. Goldstein wished Emilia luck and handed her the car keys.

"Safe journey, Mrs. Andersen. I believe you will be extremely pleased with what life has in store for you," he told her.

After shaking Emilia's hand, Mr. Goldstein turned and made his way out of the house and out of her life. She watched him go with a quizzical look on her face. What did Mr. Goldstein mean by his parting remark?

Gathering up the coffee cups and spoons, Emilia washed the pot and dishes, dried them, and put them away.

After fixing the time on the clocks, she took the watch back upstairs one more time and deposited it on the dresser next to the wedding band she'd worn for twenty-five years. Returning downstairs, Emilia carefully went from room to room to be sure everything was in order, and nothing personal was being left behind. Taking her purse, Emilia looked through the contents to be certain she had everything she needed. Removing the house and car keys and the credit card to Bain's bank account, Emilia placed them next to Bain's note on the kitchen counter. God, Emilia forgot that was there. She hoped neither Mr. Goldstein nor his associate read it while she wasn't looking. How embarrassing was that?

Grabbing her purse, the folder, and envelope full of cash that Mr. Goldstein had given her, Emilia took one last look around at the place that she'd called home for more than half of her life. Turning the lock on the door so that no one could gain access to the house, Emilia pulled the door shut behind her and walked down the porch steps for the very last time.

Placing her purse and the envelope full of money in the car, she locked the door. Going to the flower bed along the house's foundation, she picked some of the flowers blooming there. When she had a bunch, Emilia made her way along the path to the family plot. The pile of dirt covered by the tarp was gone, and Iain's grave was filled in. Once the ground had settled, Emilia knew that a stone would be placed there to mark his grave. She'd ordered the headstone herself and paid for its placement in advance. Kneeling down, Emilia arranged the flowers over the mound of dirt that covered her husband and bowed her head.

"I hope you rest in peace, Iain. I'm sorry that I wasn't a better wife. I think we would have been happier if I'd been able to share all of my love with you. Unfortunately, my heart and soul moved to Montana when I was sixteen, so they were no longer mine to give. I did love you, but I think you deserved better. I'm going away now, so I won't be able to visit you anymore. Thank you for taking me in when I didn't have a home. I'll be eternally grateful for that."

Placing a kiss on her fingers, Emilia touched the mound to transfer that kiss to her husband. Then she stood, brushed the dirt off her knees, and walked away. On her way back to the house, she let the tears that she'd refused to cry at the funeral flow silently down her cheeks.

Emilia was very impressed with the vehicle Mr. Goldstein left behind for her use. It was a late model BMW sedan. She pinched herself to check if she was dreaming. After all of the bad things that had happened in her life, was she finally going to experience something good? Not if she didn't get out of there. Shawn would be back shortly. Emilia knew that he hadn't given up.

Placing the key in the ignition, Emilia looked up at the house one last time. The clapboard siding was peeling and desperately in need of a fresh coat of paint. Some repairs to the porch and definitely a new roof were in order. She thought about Bain and wondered if he would find a woman to give him the children he wanted. She knew he wasn't a bad person and deserved a loving wife. Closing her eyes briefly, Emilia said a solemn prayer that Bain would find happiness. Then she turned the car around and began her journey to Montana and a new life. But first, to the bank where Emilia kept her money, She planned to ask for a certified check to close her account and empty the safety deposit box of its contents. The next stop would be her place of employment to let them know about her new job. Then she'd say goodbye to Pennsylvania. With no relatives, nor anyone who loved her, Emilia hoped that she'd never set foot inside the state again.

CHAPTER 4

ROGER Michael Willis stretched and yawned as he made his way across the barnyard to begin his morning chores. He hadn't slept well in days. His mind kept dwelling on his past, and Mike didn't understand why. He knew he was feeling restless. His forty-ninth birthday was coming up in September. He should be married with children and grandchildren. Instead, he was still hung up on a girl he'd met in high school that he hadn't seen in thirty-two years.

Mike always started his day at 5:00 a.m. in the stable. While he was feeding the horses, he checked the automatic waterers to ensure they were clean and working correctly. As he labored, he thought about his childhood growing up near Reading, Pennsylvania. His father, Malcolm Willis, was a ranch manager. While his mom, Ailsa, took care of her three children, Alec, Mike, and Aileen, she sewed and did mending for customers. She also made quilts to sell at local church bazaars. Mike had a good, wholesome childhood with loving parents and siblings comparable in temperament while not close in age. Everyone got along just fine, and all three children helped out with the chores.

Mike paused, took a look around him, and shook his head. What was with the nostalgic trip down memory lane? Grabbing the wheelbarrow, manure fork, and a broom, he parked them in the wide center aisle. He was thankful for that wide aisle. It made it easier for him to handle the equipment and groom the animals. Each stall had Dutch doors that led to the exterior of the building. Opening the doors, Mike turned the horses out into a small paddock. Grabbing the manure rake, Mike proceeded to clean up the soiled shavings in the end stall and place them in the wheelbarrow.

Leaving the bare floor uncovered to dry, he sprinkled baking soda on the wet patches to deodorize. As he moved on down the row, his mind turned to his junior year in high school. It was the year he turned seventeen when he lost his virginity and his heart to that young girl Mike was still in love with. Her name was Emilia Addison

Mackenzie. Mike recalled the moment they met in the library at school. Emi had dropped her belongings while trying to replace a book on a shelf above her head. As Mike reached down to help, they cracked heads. Standing back up, Mike closed his eyes and rubbed the spot on his forehead, wondering if he would get a lump or a bruise. When Mike opened his eyes, gazing back at him were the most beautiful cerulean blue eyes. Mike knew he could drown in the depths of those eyes. They were bottomless pools of wavering emotions.

Emi was a year younger than Mike. She was a tiny bit of a girl with the most glorious, dark brown hair that fell to her waist, firm breasts tipped, trim hips, and long silky legs. Mike was confident that Emi was a virgin the first time he kissed her. Knowing his brother Alec was sexually active, he took his brother aside one day when Al was home on leave from the Army, so they could have a private talk. Al gave Mike pointers about sex and his first box of condoms, plus he promised not to tell their parents. Two days later, Emi lost her virginity to Mike, and she was the most responsive woman Mike has ever been with.

Emi's mom worked for an attorney and was often late coming home. So, it was the perfect opportunity for them to get up to mischief without Emi's mother knowing. God only knew what she would have done to Emi if she found out that they had sex almost every day after school. She was a real "Bitch." She hit Emi all the time and locked her in her room. Mike wanted so badly to get Emi away from her mom, but he guessed they were never meant to be. Mike's parents moved their family to Montana at the end of Mike's junior year of high school. The last time Emi and Mike had the chance to be together they desperately clung to each other. Not being prepared, it was the only two times they made love without using condoms. Mike would never forget the feel of her sweet pussy as he slid in and out of her tight embrace. It's the only time he's had unprotected sex.

Mike's dad took a new position at a cattle ranch in south-central Montana near Billings. Mike's brother had joined the Army right after high school. So, it was just Mike, his parents, and his younger sister who made the move. His father's job only lasted long enough for Mike to graduate. Then the rest of his family moved to Utah. Mike loved Montana, so he applied to Montana College of Agriculture and was accepted. Before starting classes, he traveled back to Pennsylvania to find Emi, but she was gone. He wasn't able to find out where, either. The few classmates Mike found to ask said it was like Emi disappeared right after Mike moved away. She never returned to school for the fall semester, and no one saw her ever again.

Giving his head a shake, Mike continued to muck until all the stalls were cleaned. Starting back at the beginning, Mike took a broom to the baking soda, then spread a good thick layer of shavings. Mike appreciated how the stable was designed since mucking out was accomplished more quickly when the horses were outside. It was more dangerous to try to work around them, especially today when Mike's mind wasn't on his chores.

Most people eventually encounter a moment that forever alters the course of their lives. For Roger Michael Willis, that moment arrived on this beautiful, cloudless day in July. A moment that would bring about a set of defining revelations. The day had started like any other day on the ranch. It included a list of chores to complete that stretched the length of his arm. However, things were about to change.

Roger Michael Willis was best known to his friends and loved ones as Mike. He has worked for *Circle R Cattle Company* near Billings, Montana, for the last twenty-six years of his life. For the past twelve years, he's been proud and fortunate to be called its manager.

Mike took over from the prior manager, Taylor Morgan when Taylor decided it was time to retire. Taylor wanted to take his wife on a trip around the world before becoming too old to enjoy the adventure.

Mike would honestly say the owner, William Roberts was his best friend. Bill took a chance on the fresh-faced kid straight out of college, and Mike has always been humbled by Bill's faith in his abilities. If anyone were to ask, Mike would have to say it's been a good life so far, with only one exception.

When all the stalls were finished, Mike washed up, then made his way to the main house for breakfast with Bill and Peggy. Tim, Peggy's nephew, was visiting with his wife, Jeannie, and Jeannie's daughter, Sophie. They had come to celebrate Tim's birthday. Everyone was bustling about the kitchen when Mike entered through the mudroom, where he discarded his boots and hat.

Tim had just turned thirty-five years old. Not quite as tall as Mike at a little over six feet, he was well built, not muscle-bound. Tim had kind brown eyes and a toothy, lopsided smile. His light brown hair stuck up in a cowlick that he kept trying to tame with his hand. It refused to cooperate.

Tim met Jeannie when she visited Tim's tiny airport in Kirk, Oregon, to charter a plane for herself and her daughter, Sophie. The mother and daughter were to attend the wedding of Jeannie's brother in northern Washington, and she didn't feel like driving that distance. Tim, Jeannie, and Sophie hit it off, so Tim spent the week in Washington getting to know them. Tim fell in love that week. He and Jeannie got married at the Circle R Ranch in front of the living room fireplace. At the end of November, they would celebrate their sixth anniversary.

Jeannie was tall, about 5'10", but thin and fine-boned. She was a brunette with brown eyes and a smattering of freckles across her nose. Sophie just turned twelve years old but was a miniature copy of her mother.

Conversation during the meal was lively, with everyone joking around and getting caught up with the details of their lives. Mike felt fortunate to be considered a family member since he didn't have one of his own. While Tim was telling a story about a wealthy man that chartered a flight to Southern California, Mike's mind wandered. He scrolled through his memories of these people and his life since moving to Montana.

Bill and Peggy were in their early nineties, now. Bill was about 5'9" tall, but his shoulders had begun to stoop as if he carried the weight of the world upon them. His hair used to be light brown, but it was all gray now worn in a wave to the side. His eyes were now a faded hazel. He had a ready smile that made the skin around his eyes crinkle. He loved to wear a plaid shirt with a bolo tie, dark stonewashed jeans, and scuffed boots that looked well-worn and comfortable. Mike rarely saw him dressed any other way.

Bill was still active in ranch affairs. Until just recently, Peggy was too. Peggy was 5'6" tall, but her once snow-white hair that flowed loosely down her back had begun to lose its softness and was starting to yellow. Now it seemed more brittle. She'd always had a trim figure, but that too had changed. She'd lost weight, and her bones had begun to protrude. Peggy liked to wear comfortable-looking jeans, boots, and embroidered western-style shirts with pearlized snaps in place of buttons. Once form-fitting, her clothing had begun to hang on her slight frame. She still smelled of lilacs in springtime and freshly washed laundry, however.

Something was going on with Peggy's health. Bill had taken her for tests and several doctor's visits in the last few months. Mike was anxious. He loved that woman like a mother. He knew Tim was concerned, as well. Hopefully, Bill would clue them in as soon as the doctor had some answers.

Bill came to Montana as a young man in his mid-twenties, fresh from a horrendous divorce. Before making Montana his home, he lived in Fair Lawn, New Jersey, with his wife, Eloise, and son, James. According to Bill, he and Eloise married way too young. They were both eighteen and fresh out of high school. Too late, he discovered that Eloise suffered from mood swings. When she was having one of her spells, she became a very headstrong, bitter woman who liked to yell. Unfortunately, Bill didn't discover her true nature until she was expecting their son. Five years later, Bill couldn't take anymore. He was tired of treading carefully. Saying or doing anything might cause Eloise to spiral into one of her black holes. He moved out and filed for a divorce. A legal battle ensued that was far from amicable due to a fight over their young son's custody. He was concerned that Eloise beat the boy and locked him in his bedroom for days as punishment for wrongdoings. Not having any physical evidence to substantiate Bill's claims, the court gave Eloise full custody due to Bill's abandonment.

Bill's own father passed away not long after Bill's divorce became final. With his inheritance, Bill purchased the *Circle R Cattle Company*. With help from kind neighbors and a good ranch manager, Bill settled into the cowboy lifestyle. While learning the ropes, he also took classes in business management and agriculture at a college in Billings.

Peggy met Bill when she was a waitress at a diner in Billings. She worked the late shift, and Bill would come in a couple of nights a week after college classes. She told Mike that Bill always wandered in by himself and that he seemed sad and lonely. If there weren't many customers, Peggy would sit and chat with Bill. Over coffee and pie, they got to know each other better and fell in love. They got married not long after and have been living on the Circle R Ranch ever since.

William and Peggy Roberts were two of the best people God ever put on this planet. Not having children, they helped raise Peggy's nephew, Tim, plus provided foster care for six more kids. The foster kids were all grown now with families of their own. Having moved to other parts of the state and country, they seldom visited. Tim was the only one that took time out of his busy life to come for a visit regularly.

Twelve years ago, Bill's granddaughter, Eloise Lianne Roberts, found her way to the Circle R quite by accident. Bill never knew he had a granddaughter, and Elli didn't know anything about her grandfather. Bill told Mike that Elli's arrival was one of the best days of his life.

Elli was very pregnant when she arrived at the Circle R Ranch. She was running from her parents, Bill's son James and wife, Lilianne Roberts. Professors at a college in upstate California, they were basically holding Elli hostage in their home with plans to sell Elli's baby when it was born.

When Elli discovered their scheme, she escaped with the idea of driving to Montana. She had chosen Montana as her destination on a whim. Elli believed the sparsely populated state would be the last place her parents would look for her. Thus, an excellent place to hide. She wanted to find a women's shelter that would take her in and guide her to medical care for her child's birth. Those plans went awry when she spent her first night at a motor court in Kirk, Oregon. A patrolman discovered Elli's car parked in front of her room. Since it matched an APB on a missing vehicle, he ran the plates. Thankfully, Elli managed to sneak out through the bathroom window. Making her way on foot to a small airport several miles outside the town limits, she prayed someone there would be able to fly her to Montana. That airport belonged to Tim Jones.

The Circle R had a small airfield installed to allow Tim to fly in to visit his aunt and uncle regularly. Tim called his aunt to ask for assistance in finding Elli a shelter in Billings. When Peggy and Bill discussed Elli's plight, they decided to offer Elli the opportunity of staying with them. Peggy and Bill had very compassionate hearts.

Mike drove the jeep to the airfield to pick Tim and Elli up the day they flew to the ranch. When Elli stepped down from Tim's plane, Mike became confused and just stood there staring at her. Mike guessed he probably had a stunned expression on his face. He was in shock because Elli looked so much like Mike's childhood sweetheart, Emilia Addison Mackenzie.

As it turned out, there wasn't any way Elli and Emi could be related. Elli lived in New Jersey all of her life before her parents kidnapped her and moved her to California. Emi was born and raised in Pennsylvania.

Being unable to find Emi was that one exception Mike was thinking about to his otherwise perfect life. He'd never met another woman that could measure up to Emi. That's not to say that Mike had been celibate for the last thirty-two years. He'd dated a few women and had more than his fair share of hookups, but what his heart wanted was Emi. If he'd found her, Mike would have put a ring on her finger and never let her go.

When Bill and Peggy discovered that Elli was their granddaughter, they told her she would have a home with them for as long as she wanted. Elli Roberts gave birth to a beautiful baby girl the very next day after arriving at the ranch. She named her child Jessica Blair Whrite-Roberts. Richard Blair Whrite, Jessica's father, was Elli's childhood love. Elli met him for the first time when she was in sixth grade, and she loved him with all of her heart. Unfortunately, Rick didn't know that Elli was pregnant with his baby when he married another woman.

Right after Jessica was born, Elli's parents were killed in a head-on collision with a tractor-trailer during a freak snowstorm in

Idaho. James and Lilianne were on their way to the Circle R to see Elli, meet their new granddaughter, and try to make amends for their treachery when it happened. Tim flew Bill to Oregon, then they drove down to California to handle the details of the estate for Elli. Mike's always had his suspicions that Bill and Tim discovered something odd during that trip. Both of them acted a little weird when they got back, having discussions behind closed doors. Mike wasn't taken into their confidence, however. After a while, things seemed to get back to normal. Elli and Jessica were absorbed into life on the ranch. It was like they'd always been a part of their lives.

Elli and Jessica lived there on the Circle R for the first five years of Jessica's life. Bill and Peggy supported Elli while she attended college, where she got her teaching degree. Those five years were terrific. Mike came to love Elli like a daughter. Tim and Mike taught Elli to ride and care for the horses, ride fence lines, make repairs, and even herd cattle. They'd turned her into a real cowgirl.

While Elli was taking classes to get her degree, they all pitched in to care for Jessica. She was the cutest baby Mike had ever seen and as clever as a whip. Mike would never forget the day Jessica noticed a stallion breeding one of the mares. She asked her mom if that's how she was conceived. Mike had to admire how Elli educated her four-year-old daughter about the birds and the bees. Elli explained, then promised to get a book from the library concerning the subject suitable for Jessica's age.

Mike thought that Tim and Elli would end up married, but the day came for Elli and Jessica to leave the ranch. Elli received a call from an attorney in New Jersey concerning the death of a woman Elli had grown up with. As it turned out, the woman was the wife of Jessica's father. She'd named Elli executrix of her estate.

The night before Elli and Jessica left for Stillwater, New Jersey, Mike had a dream. Both of them were being hugged by a blond-haired, blue-eyed man. Another dark-haired young man was standing off to the side. That man stared at Elli with so much love and longing. Mike could tell the dark-haired man was hurting. Mike woke up knowing that Elli and Jessica wouldn't return to the ranch for a very long time.

Mike was jolted out of his reverie when Bill cleared his throat and said, "Mike, did you hear what I said?"

"Umm…no, sir. I guess I was woolgathering. Could you repeat what you said, please?" Mike asked him.

Bill responded, "I'd like to talk to you and Tim in my office after you've finished with the horses. Get a couple of ranch hands to take care of that long list of chores I know you have planned for yourself. After our discussion, I want you to take the rest of the day off."

Mike could feel his stomach begin to churn. Whatever Bill wanted to discuss couldn't be good if Mike was being told to shrug off his duties. Mike hoped Bill wasn't planning to fire him. The Circle R was Mike's life, and he didn't have anywhere else he wanted to go.

Nodding, Mike indicated that he understood what Bill was requesting. He thanked the ladies for the excellent meal, rinsed his dishes, placed them in the dishwasher, and then headed out to speak to Tom and Jake. Mike hired the sixteen-year-old high school students to help with summer chores, mostly cleaning, taking care of yard chores, and exercising the horses. After giving them his list and answering a few questions, Mike went to speak with the regular ranch hands. They would be riding and mending fences today and checking that none of the cattle had gotten out. Then Mike headed back over to the stable to finish up. After brushing each horse and inspecting and picking out their hooves, Mike sprayed each horse with fly spray and put them back in their stalls. Tom and Jake would give each of them some exercise on a long rein later.

Finished, Mike made his way to the little house that sat a few hundred yards from the primary home. Both buildings were designed using the same log and stone exteriors. Mike's house included two bedrooms and an open floor plan for the kitchen, dining, and living room space. With oak hardwood flooring throughout, it was easy to take care of. Mike didn't have to spend much of his free time chasing dirt since it was just him living there.

When Mike entered the kitchen, his mind wandered back to thoughts of Emi. He imagined her smiling at him across the kitchen table while they ate the delicious meal she'd prepared just for him. He'd had that vision hundreds of times before.

Removing his hat and boots, Mike made his way down the hall and entered his bedroom. Standing in the doorway, he stared at the bed, imagining Emi lying tangled in his sheets. Mike lost himself in the mirage of her shy smile as she wrapped her shapely legs around his waist, her flowing brown hair spread across the pillow beneath her head. Mike could feel her muscles tighten around his shaft as he brought them both to orgasm.

Giving his head a shake, the vision of Emi evaporated, and Mike stripped to take a shower. Of course, his daydream of Emi had him all riled up, so he took himself in hand. Mike was almost forty-nine years old but still had needs. What he needed most was Emi, but he couldn't physically make love to a memory.

After getting himself off, Mike turned the water temperature to cold. He realized it was time to take a ride into Billings to the bar where he liked to drink on occasion in the hopes of hooking up for another one-night stand. That shit was getting old, and Mike guessed he was too. Thankfully, he wasn't so old that he couldn't catch the eye of an available woman. Tall, at 6'3", Mike had blue eyes and a crooked smile. His dark brown hair only had a few streaks of gray. Working on a cattle ranch had kept his weight down, and Mike continued to have a solid muscular build with broad shoulders, narrow hips, and long legs. Wearing his Stetson, the typical jeans, plaid shirt, and boots, Mike looked like a real cowboy to most women.

Emi and Mike should have grown children with children of their own by now. Mike had always wanted a big family, so he'd been living vicariously through Bill and Peggy. Loving Elli like a daughter the way he did, Mike pretended her children were his grandchildren.

Elli was thirty-one years old now and gave birth to her sixth child about six weeks earlier. The dream that Mike had the night before she returned to Stillwater, New Jersey, proved to be prophetic. Elli married Richard Blair Whrite. It turned out Rick had been dreaming about her every night since the night they'd conceived Jessica. Right before they married, Elli got pregnant with triplets Blair, Peggy, and Logan. Unfortunately, just a few months after Elli gave birth, Rick was killed in a freak farm accident. Mike missed that young man. Rick was full of life and loved his wife and children dearly. Elli was in a very dark place after Rick's death, and Mike was worried sick about her. He went to New Jersey to convince her to pack up the kids and come home to the ranch.

That's when the second man in Mike's dream proved that love can conquer all when it's what his heart wants. The dark-haired man was named Tyler Logan Thompson. He was Rick's best friend since they were in seventh grade together. Tyler was in love with Elli since they were in tenth grade but kept those feelings to himself out of loyalty to Rick. Tyler married Elli on the same day as Tim and Jeannie's wedding in a joint ranch ceremony. Then Tyler adopted Rick's children and added two more to their brood, Billy and the new baby, Lianne.

If Elli, Tyler, and the kids couldn't visit this summer, Mike knew he would need to travel to New Jersey. He wanted to meet his new surrogate granddaughter and catch up with the rest of the family. Mike had come to admire Tyler immensely and valued his friendship. Mike was thankful that Elli had found another man to love her the way she deserved.

Toweled off, Mike headed to his dresser for a fresh pair of jockey underwear, jeans, a Henley t-shirt, and socks. Then he brushed his hair and teeth. Donning his Stetson and well-worn boots, Mike headed to the main house for that meeting with Bill. Admittedly, he was dreading the coming confrontation.

CHAPTER 5

AFTER Mike left the house, Bill turned to Tim. "Will you and Jeannie clean up from breakfast, please?" he asked. "I have something to speak to Peggy about in the study. As soon as Mike gets here, both of you should come to the study, as well."

"Certainly, Uncle Bill. Jeannie and I will be happy to do the dishes," Tim responded.

Helping Peggy from her seat at the table, Bill wrapped his arm around her waist. Then he led her from the room. Peggy was weakening quickly, and it wouldn't be long before she would probably be completely bedridden.

Bill had asked Mike and Tim to join him in the study because the news he had to tell them would come as a shock.

After helping Peggy to sit in a comfortably upholstered chair, Bill closed the door. He didn't wish for their conversation to be overheard.

First, Bill needed to make a telephone call to the detective agency in Pennsylvania for an update. He had Samuel Goldstein's private number, so that was the one he dialed.

The phone rang several times, then Bill heard, "Hello, Sam speaking. How are you doing, Mr. Roberts?"

Bill had forgotten that Sam could tell who was calling, so not needing to identify himself always surprised him.

"Hi, Sam. I'm doing okay. I'm hoping you have good news for me. I'm going to put you on speaker so that my wife, Peggy, can hear both sides of our conversation. Is that alright with you?"

"Yes, sir. Hello, Mrs. Roberts. It's a pleasure to speak to you again," Sam said.

Peggy responded, "Hi, Sam. It's good to speak to you as well. Go ahead and give Bill your update. We're both anxious to hear what you have to say."

"All right, I think you are going to be very pleased. Before I get to the part you most want to hear, let me give you an accounting of what has taken place since we spoke a few days ago. As you know, the funeral for Mrs. Andersen's husband was yesterday. Iain Andersen was buried in the family plot on the farm. The man I employ that was able to insert himself into Iain and Bain's close circle of friends was at the service and has given me a verbal report. His written report will follow, and I'll fax that over to you. Anyway, he said that Bain pulled Emilia against his body during the eulogy and whispered something to her. Emilia seemed to be very uncomfortable at Bain's proximity. Bain also grabbed Emilia after the service and proceeded to drag her to the house. My man was close enough to hear Bain tell her to keep up, or he'd throw her over his shoulder and spank her after she'd stumbled several times. During the repast, one of Iain's friends, Shawn Jameson, touched Emilia inappropriately on the backside. Bain proceeded to have a heated conversation with him. After that, Shawn left. As you know from past reports, Emilia has been a continual conversational topic amongst the brothers' close circle. The brothers and the men in that circle enjoy sharing the women they pick up or date. Iain has always been a part of sharing those women, but he's never shared Emilia, not even with his brother. It seems to be a sore point, especially with Bain. Bain's very interested in asserting his dominance over Emilia and getting to know her better if you know what I'm trying to say."

"Was Emilia left alone with Bain last night?" Bill asked, concerned about her safety.

"No, sir. Thankfully, she was not. After the repast, Bain changed into his work clothes and went out to do the milking. Shortly after he finished his chores, he went into the house for a brief time. I'd say Bain was only in the house for about ten minutes. Then he and one of his friends loaded a cattle trailer with a bull and left for Indiana. From what my employee discovered, Bain will be delivering that bull to a buyer in Indiana, then picking up another animal that he purchased at a different location in Ohio. He is not supposed to return until Friday. Bain wasn't alone in the house with Emilia long enough to have pressured her into having sex. I don't think that is what happened, but I'll get to my reasoning for that in a few minutes."

"Well, I'm thankful that she is safe for the time being. Believe me when I say that the reports you have sent me since you discovered that Emilia is Elli's mother have been very upsetting. Sadly, Emilia has lived a friendless life since she made the mistake of taking Iain for her husband. I'm worried as to her state of mind after suffering years of mental and verbal abuse at that man's hands," Bill responded.

"Well, through my investigations, I discovered that people consider Emilia to be shy and too trusting, but hardworking, compassionate, generous, and always willing to offer her assistance. She's also a gorgeous woman, so I can understand why Bain and his buddies are so interested in her sexually."

"As to my personal experience with her, I found her to be quite level-headed and emotionally stable. I find that remarkable. She was abused by her mother, and her child was stolen. Then she suffered at the hands of the man who was supposed to love and support her. I think under that shy, retiring shell is a strong, capable woman," Sam concluded.

Relieved, Bill responded, "That's excellent, Sam. I trust your judgment implicitly. So, tell me about your conversation with Emilia. Will she be accepting the position she's been offered?"

Sam said, "That's the part I think you will be pleased about, but let me finish explaining. I believe Bain did not force Emilia into a sexual encounter before leaving on his trip. I read a note lying on the kitchen counter underneath a pile of money that Bain left for Emilia. I took a screenshot of it, and I'll send that to you so that you can see for yourself what Emilia was facing if she had stayed in that house."

"As I arrived at the home this morning, Shawn Jameson, the man who touched Emilia inappropriately at the repast, was pounding on the living room door. He was yelling for her to open up, or he would break it down. He threatened rape if she didn't. When he noticed me, he got in his truck and left."

At that revelation, Peggy gasped and covered her face with her hands. "We have to get her out of there, Bill."

They could hear Sam clear his throat. Then he said, "Not to worry. After Emilia answered the door, we spoke at length about your offer of a position in your home as a home health care nurse. She invited me in for coffee, which I accepted. She makes excellent coffee, by the way."

That got a chuckle out of Bill, "That's good news. Peggy and I love a good cup of coffee. How did the rest of the meeting go?"

"Very well. Emilia was concerned about the position being in Montana because she is not licensed there. I was able to assure her that she can register after relocating. I gave her the folder with all of the information concerning the position. She read through that, as well. When she was finished, she told me this is actually an answer to her prayers. Something happened between her and Bain last evening before he left. He may have touched her inappropriately. I'm not certain, but he spooked her enough that she had already boxed up all of her belongings. The boxes were in the living room. Either way, she was planning to leave that house before Bain gets back on Friday."

"That's good news," Bill told Sam. "What did she decide? You have Peggy and me on tinder hooks, here."

Sam chuckled at Bill's comment. "She accepted the position and signed the agreement contract. I'll fax over a copy of that as well. The original will be filed with my official report. I had my associate waiting in another vehicle at the end of the drive, in case she did accept. The two of us helped to load Emilia's belongings in the trunk of the BMW sedan you had me purchase for her. I told her that the car will become her property as part of the contract. While Emilia was distracted, I read and got the screenshot of Bain's note that I mentioned. I believe his intent is to take over his brother's position as the primary male in Emilia's life. The note is very explicit as to what their relationship will entail."

"Thankfully, that won't be happening," Sam continued. "When all of Emilia's belongings were loaded into the BMW, I gave her the keys to the car and wished her well, then took my leave. I left in my associate's vehicle, and we parked in view of the end of the driveway to the farm. Approximately thirty minutes later, Emilia left the property. We followed at a discreet distance. She proceeded to a bank in a neighboring town. She was in the bank long enough to have closed out the accounts she had there. I'll double-check that. From my investigation, I know that she had a substantial amount of money totaling more than one million dollars in savings and a safety deposit box. She's managed to save half of her income throughout her marriage. Her husband didn't know about that money because, according to my source, her husband took what he thought was everything she was earning. She's not as helpless as one would perceive."

"Anyway, after leaving the bank, we continued to follow. Emilia drove to her place of employment next. I assume to advise them of her new job and that she will no longer be working for that agency. I will double-check that as well. When Emilia returned to the BMW, she made her way to I-80 W. So, she's headed to you. I do have another vehicle following to be certain she makes it to Montana safely. I'll continue to update you as to her location and potential arrival time," Sam concluded.

"Very excellent. I can't tell you, Sam, how relieved we are. It has been a pleasure working with you while you uncovered all the details for Peggy and me. Please send me your final invoice when you have it calculated and your final report," Bill told him.

"Certainly, Mr. Roberts. I'm happy to be of service and truly grateful to see this to what I hope will be a good conclusion. I'll let you know where Emilia spends the night. She may take her time driving to Montana. So, I'm estimating her arrival as sometime late Thursday. She'll probably come to the ranch on Friday morning, but I'll keep you updated. I wish all of you well." Then the line disconnected.

Bill looked at Peggy and sighed. "Peggy, do you think we're doing the right thing by withholding information from Mike, or should we just come out and tell him everything we've uncovered?" he asked his wife.

Peggy took Bill's hand in hers and gently gave it a squeeze. "I understand your reasoning, Bill. We've argued both sides of the situation repeatedly. I, for one, still don't know what the best course of action should be. Either way, I think everyone is going to be upset with us. I do think that it wouldn't be fair to unduly influence the outcome. We must allow everyone involved to work through their own feelings and then decide their own destinies. If we tell Mike everything before Emilia arrives, she won't have the opportunity to tell him herself. The same is true of Elli. We've withheld the truth from her since James and Lilianne's deaths. We wouldn't have known that they weren't her real parents if it weren't for you and Tim. You are the ones who found James' journal in his safe, plus the documents, Elli's birth certificate, and the letters from Eloise in the safety deposit box when you handled the estate. It took the detective you hired to uncover the rest of the details. We've only known that Mike is Elli's father for a few weeks. I think we should give Emilia the chance to tell Mike that she was pregnant when he moved away. If she does, we can sit down with them and give them the private detective reports to read before Elli arrives with Tyler and the children. All three of them will be angry and hurt because they've lost thirty-one years where they could have been a family. If I wasn't a good Christian, I would wish Eloise the joy of rotting in Hell for what she did."

"Well, I don't think Eloise was a particularly happy woman. Her life here on Earth was probably its own type of Hell. So, we're in agreement. We'll just tell Tim and Mike our bad news and let things progress as God sees fit," Bill replied.

Just then, there was a soft knock on the door.

"It's okay, you can come in," Bill called out.

As soon as Tim and Mike entered, Bill asked Tim to accompany Peggy to her bedroom. Peggy was clearly exhausted, and Bill wanted her to rest. She didn't need to be here for the meeting. Dealing with the emotions of Bill's revelation would be too much for her. Before she left the room, she placed a hand on Mike's arm, leaned in to place a kiss on his forehead, and told him she loved him. Startled, Mike looked at Bill questioningly.

Mike took a seat to the right of Bill's desk and cleared his throat as he watched Peggy and Tim leave the room. Then he turned to Bill. The expression on Mike's face was the same look he'd gotten at the breakfast table when Bill asked him to come to the study after finishing with the horses. Telling Mike to take the rest of the day off had him worried. He probably thought Bill intended to fire him.

Mike never neglected his chores in all the years he'd worked for the Circle R. He had grown into a fine man and a good manager. Bill would never let him go. Mike had taken the place of the son that Bill never got to love. Bill's only regret was that Mike never found the love and devotion of a good woman like Peggy. Bill believed Mike's heart still belonged to the young girl he'd left behind in Pennsylvania when his parents moved him to Montana. Hopefully, Bill could fix that with what he had planned.

CHAPTER 6

WHEN Tim returned to the study, Bill indicated that he should take the chair on the left side of the desk. After Tim was seated, both men looked at Bill expectantly.

Clearing his throat, Bill began, "I'm quite certain that you've both noticed that Peggy is not her usual energetic self. Anyone who knows her can see that something isn't right. You know that I've been taking her to the doctor. We've really been going to a specialist in Billings since just after Elli, Tyler, and the children visited in February. Peggy had noticed changes in her health last November, but she thought it was just due to getting old."

Stopping, Bill went over to the cooler that sat in the corner of the room to get some cold water. His throat was parched, and the pause gave him time to bolster his courage. What Bill had to say was going to cause both of these men a great deal of pain.

Tim and Mike both stared at Bill intently, but neither said a word. They were waiting for Bill to continue.

"Since Peggy was going to get a complete physical, she insisted that I get one as well. She said it had been too long, and if she had to get one, so did I. The specialist did a thorough examination and ran numerous tests. The results were not good for either of us."

At that, both men jumped to their feet. Mike started to pace back and forth in front of the desk.

Tim mumbled, "Shit, I need a drink, and it's not yet lunchtime, and I don't drink anyway. I'm not certain I want to hear this."

"Mike, will you get us all some coffee, please?" Bill asked him.

After Mike left the room, Bill stood and wrapped an arm around Tim's shoulders. Tim had always been a good person, and Bill knew Tim loved Peggy and him like they were his real parents.

Patting him on the back, Bill told him, "Sit, Tim. Telling you this won't be easy for me, but you have to prepare yourself. Peggy and I will need your strength to be able to get through what is to come."

Tim swallowed the lump in his throat, nodded and returned to his seat, then hung his head between his splayed knees. When Mike returned with a serving tray loaded with mugs, sugar, creamer, spoons, and the coffee pot, he placed them on Bill's desk. Then Mike proceeded to pour for all three of them. Each prepared their mug according to how they preferred their coffee and sat there quietly drinking while silently prolonging the inevitable.

Finally, Bill looked at Mike and then Tim. "Alright, there isn't any sense in putting this off any longer. Peggy has been diagnosed with pancreatic cancer. The doctor gave her three more months to live. That was two months ago."

Tim shouted, "No. That is not acceptable. We'll take her to another doctor or ten more doctors if we need to."

Mike hadn't said anything, but being fourteen years older than Tim, he had the added maturity to help him deal with what they'd just been told. He sat there glassy-eyed because he knew there was more bad news coming. Then he cleared his throat and asked, "What was your diagnosis, Bill?"

"I have slightly longer. Maybe a year if I am lucky. I have kidney cancer, and it has spread. There's nothing the doctor can do for either of us."

Tim was sobbing now, and Mike rested a comforting hand on Tim's arm. Bill knew he could count on Mike to be the strong one. Mike had been the strength and backbone of the ranch for a long time. Bill didn't know what he would have done without Mike. Having him apply for a position as a ranch hand when he was fresh out of college had been a blessing.

"What do you need us to do?" Mike asked. "We'll do whatever you need us to do."

"A woman will arrive in a couple of days, who is a certified home health care nurse. She lived in Pennsylvania before agreeing to take this assignment, so she will need to register in Montana to practice. She will be caring for Peggy's and my physical and medical needs. Both Peggy and I wish to die peacefully in our home, surrounded by the people we love, not in some facility. You will take your orders from her concerning any changes made for our care and comfort."

"Why didn't you find a nurse that is already licensed to practice here?" Tim questioned Bill.

"I have my reasons. All will become clear," Bill told him.

"Now, as to what will become of the ranch," Bill continued.

"No, we aren't going to discuss that. It's not something we need to discuss, ever," Tim demanded.

"Tim, that's enough. I want to discuss this, and you will certainly understand why since you know part of the story. Now sit there and listen," Bill admonished him.

Chastised, Tim fell silent.

"Mike, I imagine you probably think the ranch will be left to Elli," Bill said as he looked at Mike directly. "Elli will inherit eventually, but not at first. Elli is not my real granddaughter."

Mike's eyes went wide, and Bill could see Tim blanch. It was time for the big reveal. Tim was with Bill when he'd discovered the truth.

"When my son James and his wife Lilianne died in that car crash, Tim went with me to northern California to handle the details of their estate for Elli. She had just given birth to Jessica and wasn't physically or emotionally capable of handling that. You know James beat Elli when she was a child. When he found out Elli was pregnant, he moved them to California to avoid embarrassment due to the child's illegitimacy. His intention was to sell the baby so that Elli could get on with her life without the stigma of being an unwed mother."

"Yes, I know all of that, Bill. What makes you think Elli isn't your granddaughter? Did James' wife have an affair with another man?" Mike asked.

"No, neither James nor Lilianne were Elli's parents. Nor was Elli adopted," Bill responded. "When Tim and I opened my son's safety deposit box and the safe in the house, we found correspondence and a copy of Elli's birth certificate. We discovered the partial truth of Elli's parentage."

"Tim, you know the details of what we discovered. I want to thank you again for keeping this quiet until now. If you don't feel that you have anything you can add to what I'm going to tell Mike, you should go and spend time with your wife and daughter. I'll have Mike come to get you when I'm ready to finish discussing the ranch's disposition. Maybe we'll talk about that after lunch."

"That's a good idea. I need some time alone. I'll see you at lunch. Love you, Uncle," Tim told Bill. Then he rushed from the room, closing the study door quietly behind him.

"I knew Tim would have trouble dealing with this," Bill said to Mike.

"So, where were we? Oh, yes, Elli's parents. As it turns out, my ex-wife Eloise moved to Pennsylvania. She took a position at a law firm near Philadelphia after James went off to college. Eloise would have been thirty-seven at the time. Apparently, she had an affair with a senior partner of the firm and got pregnant. The child from that liaison was a girl. Later, Eloise moved to a smaller town. When her daughter was sixteen, the girl got pregnant. Her baby's father moved away before the girl realized she was pregnant, so he never knew he had a child. Eloise's daughter didn't know how to find him, either. When Eloise discovered her daughter was pregnant, she moved them again to western Pennsylvania. Apparently, she locked the girl in her bedroom for the duration of her pregnancy. Eloise had a midwife deliver the baby. Then Eloise gave the baby away. The poor girl never even got to see the baby she'd given birth to."

Mike interrupted, "Are you telling me that baby is Elli?"

"Yes, Eloise gave the baby to James and Lilianne. James had his corrupt attorney file a birth certificate naming James and Lilianne as the baby's birth parents. Eloise paid James one thousand dollars every month while Elli was growing up for her care."

"This is unbelievable. Now I understand why you and Tim acted funny after returning from your trip to settle your son's estate. You knew Elli wasn't your flesh and blood, but you've continued to treat her and Jessica and the rest of her children as if they are. Elli doesn't know any of this?" Mike asked.

"No, but she will learn the truth soon. There is a lot more to the truth concerning Elli's parentage, but I'm not ready to discuss those details yet. I've spoken to Tyler by phone and asked him to bring Elli and the children to the ranch for an extended stay. He promised as soon as Elli and the baby are up to taking a trip. He needs to make arrangements concerning everything that is going on with the farms, as well. So, it may be a few weeks. Now, let's go see how Peggy is doing, and prepare lunch. Then, we'll finish our discussion."

Mike asked, "Bill, can you give me some time before I come into the kitchen?"

"I know this is a lot to take in, Mike. Take all the time you need." Then Bill patted him on the back and went off to find his wife.

CHAPTER 7

PEGGY was lying on the bed they'd shared all of their married lives. When Bill entered the bedroom, she struggled to sit up. Bill's heart broke at how weak she was becoming and how little time they had left. Bill wouldn't change their lives together for anything except to ask for more time.

"Have you finished telling Tim and Mike?" Peggy inquired.

"Not everything. Mike and Tim now know about the diagnoses we've been given. Tim is taking the news much as we expected. Mike is shaken, but he's keeping his grief locked inside. I'm certain he'll let it out when no one is around to hear. Mike now knows that Elli is not our granddaughter by blood. I told him that Elli doesn't know anything yet, but will soon and that Tyler will be bringing the family to the ranch in a few weeks. I've asked Mike and Tim to meet me in the study again after we've eaten lunch, so I can advise them concerning the disposition of our assets. They've agreed. Tim is off somewhere with Jeannie and Sophie. Mike asked for some time alone in the study."

Peggy sighed and squeezed Bill's hand. "I'm sorry, my love, that I didn't stay with you. You shouldn't have been burdened with telling Tim and Mike all by yourself."

"You're not to worry about that. It gave me peace of mind that you were resting. Are you up to eating some lunch, my dear sweet girl? What can I get you to tempt your appetite?"

"How about a kiss," Peggy giggled.

"Ah, you still giggle like the young girl I fell in love with. Now, up you go. Let's spend some time with the people we love." Then Bill kissed Peggy and helped her to her feet.

Tim and Jeannie were placing fixings on the counter for sandwiches when Peggy and Bill entered the kitchen. Sophie was busy setting the table.

Peggy said, "Sophie, you come and sit by your great aunt and tell me all about your friends at school. Any young man catch your eye yet?"

Sophie blushed, "Well, Aunt Peggy, there is one cute boy named Jimmy, but Tim said I can't date yet. He said maybe when I finish college. Then the boy will have to pass Tim's interrogation while he's cleaning his shotgun at the kitchen table."

That pronouncement had everyone laughing and helped to lighten the somber mood.

After that, they all talked about politics, an upcoming meeting at the grange, some ideas for the ranch's website, and Tim's business. He was hoping to expand so that he could take on more customers. There seemed to be a growing need for his services. He was excited, and they all offered suggestions.

When lunch was concluded, Jeannie offered to take Peggy out to the garden to sit in the shade. Sophie was taking flute lessons and wanted to play some music for them while they relaxed.

"I think that is an excellent idea. Mike and Tim can help me clean up, then we'll be in the study if you need us for anything," Bill told everyone.

Tim grimaced because he didn't want to have a discussion about the property. That would mean that all of this was real and that

Bill and Peggy would die soon. He'd have to listen, though, because he couldn't bury his head in the sand.

Mike told Bill to sit at the table and relax. "I'll wash, and Tim can dry. Would you like some coffee, Bill? I can make a fresh pot," he offered.

"That sounds excellent. I think I'd like that. Thank you, Mike."

While the young men were working, Bill watched Mike move around the kitchen. Mike's eyes were red-rimmed when he came out of the study earlier. Bill was worried about how Mike would react when Emilia arrived. Then, at the revelation that Elli was his daughter. Mike would have a lot on his plate in the coming months. Peggy and Bill were praying that the love Mike and Emilia had once shared could be rekindled. Mike needed that.

When the last dish was back in the cabinet, Bill said, "Okay, enough procrastination. Back to the study with you. Let's get this over with. I want to spend time with my family. Maybe we can play some games with Sophie, then watch a movie. How does that sound?" When Bill looked at each of them, they nodded and followed him down the hall.

Tim closed the study door, and they all got comfortable.

"Alright. So, this is what I am thinking. Tim, you have your business in Oregon, and that is where Jeannie's family is and Sophie's father. I'm going to parcel off some acreage with the airstrip here on the ranch. That will be deeded to you, and I'll supply funds so that you and Jeannie can build a house on the property. This ranch has been part of your life for many years, and I know part of your heart is here. I'll also give you money to help grow your business. How does that sound?" Bill asked.

"That's too generous, Uncle Bill. I don't deserve that." Tim shook his head at Bill when he said this.

"Nonsense, I won't hear any argument on the subject," Bill responded. "You've done your fair share of chores around the ranch over the years, and Peggy and I both love you like a son."

"Now, Mike. As I mentioned earlier, Elli will inherit the ranch eventually from you. Until that day, you will own the ranch."

"No. I don't have any right to inherit the ranch from you, Bill. I'm not your flesh and blood." Mike jumped to his feet and stormed over to the door.

101

Bill yelled at him, "Sit down, now, and behave yourself. I'll leave my property to whom I see fit. Peggy and I love you like a son as well. You've been more son to me than James ever was. Peggy and I want you to continue our legacy. If you decide to retire, you can turn it over to Elli then. Otherwise, it will go to her upon your death. I expect you to take good care of the ranch and help it to grow. I'm also hoping that I can convince Elli and Tyler to move here with the children. They can live in the main house since there are so many of them, and you can continue to live in the manager's house. You can add onto that if you need more room."

Mike resumed his seat when Bill expressed his displeasure at Mike's attempt to leave the room. He looked at Bill, then scrubbed at his face with his hands. His eyes red-rimmed and his emotions raw, he finally said, "I don't know what to say. When you told me to take the afternoon off and shirk my chores, I thought you were going to fire me."

Laughing, Bill winked at Mike and told him, "I had a feeling that's what you were thinking. I saw the look on your face."

"Well, gentlemen, I think that concludes our business. I don't want any sad faces around here. Is that understood? It will be business as usual. I'll continue to make decisions concerning the ranch until I don't feel up to it, and then Mike will take over. Let's go join the girls. Maybe we can talk Jeannie into making some of her wonderful lemonade. I can go for some of the cookies she baked, too."

Mike and Tim chuckled, and they all traipsed out to the garden.

CHAPTER 8

THE car Emilia was driving was a dream come true. While the compact vehicle Iain had purchased for her use had all manual features, this BMW had so many bells and whistles Emilia was intimidated. Afraid to touch most of the buttons or knobs, the only things she was confident of were how to start the engine and turn on the lights and the wipers. The leather driver's seat was so comfortable, Emilia risked falling asleep at the wheel. When she stopped for the night, Emilia planned to check the glove compartment for a car manual. She wanted to learn about the various controls before doing something idiotic like setting off an alarm. Maybe she should have done that first before leaving the farm, but she'd been anxious to get away in case Shawn showed back up.

She'd been driving for several hours and was now in Ohio. The route had changed from I-80 W to I-90 W. Since Emilia was up half the night, she planned to take the next exit for Toledo and try to find a motel room and something to eat. Her eyes were bloodshot, and they felt like she's been caught without protection in a sandstorm. She also didn't enjoy driving after dark, so she hoped to only travel during daylight hours for the remainder of her trip to Montana. Emilia was estimating that she would arrive in Billings, Montana, sometime on Thursday, after which she planned to get her bearings. After a good night's rest, she would present herself to her new employers on Friday morning.

She also wanted to reread the contract she'd signed and look at the photographs of her daughter. Emilia hadn't seen them since she put the envelope in the safety deposit box. Wondering where her daughter was right now, Emilia let her mind wander. Did Elli have a good childhood? Her birthday was in February, and she would be thirty-one years old now. Did she have a husband who loved her and treated her well? Did they have children? If they did, that meant Emilia was a grandmother, and the thought made her feel old. She was forty-eight now and still capable of having children, but any pregnancy would be considered high risk at her age. Was forty-eight old enough to be a grandma? Emilia guessed so since she was very young when she gave birth to Elli.

God, she missed Michael! Emilia hoped his life had been a good one so far and that it had been filled with love. Since she would now be living in Montana, maybe she would find out what became of him. At that thought, she gave her head a shake and groaned at her own stupidity. Michael might not appreciate that. He probably had a wife and several children and grandkids, too.

Emilia guessed she wouldn't look for him after all, and she'd stop thinking about him now. She couldn't see to drive when she was crying over what was and what could never be.

Fortunate to find a room available at a motel just off the interstate, Emilia registered. Then she got back in the car and drove to a mini-market-style gas station up the street. Not wanting to take advantage of her employer's hospitality by wasting the funds she was given on expensive room service Emilia went inside to look for something to eat. After scanning the choices, she purchased a chef's style salad and mineral water for her supper. Taking the small case, she'd packed some clean clothes and toiletries in from the trunk of the car, she added her food purchases. Then, Emilia placed the case in the passenger seat for easy retrieval upon arrival back at the motel parking lot. After filling the gas tank, she made her way back to the motel and then up to her room.

Deciding on a hot shower first, Emilia scrubbed her body, then lathered her hair using the motel's complimentary shampoo. Breathing deeply, she took in the delicate floral scent. She used the conditioner, as well. When she was finished, Emilia donned her pajamas. Then she climbed on the bed with her salad and the photo album containing her daughter's pictures.

Emilia wondered what Elli was like as a child. Was she outgoing or shy like Emilia was and still is? Did the girl do well in school? Did Elli have lots of friends, or did she keep to herself? Emilia sighed, frustrated that she would never know. Closing the album, she placed it back in the envelope and set it aside. Climbing under the covers, Emilia cried for a little bit, then drifted off to sleep.

Her dream that night was of Michael holding out his hand to her. He seemed older and taller than she remembered. As Emilia placed her hand in Michael's, he pulled her tight and nuzzled the side of her neck. After nipping her earlobe, he whispered in Emilia's ear,

"I still love you, Emi. Will you marry me? I think we've waited long enough, don't you?" When he tilted her chin up and slid his tongue over her bottom lip, just like he did the first time he kissed her, Emilia woke to the sound of the alarm on her phone. It was 7:00 a.m. Time to get back on the road. It was Wednesday morning, and she had a ton of miles to cover.

After stopping at the mini-market for an egg-and-bagel sandwich and a cup of coffee, Emilia got back on the interstate and headed west. Two more days, and she'd meet her new employers. Emilia prayed they were good people. This was definitely the scariest chance Emilia had ever taken if she didn't count the stupid mistake of marrying Iain. "Montana, here I come, ready or not!" she thought.

CHAPTER 9

ON Tuesday evening, Sam Goldstein called, as promised, to give Bill an update on Emilia's progress.

"She's stopped near Toledo, Ohio, just off the interstate to spend the night at a motel. I'm still projecting that she will arrive in Billings on Thursday evening. She'll probably come to your home on Friday morning, barring any unforeseen developments, that is," Sam said. "I still have my associate keeping an eye on the Andersen farm. Shawn Jameson showed back up to do the afternoon milking. I assume he will continue to do that until Bain Andersen returns on Friday. Unless Emilia left some clue to her destination in the house, I don't believe Bain will be able to discover her whereabouts. That's even if he's interested since she's no longer living in his home. Hopefully, he'll get on with his life and forget about her. Do you want me to do any further surveillance?"

"No, I think we can conclude our business association as soon as Emilia has safely arrived here. Please continue to have the man trail her until then. I'll pay for him to fly back to Pennsylvania. Then you can send me your final report and invoice," Bill told Sam.

"Very good. I'll only call again if it appears that Emilia will arrive earlier or later than estimated. Thank you for your business. Have a good night," Sam replied, then disconnected.

After speaking to Sam, Bill headed to the bedroom to get ready for bed. Peggy was already snug under the blankets, propped up against the pillows and reading a book. Bill told her about Sam's update on Emilia's progress.

Peggy said, "I can't wait to meet her. In the pictures Sam has sent us, she looks just like an older version of Elli. It's going to be unbelievable when Mike gets a look at the woman who we've hired as our nurse. He's highly intuitive. He's going to realize that something is fishy. I'm certain of it. I can only hope he will forgive us for not telling him anything about what we've discovered."

"Well, have you changed your mind? Do you think we should tell him before Emilia gets here?" Bill asked quizzically.

"Maybe we should. Tim, Jeannie, and Sophie are flying out in the morning. Tim has promised to fly back every other weekend, work schedule permitting. We can tell Mike after they leave," Peggy responded, then gave Bill a gentle kiss on the cheek. "Call Mike and tell him to take tomorrow off. He'll need to read all of the reports and take the time to absorb everything. At least he'll have until Friday morning to prepare himself for the monumental changes that will be taking place in his life. He's going to think we're meddling, old fools."

"I think I'll take a walk over to the house and tell him in person about the day off. Maybe the fresh air will help me sleep," Bill responded. "You need to get some rest. I'm going to turn out the light."

After placing a kiss on Peggy's forehead, Bill tucked the blanket gently under her chin and told her he'd be back soon.

Slipping his feet into his well-worn but comfortable boots, Bill quietly closed the front door behind him and made his way to the stable. He wanted to visit with the horses to calm his racing thoughts.

As fate would have it, Mike was in the stable brushing Bill's prized registered American quarter horse, Midnight Blue. Known for his ability to run a super-fast quarter-mile, people from all over the country brought their mares to the Circle R for stud service.

"Bill, what are you still doing up?" Mike asked him.

"Have things on my mind and can't sleep. I was headed over to your place but made a detour to visit the horses," Bill responded.

"What do you need to tell me, Bill? You've been preoccupied since our meeting this morning. Spill. What else haven't you told me? Get it off your chest so you can sleep," Mike replied.

"You probably won't sleep after I tell you. I wanted to wait until tomorrow. I was coming to tell you to take the day off tomorrow after Tim leaves," Bill said.

"Okay, that alone would have kept me up all night. I've never taken two days off in a row, and you know it. Let me have it. I'd rather be awake over whatever it is you're going to tell me than over the fact that I need to take tomorrow off waiting for you to tell me. Give it up."

"Let's go to the house. You're going to need to sit down," Bill said with a grimace.

CHAPTER 10

"ARE you worse than you led Tim and me to believe, Bill? You have to come clean, so we know what to expect, and be there for both you and Peggy. I'm worried. Please tell me what's going on," Mike demanded.

"No, I've told you everything. The home health care nurse that is coming will know how to handle the situation. It would be best if you took your cues from her," Bill responded. "Look, I don't know how to tell you this. You're going to be very angry and hurt. Just remember, Peggy and I haven't known about your part in this for very long. Get us a beer. We're going to need one."

After Mike grabbed a couple of bottles out of the refrigerator, he handed one to Bill. "You said something about my part in whatever you're going to say. Do you think I've been embezzling from the ranch? Are you going to fire me after all?"

"No, absolutely not. All right, stop trying to guess. It's about the woman who is coming, and about you, and Elli," Bill said. Then he sighed.

"I don't understand. What would some nurse you hired from Pennsylvania have to do with Elli or me, for that matter?" Mike questioned.

"You already know that we discovered that Elli's parents weren't my son and his wife and that my ex-wife Eloise's daughter gave birth to Elli."

Mike nodded his head, yes. He was more confused than ever. "What does that have to do with the nurse and me?" he asked.

Bill cleared his throat, then admitted, "The sixteen-year-old girl who gave birth to Elli thirty-one years ago was Eloise's daughter. Her name is Emilia Addison Mackinsey."

Jumping to his feet, Mike started to pace and pull at his hair. He was smart enough to be able to do the math. "Are you telling me that Emi had my baby and that baby is Elli? She is my daughter, Bill?"

"Yes, Elli is your daughter. Now, before you slug me for not telling you, remember I said that I've only known for two weeks that you are Elli's father. Now, sit down and drink your beer, Mike. There's more to the story."

"More? How could there possibly be more? Elli's going to be devastated when she finds out James and Lilianne weren't her real parents and that her grandmother threw her away to save herself some embarrassment. That's the same thing your son and daughter-in-law tried to do to Jessica. This whole situation sucks, Bill. What's the rest of it? I need to know. Don't hold back."

"Let me drink my beer first in case you decide to toss me out when I've finished saying my piece," Bill grimaced. As he lifted the bottle to his mouth, he said, "I enjoy a nice cold beer. I hope it helps me sleep tonight."

Mike sat there stunned, and his mind was racing. Emi had his baby because he didn't use protection the last time, they were together. Mike got her pregnant, and he wasn't there to take care of her and be a father to their baby. What kind of man did that make him? Mike refused to look at Bill. He hung his head in shame and tried not to cry out of frustration and humiliation.

As Mike fought to get his emotions under control, he cleared his throat, "This has been an unbelievable bitch of a day. I found out the woman and man I love most in this world are both dying and that I'm the lowest kind of vermin for abandoning my pregnant girlfriend when she was sixteen years old. I've come to love a young woman as a daughter. Now I find out she is my real daughter, but she doesn't know that. When she finds out, Elli's going to hate me. Can there be anything else? Wait. How does your home health care nurse fit into this? Is she the midwife who delivered Elli?"

"Ummm…are you certain you don't want to drink that beer?" Bill responded.

When Mike shook his head vehemently, Bill said, "Well, it was worth a try. Remember, no hitting a dying old man."

"That comment is in poor taste," Mike groaned. "Get on with it before I actually consider punching you."

"When I discovered that Elli wasn't my granddaughter, I hired a private investigator. I've been receiving regular reports. It took a while for him to track Eloise's movements and discover her daughter's name. Once he knew the girl's name, he had difficulty finding anyone who went to school with Emilia that remembered any details about her. Also, Eloise had moved several times. The private eye finally discovered that she'd moved to a small town in western Pennsylvania north of Pittsburgh in Butler County when she found out Emilia was pregnant. Emilia was locked in her bedroom for eight months until she gave birth. Eloise hired a midwife to deliver your daughter, Mike. That meant that no one knew anything about the baby's existence except that midwife."

At that, Mike was on his feet again. "I knew Emi's mom was a bitch. She wouldn't let Emi have any friends. God, I loved that girl. I promised I'd come back for her after I graduated, and I did try to find her. I told her I'd love her for the rest of my life, and I meant it. She's the reason I've never married another woman."

Bill nodded his head in understanding before continuing, "When the private investigator finally found the mid-wife in question, what she told him came as a shock. She said that Eloise paid her extremely well to keep her mouth shut, but the woman has always been ashamed for not telling the authorities. She said that as soon as

Emilia gave birth, Eloise took the baby away. The mid-wife saw James and Lilianne leave the house with the infant. She told the investigator that Emilia never got to see the baby and didn't even know what sex the child was. When James returned to New Jersey, he had his attorney file a fraudulent birth certificate showing James and his wife as the birth parents. Eloise agreed to send James one thousand dollars every month for Elli's care. I think he was in it for the money. He was extremely avaricious. So, I doubt very much that James spent the money on Elli. Anyway, in exchange, Eloise figured her daughter got her life back on track minus the stigma of being branded an unwed mother."

"This story gets worse and worse. I feel like a worm. Emi should never have needed to deal with any of that. All of this is my fault," Mike winced.

"No, it's not. Would you please sit? You're making me dizzy with all the pacing around the room," Bill admonished. "Let me tell you the rest, and then I'll get out of your hair. I'll give you all of the official reports from the private investigator tomorrow so that you can read them."

"Okay, tell me the rest," Mike pleaded.

"After Emilia gave birth, she went back to school and graduated when she was nineteen. To hide the pain of her loss, she threw herself into her studies. As a result of her excellent grades, Emilia received a scholarship to a local college. She got her degree at the age of twenty-three. Unfortunately, Eloise made Emilia move out of her apartment the day after Emilia graduated. With no money or job, Emilia had nowhere to go. So, she was ripe for the man she ran into in a grocery store. His name was Iain Andersen. According to the detective, Iain owned a dairy farm with his brother. He took Emilia to his home and convinced her to marry him. It was probably the worst mistake of her life."

"Oh, what could be worse than me abandoning her at the most important time in her life? She must hate me, too," Mike declared.

"Andersen was much worse. Emilia has spent the last twenty-five years being verbally and mentally abused and isolated without friends. Her husband and brother-in-law shared women with their friends. Andersen's only saving grace is that he refused to share Emilia until he died four days ago. Before he passed away, he gave her to his brother."

"What the hell! What do you mean he gave Emi to his brother? Where is she? I have to go to her, Bill."

"That's the other part of what I have to tell you. Emilia is the certified home health care nurse that I've hired to take care of Peggy and me. She's on her way here from Pennsylvania. According to the private investigator following her, Emilia stopped near Toledo, Ohio, this evening. He estimates that she should arrive in Billings on Thursday evening. He believes she'll come to the ranch on Friday morning."

"I can't believe this. Emi's on her way here? What about the brother-in-law? He just let her go?" Mike was back on his feet again and pulling at his hair.

"The brother-in-law's name is Bain. He left right after the repast for Iain on Monday to deliver a bull to an Indiana farm. He won't be home until Friday. So, he doesn't know that Emilia has left. She's safe, Mike. We got her out of that bad situation just in time. Now, I'm going to bed. You get some rest. Things are going to be a little bit crazy until we get everything sorted out. I'll get you those reports tomorrow. They go into more detail. I just gave you the highlights." Then Bill left Mike alone with his thoughts and emotions all tangled up in knots.

After dumping his beer down the kitchen sink, Mike poured himself a shot of whiskey. He felt like getting drunk to drown his feelings of inadequacy. He considered himself the lowest life form on the planet. Emi was on her way here, and Mike had caused her years of heartache. Then there was Elli. Finding out about all of this was going to blow up her world. Nothing was what she believed it to be. Mike shook his head, "Man, I've fucked up! I think I'll go crawl under a rock."

After a few more shots, Mike had numbed his brain sufficiently that he thought he might be able to get a few hours of sleep. Stumbling to his bed, Mike flopped face down. He didn't feel that he deserved to be comfortable, so he'd just lie there fully clothed, smelling of the horse he groomed before Bill blew up his life.

After tossing and turning, Mike finally fell into a deep sleep and dreamed of Emi lying broken against a pile of rocks. It reminded Mike of the outcropping behind the line cabin. Mike heard Emi groan in pain as some guy lifted her gently into his arms and carried her down the slope. Once inside the cabin, he laid her on one of the bunks.

Mike made a grab for the guy in his dream, but the man pushed Mike away and yelled, "Emilia's mine, so fuck off! If I can't have her, nobody can." Mike woke up soaked in sweat and screaming, "Noooo!"

CHAPTER 11

PRAYING that the nightmare he'd had wasn't a foreshadowing of events, Mike decided not to go back to sleep. It was already 4:00 a.m. Another hour wasn't going to help, and he was not interested in having another bad dream. Mike's stomach was sour from the whiskey he'd polished off, and his head was pounding. It wasn't anything Mike felt he didn't deserve, however.

After drinking a full glass of water and downing several pills for his headache, Mike tugged on his boots and hat and headed over to the stable. It was still dark out, but the moon cast enough light to ride the trail towards the ranch hands' line cabin. It sat in the foothills, and there was a pristine pond nearby.

When Mike reached the cabin, it was almost 5:00 a.m. He decided to make a quick perusal and then head back to the house. He wanted to spend time with Tim before he flew his family back to Oregon. Then Mike would talk to Bill, grab those reports from the detective that Bill promised him, and gather up some supplies for a couple of days. When he knew that Emi had arrived safely in Billings, Mike would return to the cabin to hide.

Mike was acting cowardly, but he wanted to give Emi a few days to establish a routine before facing her. Mike needed to remember to tell Bill to hide the photographs of Elli until they had a chance to sit down with Emi and explain. What a mess!

Mike checked the shelves in the cabin to see what provisions he'd need to bring, then grabbed a towel and shucked his clothes. Running down the slope, buck-ass naked, Mike dropped the towel and hit the water. The pond was spring-fed and ice-cold. Coming to the surface, Mike let out a whoop. After swimming several laps, he climbed out, toweled off, and nonchalantly headed back to the cabin to get dressed. That swim cleared out the cobwebs in his brain, and the ice-cold water cured his raging libido. Mike believed he was prepared for what was to come. Or so he thought!

Mike took his time riding back to the ranch house. The horse knew the way, so Mike let his mind wander. Maybe, if Emi forgave him, he could convince her to spend some time alone so they could get to know each other again. He wouldn't mind getting her to skinny-dip in the pond, either. That's if she didn't hate Mike's guts. He couldn't imagine what her life had been like being married to a man who controlled her just like her mother had. Would there be anything left of the shy, sweet girl that Mike fell in love with, or did her husband destroy her?

After Mike arrived back at the stable, he dismounted and tied up the horse to remove the saddle. She was the gentle sorrel mare that Mike taught Elli to ride on. Mike would love to be able to teach his grandchildren. Wow! It just hit him. He had grandchildren and a son-in-law. He was a grandfather. That knowledge made him feel old. Mike had so much to make up for. Unbelievable! While he was at the cabin, he'd have even more to think about. Plus, he'd be pining for Emi while waiting for an opportunity. He wanted to claim her and make her his wife.

Jake showed up while Mike was lost in his thoughts. "Good Morning, boss. Let me take care of Cheyenne for you. I've done most of the chores in the stable already."

"Thanks, Jake. I appreciate that. I'm afraid my mind is on other things right now," Mike told him.

"Mr. Willis, is everything all right? Mr. and Mrs. Roberts seem off somehow. They don't seem like their normal selves. Do you know what I mean?" Jake asked.

"I can't talk about that right now, Jake, but I'll be having a discussion with the ranch hands in a few days. Try not to worry. All right? There'll be a few changes around here, but your summer job is safe. You're a good man and a hard worker."

"Thank you, Mr. Willis. If there's anything I can do to help, please let me know. Tom feels the same way, I'm sure."

"Your offer is much appreciated, Jake. I'm going to head up to the main house. Take good care of Cheyenne. I'm going to be spending a few days at the line cabin, so I would appreciate it if you and Tom could take care of the stable while I'm gone."

"Yes, sir. I'd like that. Thanks again, Mr. Willis. I love working here."

126

Nodding his head at the young man, Mike turned and strode away.

Tim and Jeannie were making breakfast when Mike entered the kitchen.

"Good Morning. What time are you heading out?" Mike asked.

"Just as soon as we finish eating. Sophie is getting a shower and packing up. Bill and Peggy haven't come out of their room yet," Jeannie responded.

"I'm worried sick. I don't know if I'm strong enough to watch both suffer and die," Tim told Mike. "This isn't fair. They have been so good to me."

"We'll be there for both of them, Tim. It's all we can do. What can I do to help with the meal prep?" Mike asked to change the subject.

Jeannie spoke up, "You can put the silverware and napkins on the table. Things are almost finished. Tim, maybe you should check on your aunt and uncle to let them know that breakfast is ready. Oh, and tell Sophie to get a move on, too."

Everyone was somewhat subdued and lost in thought during the meal. Finally, Tim told them, "We hate to eat and run, but we need to get a move on."

"That's fine, Tim. I'll clean up. You should spend some time with Bill and Peggy with just your family before you head out." Shaking his hand, Mike pulled Tim into a man-hug and whispered, "We'll get through this."

After Mike cleaned up from breakfast, he went in search of Bill. He found him sitting with Peggy in front of the fireplace in the living room. Peggy was bundled up in a blanket.

"Is there anything I can get either one of you?" Mike inquired.

"No, Mike, I think we're both good. Did you sleep at all last night?" Bill asked.

"Maybe two hours. I had a bad nightmare that woke me up at four. Took a ride out to the line shack. If it's all the same to you, as soon as your detective calls to let you know Emi is in Billings, I'm going to spend a few days at the cabin. Give Emi a chance to settle in and get a feel for how she will manage your care before she has to deal with seeing me again after thirty-two years. I don't want to overwhelm her."

Bill seemed to be thinking about Mike's suggestion, then replied, "I think that may be a sensible course of action. Here are all of the files on Sam Goldstein's investigations. Take them with you and read them over. Let me know if you have any questions or anything else you think Sam should check. If you ride out Friday morning, how long do you intend to stay away?"

"Sunday night sound good? I'll come to the house after breakfast Monday morning. What do you think, Peggy?"

"I think that's a sound plan. I'm tired. I'm going to go lie down. There's been too much excitement. Come get me when you're ready for lunch."

"Come on, my love, I'll tuck you in," Bill responded as he took Peggy's hand and helped her from the room.

CHAPTER 12

"FINALLY, Billings, Montana." Emilia breathed a sigh of relief. "I've made it!" It was Thursday evening. She was hungry, tired, and felt grimy. A hot bath, a good meal, and a soft bed would feel good, but not necessarily in that order.

Having spent very little of the money that Mr. Goldstein gave her, Emilia intended to splurge. Room service. Maybe a nice steak and baked potato with sour cream and a sundae for dessert.

Dinner finished, Emilia licked her spoon clean to get the last bit of chocolate syrup from her ice cream sundae. Eyeing the bowl, she wondered if her tongue was long enough to lick that, too. No, maybe not. She was forty-eight years old, after all. Only children would do that, right? With a giggle, Emilia thought, "What the heck," licked the bowl and managed to smear chocolate on the tip of her nose. That made her laugh outright.

This was the happiest Emilia had felt since she was sixteen and spending time with Michael. She remembered, "That's the last time I had an ice cream sundae, too. Michael bought one for me after school, and then we went to my house and made love."

Flopping back on her pillow, she stared at the ceiling and let her mind wander to that moment in time. Michael had just made love to her. They were spooned together on her bed, and he was running his fingers through her hair over and over. Leaning in, he whispered, "I love how you feel, Emi, tucked up next to me. Will you marry me? I want you to be mine for always?"

As a tear slid down her cheek, Emilia murmured, "But you left me, Michael. I wanted to be yours for the rest of our lives."

Taking the photo album out of the manila envelope, she worked her way through the pages, gazing upon the face of the beautiful baby girl she and Michael made together.

Then Emilia cried herself to sleep.

CHAPTER 13

S AMUEL Goldstein called William Roberts at 7:45 on Thursday evening with an update. "Hi, Mr. Roberts. I hope that I'm not calling too late or at an inconvenient time."

"Oh, for heaven's sakes, Sam," Bill admonished. "I think after all these years, you can call me Bill. I have you on speaker. Has Emilia arrived in Billings?"

"Yes, sir, she just checked into a room at an inn on Airport Road. My associate said she looked exhausted when she exited the vehicle in the inn's parking lot. I've run a check. She's in room 302 and has ordered room service. So, I'd venture to say that she's settling in for the night."

"All right, Sam, thank you for the update. Is your man spending the night, or is he already on his way to the airport for a return flight to Pennsylvania?" Bill asked.

"He's taken a room at the same inn as Mrs. Andersen, and he has a flight out in the morning," Sam replied.

"All right then, add the cost of his meals and hotel room to my invoice. Have a good night, Sam, and thank you again for everything you've done for me and mine," Bill responded, and then the call was disconnected.

Bill turned to Mike and asked, "Mike, you caught all that. Are you still headed to the cabin in the morning?"

"Yes, sir, but I can't promise that you won't catch me skulking around trying to catch a glimpse of Emi," Mike returned with a grin.

"Hah, you're funny. I'll tell the ranch hands to shoot on sight," Bill laughed.

"I'll have to remember to wear my bulletproof Stetson, then. I'm off to check the horses, and then I'm going to hit the sack. I haven't been sleeping well. You can only imagine why," Mike said.

"Mike, you need to stop beating yourself up over what's happened. It's what it was supposed to be. All will come right. I have every faith. Now go rest and enjoy your couple of days at the cabin."

Mike bid Bill good night and wandered out to the stable. The horses never ceased to calm his racing thoughts when he was stressed. He took Cinnamon out of her stall, secured her halter, and crooned to her in a soothing voice as he ran the brush over her sides. Finished with the rest of the body, he used soft strokes over the cheeks, ears, nose, and the top of the head. After separating some tangles in the mane and tail with his fingers, Mike groomed the mane with a wide-toothed mane comb and used the dandy brush on the horse's tail.

After leading Cinnamon back into her stall, Mike leaned his head against her flank and stroked her gently. Then, he thanked the horse for helping to soothe his mind. Latching the stall door, he turned out the light and made his way to the house he'd called home for twelve years.

Mike spent the next several hours cleaning the rooms from top to bottom. Even though the house was always neat, Mike didn't want Emi to think she was getting involved with a slob. That was if he got the chance to invite her into the house and hopefully into his bed.

Thoughts of Emi had him all worked up, as usual, so he let his mind wander to thoughts of her naked beneath him while he eased the painful erection, he was sporting. Then he took a shower, fell into bed, and slept like a log for the first time in days. When the alarm went off at 5:00 on Friday morning, Mike grabbed his pack, saddled up Cheyenne, and headed out. He'd spend the next few days reading over Samuel Goldstein's reports about Emilia and Elli and taking cold baths in the spring-fed pond. That alone should keep his raging libido in check. He hadn't been this horny in years.

Mike held the horse to a walk as he pondered the changes he was facing. He now had a daughter, a son-in-law, and six grandchildren, thanks to Emi. Mike owed her so much and was so very sorry for leaving her behind. He'd spend the rest of his life making it up to her if she'd let him.

CHAPTER 14

EMILIA'S alarm sounded at 6:30 a.m. on Friday morning. Having slept fitfully, she groaned and pulled her pillow over her head for a few moments. She'd tossed and turned all night. The few hours of sleep she'd gotten were filled with nightmares about Bain, the very last person she wanted to think about. Then she realized it was Friday and Bain would be home today. He'd discover that she was gone. Panicked at the thought, her mind raced over everything she'd done before she left the farmhouse in Pennsylvania for the very last time on Tuesday. Did she forget anything that would give Bain a clue as to her current whereabouts? No, she didn't think so. Then she chided herself for being silly. Why would Bain even care that she'd left?

It was time to get up and get going. Emilia had people waiting on her who needed her help to manage their illnesses. She'd been helping people for twenty-five years. Some had suffered injuries who just required her assistance until they could get back on their feet. Others had debilitating illnesses or were facing the end of their lives. The couple she was now employed by were facing this last situation. Emilia vowed to make their final days as comfortable as possible and to help their loved ones cope with what they were going to face during the process, too.

Emilia had ordered breakfast through room service to be delivered at 7:30, so she hopped off the bed and slipped into the bathroom. The quick shower helped wake her up. Then, she straightened up the bed and the room. Emilia knew that it was silly of her. The hotel staff would be stripping the bed and cleaning the room after she vacated. Doing it out of habit, Emilia couldn't help herself. She would be mortified if anyone thought she was a slob, anyway. Emilia also tidied up the bathroom and placed the used towels in a neat pile on the sink. She didn't have any experience, having never stayed in a hotel before. Believing the hotel staff probably worked very hard, Emilia wanted to make their jobs easier for them. Then she packed up all of her belongings so she'd be able to leave as soon as she was finished eating.

Her meal was delivered promptly at 7:30, and she left a generous tip. The food was excellent. She had ordered scrambled eggs, sausage, toast, tea, and orange juice. That was way more food than Emilia typically ate, but she didn't know what the day would bring, and it felt good to pamper herself for the first time ever. After all, she was no longer controlled by anyone. She would be making the decisions about her life from now on, not her mother or her controlling husband.

Having read the manual for her new car, she was confident that she understood how to program the Circle R Ranch address into the navigation system. She didn't want to get lost in Billings. She would probably never find her way out of the city if she did. That meant her nightmare the previous night would come true. She didn't want to end up going the wrong way on one-way streets, running stop signs, and have people yelling and swearing at her when she narrowly missed running them down.

Finished with her meal, she stacked the dishes on the tray, used the bathroom, and brushed her teeth. Taking one last look around the room and peeking under the bed to be sure she hadn't dropped anything she grabbed her purse and suitcase and made her way to the lobby of the hotel. After returning her keycard, Emilia found the BMW in the parking lot. She took a few minutes to program the GPS with her destination, and then she was on her way.

Emilia found the drive enjoyable while taking in the beauty of the countryside. In no time at all, the GPS said she had reached her final destination. The pleasant computerized voice told her that she was supposed to make a turn fifty feet on the left. Turning into the gravel drive as directed, the road took her under an arched sign confirming that this was indeed the Circle R Ranch. Fenced fields on each side of the driveway contained cattle grazing in the sun. She slowed her car to get a better look. Then stopped to get out when she noticed a couple of men working on a section of the fence's railing. The sight made her blood hum. Boy, they grew them tall and handsome in Montana. One of the men paused and made his way over to where she stood admiring the view.

"Good Morning. I didn't mean to interrupt your work. I just stopped to admire the animals," Emilia fibbed. She didn't want him to know she was actually ogling him. He was tall, very tall, with light brown hair covered by a cowboy hat with a wide brim, jeans, short-sleeved Henley shirt, and scuffed boots. The jeans and shirt hugged a well-muscled, lean body. He looked to be slightly younger than Emilia's forty-eight years. She wondered if he liked older women.

"Morning, beautiful. Are you lost?" the cowboy asked. His blue eyes twinkled, and he grinned mischievously.

Taken aback at being called beautiful, Emilia blushed, "Umm…No. Not lost. At least, I don't think so since the sign said this is the Circle R. I've been hired by the Roberts as a home health care nurse. So, I hope to be staying here for a while. My name's Emilia Andersen."

"Ah, yes, I'm Sean Hannity, one of the ranch hands. Mike told us you would be arriving this morning. Just follow the drive. It'll take you right to the main house. I think Bill and Peggy are expecting you. Have a good day, little lady."

Then he tipped his hat, gave Emilia a brilliant smile, and turned away. When he swaggered back to where the other ranch hand was leaning against the railing, the guy poked Sean in the ribs and started to tease him. Emilia could hear Sean say, "Well, she is beautiful. I'll need to get to know her better if the boss doesn't nix it." When he noticed that she was still standing there gazing at him quizzically, he tipped his hat at her in acknowledgment.

Blushing at the comment and being caught eavesdropping on their conversation, Emilia hastily got back in the car, waved, and continued down the drive. She looked in the rearview mirror and noticed Sean watching her progress as she drove away. Having a man admire her gave her low self-esteem a boast. No one had appreciated her looks in a long time if you didn't count Bain, and she definitely wasn't going to count him.

When Emilia pulled up in front of the ranch house, she was confident that her jaw dropped. Her mouth agape, she took in the home made of logs stained a honey oak color and its beautifully arched entryway surrounded by cut stone. Large arched stained-glass windows flanked both sides. Carved oak doors with brass knockers provided entrance to the interior. She couldn't imagine living here all the time. The place was extraordinary.

Making her way to the door, she used the brass knocker to announce herself. As she stood there glancing around, a man who looked to be in his late eighties opened the door and said, "Hello, you must be Emilia Andersen. I'm William Roberts. You can call me Bill. Please come in. We've been expecting you." Then he stood aside so that Emilia could enter.

As she stepped into the foyer, Emilia took in the richness of the interior. The entryway opened on both sides to huge rooms. There was what appeared to be a living room to the right. On the left was a dining room with an ornate table with massive carved legs and upholstered chairs. The rooms had vaulted ceilings adorned with antlered ceiling fans, and hardwood buffed to a high sheen covered the floors. Magnificent stone fireplaces graced the sidewalls.

Bill placed his hand on Emilia's arm and guided her to the right towards the living room. It contained comfortable looking burgundy, tufted-leather sofas, and armchairs adorned with wood trim. Gray accent rugs lay scattered on the floor. Numerous pale almond throw pillows would make the room look very casual if it weren't for the beautiful baby grand piano that graced the corner of the room.

Leading Emilia to an elderly woman sitting on the sofa, Bill introduced her as his wife, Peggy. As Emilia clasped the woman's frail hand in hers, she noticed the jaundiced look of Peggy's skin and eyes. She looked like she had recently lost a lot of weight, and her hair looked lifeless. Emilia also noticed that Peggy had been scratching at her skin. Emilia acknowledged these signs of pancreatic cancer the woman had been diagnosed with.

"Welcome to our home. May I call you Emi?" Peggy asked.

"Only one other person has ever called me Emi. He was a young man that I knew in high school. I was very much in love with him, but then his family moved away. I never got to see him again. Actually, they moved to Montana. So, it's a small world." Emilia winced, "Sorry, I'm nervous and babbling. Emi will be fine. Thank you. Oh, before I forget, I want to return the balance of the money you advanced for my trip. I will expect to reimburse you for what I actually spent, as well."

"That is not necessary," Bill spoke up. "That belongs to you in addition to the car."

"I don't know what to say," Emilia responded. "Other than I wish we could have met under better circumstances."

Peggy, Bill, and Emilia spent the next several hours getting to know each other. She told them about her life in Pennsylvania and some of the patients she'd had the privilege of taking care of. Emilia glossed over her early years as a child and her marriage, mainly because those subjects held painful memories that Emilia didn't wish to share. Although she did tell them about her husband's cancer and her need to care for him as the illness progressed.

Peggy and Bill both expressed their sentiments for Emilia's recent loss. They thanked her for coming so quickly to assist them because they were very grateful.

"I'm the one who is grateful," Emilia responded. "The home I was living in belongs to my brother-in-law. He's not married, and I did not feel comfortable staying there alone with him. The timing of your offer of employment was very fortuitous. I intend to work very hard to meet any expectations you have in helping both of you deal with your illnesses."

Then they discussed what Emilia's role would be in their care and duties. They also hoped she would consider managing the running of the household. After, Bill showed Emilia where she would be sleeping.

"Do you need assistance with moving your belongings into your room?" Bill asked. "I can get one of the ranch hands to unload the car if you'd like."

"I think I can handle that. I don't have much. Should I come in through a different entry?"

"There's another door behind the house. That one is closer to the bedroom you will be using. You can just pull around back." Bill told her. "I'll take Peggy to our room for a nap while you take care of your things. Then we can eat lunch, and I'll tell you a little about some of the people you'll be meeting in the next few weeks. After, I'll take you on a tour of the house and the grounds. How does that sound?"

"Very good. Again, thank you for allowing me into your home," Emilia said. Then she went out to the car and drove around back to begin unloading the trunk. She couldn't believe she was being given a chance to live here.

CHAPTER 15

AFTER dropping his friend, Harry, off, Bain pulled into the drive next to the barn at 2:34, Friday afternoon. He'd made good time, urged on by the need to get back to Emilia. Just thinking about her had him so riled up while he was away that Bain was in danger of dying of blue balls. He had to keep a sweatshirt draped over the tent in his pants to hide his erection from his friend.

Bain had spent much of the trip remembering his childhood growing up on the family farm with his twin brother, Iain. Only twenty-four minutes apart in age, they were close. Iain was great at getting into mischief while growing up, most of which Bain took the blame for. After their mother and baby sister died while their mother was in labor, their father became very withdrawn and full of anger.

So, he wasn't lenient when it came to doling out punishment for transgressions.

When Iain brought Emilia home, Bain wished he wasn't so fond of his little brother. Bain wanted the woman badly. She was everything Bain knew he wanted for his wife but had never found. It was his own fault since most of that looking was done in barrooms. When the little shit snuck off to marry Emilia at the Justice of the Peace, Bain knew he'd lost his chance. He wouldn't do anything to hurt Iain and interfere with his marriage.

Swinging the truck and trailer around, Bain backed up to the holding pen to unload his new bull. The bull had an excellent lineage and good conformation, so Bain was pleased with his purchase. Grinning, he whistled while he got the bull settled into his new pen. Bain expected to earn a lot of money with the sale of the animals produced from his breeding program.

As soon as he was finished, Bain planned to take a shower and then get better acquainted with his sister-in-law, or should he say his bride-to-be? Shawn Jameson was supposed to take care of the milking for the rest of the week to allow Bain some time off, supposedly to mourn his brother's death. Bain intended to do that mourning by making love to his brother's widow.

Fed, watered, and bedded down, Bain left the bull in his stall. After checking the dairy herd, the milk house, and the barn to be sure Shawn was doing a good job, Bain made his way to the house. Surprised to find the door locked, Bain fished the keyring out of his pocket and unlocked the door. He toed off his work boots against the baseboard in the entryway and yelled out.

"Hi, honey! I'm home."

Bain was met with silence and stale air as if the house had been shut up for days. Frowning, he moved further into the kitchen, where he discovered the note and money he'd left for Emilia. They lay exactly where he'd placed them Monday night. Next to them was a pile of keys and a credit card. Picking the keys up, he turned them over in his hands. Then the significance of the additional items laying on his kitchen counter registered.

"Son of a Bitch!" he yelled. "Emilia, where are you? Don't hide from me."

After taking the stairs to the second floor two at a time, Bain stormed down the hall and threw open the door to the master bedroom.

The room was neat but empty of the woman he sought. Tearing open the dresser and closet doors, Bain was met with empty hangars and drawers devoid of feminine clothing. Then he noticed the ring and Emilia's watch laying on top of the dresser. He recognized the wedding band as the one that belonged to his grandmother and then his mother. That ring had graced the hand of Emilia Andersen for the last twenty-five years. The watch was the only gift that Bain knew his stingy brother had ever given his bride. By this point, Bain's emotions were in turmoil. He was a fool, leaving right after the repast. He should have claimed Emilia first, but now he'd lost his chance. Emilia had slipped his grasp and gotten away.

Letting out a bellow, he screamed, "EMILIA!"

Rushing from the room, he slammed the door behind him. He would find Emilia if it was the last thing he ever did and bring her home. She belonged to him now. It was time she realized that.

Searching the rest of the house produced the same results. Emilia's few possessions were gone. She hadn't taken anything else. Bain could see the car she used for work sitting in the driveway.

When Shawn Jameson pulled into the farmyard to do the milking chores at 3:37 p.m., Bain ran out the door, slamming it shut behind him. By the time Shawn had exited his vehicle, Bain had him by the throat and pushed up against the door frame.

"Where's Emilia? What did you do with her? I told you she's mine now and not to touch her," Bain bellowed as spittle flew from his mouth.

Shawn was four inches shorter than Bain and forty pounds lighter. Shawn had to push against Bain's arms to get him to loosen his hold enough so Shawn could drag some air into his lungs.

"I haven't seen Emilia since the repast, and there haven't been any signs of life in the house since Tuesday morning when I did the milking. I knocked on the door to check on her and to find out if she needed anything, but she didn't answer. Some fancy suit showed up in a BMW sedan when I was leaving," Shawn quavered.

"Fuck!" was Bain's response. "Who would be coming to the farm in a BMW? She wasn't supposed to work again for a couple of weeks to give herself time to grieve. She doesn't have any relatives to go to, and she didn't take the car. Where the fuck can she be?"

"Don't ask me. Did Emilia even have any money? I know your brother was tight-fisted and took everything she made. Maybe you could start with her place of employment? If she told anyone where she was going, I would think they would be the ones to ask," Shawn stammered. He was afraid of Bain for an excellent reason. Bain was a huge man. Shawn didn't blame Emilia if she took off for parts unknown. He'd heard about the size of Bain's dick from some of the women they'd shared. Emilia was tiny. There was no way she'd be able to service someone that big and be able to walk straight afterward.

Bain let go of Shawn and stepped back. "Sorry, I got rough. Went a little crazy for a minute or two. I have to find her. She's going to be my wife, whether she likes it or not. That was a good idea you had. I might need you to take care of things around here for a while. Can you handle that, Shawn? You can stay in the house and take care of that, too, until I come back with Emilia. That will save you the bother of driving back and forth from your Mom's place."

Shawn nodded his head, yes. "I can do that for you, Bain. Your brother was my best friend. I'll go milk the cows now. Go and find your woman." Then Shawn headed for the barn, relieved to put some distance between himself and Bain. He felt kind of bad for Emilia in giving Bain an idea where to start his search. Shawn wouldn't wish Bain on any woman. Maybe he shouldn't share the women he picked up in bars anymore, either. If Shawn got out of this situation without taking a beating, he'd avoid Bain's company from now on.

Bain went back into the house. Grabbing the note, he'd left for Emilia on the kitchen counter, he balled it up angrily and tossed it in the trash. Bain was so looking forward to making love to Emilia. Maybe he should have taken things slowly and not pushed her. Bain had scared her off. He'd been in love with Emilia since the minute his brother brought her home. Bain spent the last twenty-five years of his life watching his brother treat Emilia like shit. He'd had to listen to Iain banging her in the next room every single night while Bain was forced to jack off to the thought of having Emilia beneath him, instead. Iain cheated on her, too, and never gave her any children. Bain knew Emilia was meant to be a mother. She had so much love to offer. Bain never intended to cheat on Emilia if he was afforded the opportunity of marrying her.

Bain grabbed the phone off the hook and dialed information. He knew the name of the agency that provided Emilia's clients. When a young woman answered the call, Bain grinned because he knew he was in luck. She didn't sound very bright.

"Hello, this is Bain Andersen. I need some information concerning my sister-in-law, Emilia Andersen. I need to know her current address. My attorney has some documents that she needs to sign concerning her late husband's estate. He needs to mail those documents to her."

The woman was delighted to supply the information Bain had requested. After writing the address on a piece of paper, Bain thanked her and hung up.

"What the fuck are you doing in Montana, Emilia?" Bain questioned the silent house.

His next call was to an acquaintance who dealt in drugs and guns but was good at getting whatever a client required. Bain asked him about chloroform, but the dealer laughed.

"It doesn't work like the utter nonsense you see in the movies. You have to place a chloroform-soaked rag over your victim's nose and mouth and hold it there for more than five minutes to knock them out. Then it only works for as long as it's applied. I have something that'll work really fast. It's considered a date rape drug, but it can be injected, and it works, instantly."

When the dealer told Bain he could supply him with just what he needed to get the job done, Bain smiled. "I'll be by to pick it up in a half-hour."

Bain's final call was to the airport to book a flight to Billings, Montana. He was in luck because there was a flight leaving in three hours. Bain booked the last available seat. After hanging up, he ran upstairs to throw some clothes and toiletries in a backpack.

Then he went out to tell Shawn that he wouldn't be home for a while and handed him the key to the house. "Take care of things until I'm back," he said.

After a stop at the bank, Bain picked up a small package from the drug dealer containing what looked like an insulin kit for diabetics. Then, he was on his way to the airport to catch his flight.

CHAPTER 16

ELLI startled awake. It was early. Very early. She glanced at the clock. Yup! It was 3:30 a.m. Elli realized that it was Saturday morning. It was a day for sleeping late, not waking up early. So, what the heck!

Blair used to get up to milk the cows at 3:30 and always kissed Elli awake to make love before he went out to do the chores. The dairy herd was gone now, and so was Blair, but Elli often woke up, anyway, just long enough to realize she would always miss her late husband. Then she usually went right back to sleep. Not today!

This time she'd had another one of her dreams or visions or nightmares. She wasn't sure what she should call them. This one was much like the first one she'd had in February, right after the family returned from a visit to Montana to see her grandparents and Mike. In each, Blair was making love to her. He told her how much he missed her, the children, and Tyler. Then he warned her to rely on Tyler's love. That would give her the strength to deal with what would be happening soon. Truth be told, Elli was very terrified. What was going to happen? Was she going to lose another one of the people she loved? She couldn't deal with the thought of that happening. She might not survive emotionally.

Blair was so real in the dreams. Elli was positive. If the visions lasted just a little bit longer, she would be able to grab him, hold on tight, and pull Blair right back into this world of the living. That might be a problem, though. She was married to Tyler now and loved him as much or more, if that was even possible. Tyler and Blair may have been best friends from seventh grade until Blair's untimely death, but Elli didn't think they would be willing to share her.

Elli was certain the real reason for the dream was because she was so horny. She hadn't bounced back after her daughter's birth the way she did from the three prior pregnancies. Tyler was being overprotective, as usual, and doing everything possible to make her rest, including withholding sex. Elli was tired of being pampered, and she needed her husband. Not wanting to disturb his sleep, she snuggled in against him and let her mind wander to thoughts of her children.

Her oldest daughter, Jessica Blair, was a bright ray of sunshine in her parents' lives. Although only twelve years of age, she was brilliant. Elli was amazed that her beautiful baby girl would be a freshman in high school at the end of August. The triplets, Richard Blair, Peggy Lynne, and Tyler Logan, were six. The boys looked the most like their father, Richard Blair Whrite, but all four children had their father's blond hair and blue eyes. The boys had also inherited Blair's cleft chin. Elli's first husband may have been Rick to everyone else, but he would always be her beloved Blair.

Elli's fifth child, William Timothy, looked just like his father, Tyler Logan Thompson. At five years of age, Billy was as tall as the triplets and weighed just as much. Elli was confident that Billy would be into sports in high school. Tyler threw the football to all of the children, but Billy showed the most interest. That seemed strange. Tyler had been on the team, but it was Blair who was offered a football scholarship in college. A scholarship which he'd turned down because he wanted to be a farmer. If Billy wanted to join the football team in high school like his dad, Elli would be sitting in the stands cheering him on at the games.

Billy was also as intelligent as Jessica, having exceeded the typical milestones for children his age. He was usually in charge of any imaginative play that required constructing or building forts, tunnels, bridges, and treehouses. The triplets were happy to follow his lead.

On the other hand, the triplets adored tossing a baseball to each other. Tyler, noticing, purchased gloves for them. Then showed them the proper technique for throwing and catching. Logan seemed the best at catching, so his glove changed to a catcher's mitt. Tyler drove the family to the elementary school at least once a week, so the kids could get used to an actual ball field. Mrs. Simon would watch the baby while Elli and Jessica fielded stray balls.

So, began the huddle around the television screen during baseball and football seasons that led to spirited discussions at mealtimes about baseball or football stats and team preferences, depending on the season.

Elli felt a little left out and secretly thought, "Thank heaven, they aren't interested in soccer and hockey, as well."

Lianne Susanna, Elli's sixth child, was born seven weeks earlier, on what would have been Blair's thirty-first birthday. The family had been celebrating Blair's life by visiting and tending his gravesite. Then reminiscing by telling the children about Blair as a child and about the practical jokes he used to play on people, with Tyler's help, of course. The picnic they'd planned as a culmination of their celebration ended abruptly when Elli went into labor. The family would now have two birthdays to celebrate on that day, Lianne's and Blair's.

Remembering the day Blair was killed in a freak farm accident caused Elli to stifle a sob. She lost one of the men she loved that day, but she found the other. Elli would always be thankful that Tyler asked her to marry him. She and Tyler would be celebrating their fifth anniversary this coming November.

Elli was very much in love with her husband. Tyler was her best friend, confidante, business partner, and Elli's heart and soul. Elli thought about the day Tyler proposed to her, then asked if he could adopt Blair's children. She would never deny Tyler anything because she knew he loved Blair's children as if they were his own. When

Tyler insisted that they all share the same last name, Whrite-Thompson, to honor Blair and keep his memory alive, Elli lost her heart to Tyler even more.

It has been more than a week since Elli's six-week check-up with her doctor, and she's finally sick of being coddled. Glancing at the clock again, Elli realized that she must have dozed off while thinking about her children. It was now almost seven o'clock. Tyler was spooned around her with one hand cupping her breast, a muscled thigh draped across her legs, and his glorious wood pressed into her backside. Trying to be very quiet, Elli slipped out of bed to relieve herself. Then she snuck back and burrowed beneath the sheets. Wrapping her hands around Tyler's engorged shaft, she proceeded to pleasure her unsuspecting husband.

When strong hands grabbed her, plopped her on her back, and she was covered by a muscular body, Elli let out a surprised squeak. The squeak turned to moans as Tyler proceeded to pleasure his wife. He'd missed making love to her. It had been almost three months since he'd been inside her. That was a damn long time when you needed the woman you loved like you needed air to breathe.

"God, I've missed you," Tyler whispered against Elli's ear before he entered her. "Mmmm…you feel so good."

Elli wrapped her slim legs around Tyler's waist and arched her back. Rocking together, they found a rhythm. Tyler could feel when Elli was getting close. Her inner muscles clamped down and squeezed him tight. Reaching between them, he rubbed her swollen clit to heighten her pleasure, and she dug her nails into his back. Tyler pumped harder, and with one last thrust, they both came. Tyler with a groan and Elli with a moan. Then, he kissed her hard and collapsed his weight onto her perfect body.

Rolling his weight off his wife, he pulled her with him and nestled her against his side. Kissing the top of her head, he said, "Love you, sweet girl, so much! I guess this means you're feeling better. Are you rested enough to take a trip?"

"We're going on a trip?" Elli asked with an arched brow. This was news to her.

"Yes, we need to go see your grandparents. Bill called right after Lianne was born. I told him as soon as you were up to traveling," Tyler responded.

"What about the construction?" Elli asked him. "Don't you need to be here to keep an eye on things?"

"Dad's going to oversee everything. He's tired of his rat race life and living in New York City. He's planning to retire and come live in Stillwater," Tyler said. "Dad will stay here on the farm and give me updates. Mrs. Simon won't have to stay here alone, and I'm certain Dad will enjoy her cooking."

"Okay, I guess we'd better get up." Elli kissed him on the cheek and rolled over to throw her legs over the side of the bed. "I'm going to take a shower before the kids want breakfast and the baby wakes up."

"Do we have time for a quickie in the shower?"

Elli gave Tyler a coy smile and ran into the bathroom. Tyler wasn't far behind. Shower sex was one of his favorite forms of lovemaking. It reminded him of the first time he'd made love to Elli, and she'd gotten pregnant with Billy.

Stepping into the shower, Tyler pressed Elli against the tile wall, and she gasped out an "Eeeek. The tile's cold."

"Well, then I'll just have to warm you up," Tyler warned as he lifted her so that she could wrap her legs around his waist.

Slipping his fingers between her folds, Tyler lined himself up and thrust inside. Elli gasped again as he filled her to the hilt. Leaning in, Tyler nipped at her shoulder, then suckled and nuzzled the side of her neck, marking the tender flesh with his love bites. Nibbling on her earlobe, he stopped long enough to whisper, "Can't get enough of you, sweet girl. I could stay right here sheathed in your sweet pussy forever. I love the sounds you make when you're getting close and the look on your face when I make you come. I love you, Elli."

Elli moaned as Tyler increased the force of his thrusts, and she sucked his bottom lip into her mouth. Then she swiped her tongue inside and began an intimate exploration of his mouth. When she paused to allow them to catch their breath, she said, "I love you so much, Tyler. I'm the luckiest woman in the world, and I'm getting close. I need you to push harder."

Tyler would always give Elli whatever she needed, so he did as she requested.

After, they took turns washing each other. That was another of Tyler's favorite pastimes. When they were finished getting dressed,

Elli swept her long dark hair into a ponytail to keep it out of the way while she nursed the baby.

"You look just like the young woman who stepped out on the deck at that graduation party," Tyler told her. "You haven't changed one bit. You're still so beautiful. I can't believe how lucky I am." Then he pulled her close and kissed her breathless.

When Tyler stepped back, Elli said, "I think we both need a cold shower now," and giggled.

Tyler laughed. He could feel things stirring in his jockey shorts. "Guess we'd better go feed the kids before we get carried away and add to our brood. I don't think you're up to that yet."

Elli grinned and told him, "Well, I think you should bear the next one."

That statement only succeeded in making Tyler laugh harder. "Honey, if I had to give birth to our children, we'd be childless right now." Then he waggled his eyebrows, and with a cheeky grin, said, "Don't forget, I've seen what you have to go through. I'll stick with making them. That's more fun."

Elli kissed her handsome husband hard on the mouth, took him by the hand, and said, "Come on, wimp. You go down and help Mrs.

Simon with breakfast while I change your daughter and feed her. I'll be down in a little bit. After breakfast, we'll start making plans for the trip."

"I love it when you're forceful," Tyler chuckled as he smacked his wife on the butt and headed off to make breakfast. He knew he was the luckiest man on the planet.

CHAPTER 17

FTER arriving at the airport in Billings on Saturday, Bain leased a four-wheel-drive jeep for off-road use. It had a GPS, so he loaded in the Circle R Ranch address he was given by the woman at the agency that employed Emilia in Pennsylvania and hit the road. When he was about five miles from his destination, he noticed a board nailed to a post in front of a dilapidated two-story house that said, *"Room for Rent, Cheap."* He couldn't believe his luck and took it as a good sign that he would succeed in his mission to bring Emilia home.

Checking out the room, he dropped off his bag and paid for a week's rent. Though the furnishings were old and tired looking, everything in the room was clean and neat. The attached bath had an old claw foot porcelain tub that looked big enough for two people to bath simultaneously. Being a big man, it was just the right size for Bain to stretch out in, instead of sitting with his legs bent.

Bain made his way back to the jeep. Gunning the engine, he pulled out onto the country road to continue the final five miles to his ultimate goal, check out the Circle R ranch, find Emilia, and take her home. After doing a drive-by, he turned back and found an excellent place to park where he would be undetected. Grabbing the pair of binoculars he'd brought with him, he scoped out the property from a distance. Sighting a kennel containing several working dogs that Bain assumed were used when herding the cattle, he knew he'd need to take care of them. Otherwise, they'd sound an alarm and give away his presence on the property.

Satisfied with what he could glean through a pair of binoculars, Bain returned to the rented room. Knocking on the door to the landlord's part of the house, Bain got directions to the closest grocery store. It was about five miles away. Parking in the lot, he was pleased that there weren't many other customers because the fewer people that noticed him, the better. Going inside, he purchased a package of ground hamburger, over-the-counter sleeping aids, and some food to tide him over.

Saturday night, Bain entered the Circle R property on foot and made his way to the kennel first. He let the animals get the smell of the hamburger in the bag he carried, then petted them to be sure they recognized his scent. Happy that the dogs were friendly, Bain offered them the drug-laced hamburger. Bain grinned as he watched them gobble the hamburger down. With full bellies, the dogs were content and soon laid down to rest.

When the dogs were snoozing quietly, Bain kept to the shadows and took his time snooping around the main house, peeking in through the windows wherever possible. The windows to the rooms at the front of the house were stained glass, so it was difficult to see if anyone was inside. They should effectively prevent anyone from getting a glimpse of him, as well. The rooms at the back of the house were dark. He tried the knob on the back door but found it locked. It looked like it would be easy to pick, however. After finishing his perusal of the main home, Bain made his way to the smaller house that sat off to the side about two hundred feet away. That one seemed dark and deserted. After circling the horse stable and hay barn, he turned towards the cabins. Bain assumed they were housing for the ranch hands. Bain could hear the voices of a couple of men. So, he hid under one of the cabin windows to listen to the conversation. Bain growled under his breath and clenched his fists when one of the ranch hands mentioned the plans he had for Emilia if she agreed to date him. When the conversation ceased and the cabin's lights went out, Bain went to hide in the shadows between the stable and an outbuilding to watch the main house. He couldn't believe that luck had smiled on him again when Emilia emerged through the front door at about 11:00 p.m.

When Bain was confident that no one was with her, he followed Emilia to the horse barn entrance. Slipping inside, he hid behind some bales of hay to wait for his chance. While Emilia inspected the horses one by one, a ranch hand came into the stable and stopped to chat. Bain realized his opportunity was lost when, soon after, the two said good night to each other, and Emilia made her way back to the house. Keeping still, Bain watched as the cowboy made a pass down the row of horses, then turned out the light and left.

Frustrated at the near miss, Bain decided he needed to take his time to discover how many employees actually worked and lived on the premises and to learn their routines. Still, he ached to storm into the main house, grab Emilia, and take her home. One thing was for sure Bain wouldn't be waiting until they arrived back at the farm for him to mark her as his. He'd brought the wedding band with him, too. She would be wearing it for the rest of her life, this time as his bride.

After Bain returned to his room late Saturday night, he called home. Shawn finally answered and told Bain that everything was going well. Shawn asked some questioned about caring for the new bull, but other than that, he was good with the job until Bain would return to the farm. When Shawn asked about Bain's location, Bain lied about being in Bethlehem, Pennsylvania. He said he had a lead on Emilia but hadn't found her yet.

After sleeping late, Bain spent Sunday in his rented room thinking about Emilia and dreaming about their life together. He couldn't wait to get her pregnant. She'd be beautiful with her abdomen swollen with his child. When the baby was born, he'd take good care of both of them. Maybe they'd have twins. That would be awesome.

On Sunday night, Bain parked his jeep in a turnout a mile from the Circle R property entrance. Slipping through the fence that bordered the main road, he made his way along the fence line to the outbuildings surrounding the barn. Bain didn't have the opportunity to check them out the night before. He wanted to determine what they contained or if they could be used for hiding.

While Bain was busy snooping around the buildings, Mike took one last dip in the pond near the line shack. Then he placed his dirty clothes and the reports prepared by Samuel Goldstein into his saddlebags. He'd read every word of those reports several times. There were several photographs of Emilia in the file, as well. She was as gorgeous as Mike remembered, and she looked just like Elli. He couldn't believe what Emi had gone through since the last time he'd seen her. Mike knew he had a lot to make up for.

Donning his Stetson, Mike saddled Cheyenne and headed for home. It was time to present himself to the woman he loved. That meeting would determine the course of their lives. Either she would reject him or forgive him. He hoped for the latter because he had never stopped loving Emi. They would need to present a united front when Elli arrived at the ranch with her family. Elli was their daughter and would need all the support they could provide her. Mike loved Elli and wanted to do everything he could to help her adjust to her new reality.

When Mike arrived back at the stable, it was after 9:00 p.m. He took care of the mare, fed and watered her, then cleaned the tack. After he was finished, Mike wandered to the house to eat and grab a shower. He didn't want to smell like his horse when he saw Emi for the first time in thirty-two years.

Before eating, Mike called to inform Bill of his return. Mike also wanted an update on the situation. Excited, he didn't stop to take a breath as he fired off question after question at Bill.

"Hi, Bill. It's Mike. I'm back. Are you and Peggy alright? Did Emi arrive on Friday? Do you like her? Do you think she will stay? Do you think I have a chance?"

Bill laughed. "Calm down, son. You're going to pass out. Breathe. Peggy and I have nothing but praise for Emi as a person and her abilities as a nurse. She's extraordinary, Mike. I can see why you fell in love with her. She seems shy but has a sweet personality. She's already taken charge of our care, including making meals, doing laundry, and housework. Emilia's an excellent cook, by the way, and make's a fantastic cup of coffee. Peggy's eaten more in the last two days than in the prior week, which makes me happy. I think Peggy's fallen in love with her as a daughter."

Bill sounded like he thought Emi hung the moon. That told Mike that Emi hadn't changed one bit. She was still a loving, caring person despite everything she'd been through over the years.

"Mike, I think you may have some competition. Sean seems to have taken a shine to Emi."

"Uh, no way. Emi's mine," Mike growled. "He'd better keep his hands and his dick to himself."

"Well, just a heads up. You never know with women. Anyway, Emi took a walk after assisting Peggy with her nighttime routine last night. I think she went to the stable to check out the horses. If she does the same thing tonight, I'll call as soon as she leaves the house. You can reintroduce yourself, then."

"That works. Thanks, Bill. Has she mentioned anything at all about me?" Mike anxiously inquired.

"Well, she did mention a boy she loved when she was in high school when Peggy asked her if it would be permissible to call her Emi," Bill responded. "She said he was the only other person to call her that. Otherwise, she glossed over her childhood and marriage when we were talking about her life. I got the impression that those years held a lot of bad memories."

"Well, the boy that called her Emi would be me. All right, I smell like the horse, and the only baths I've had were in ice-cold water. I'm going to shower, shave, and put on some clean clothes. I have a date with an old flame. Wish me luck, Bill."

While Mike was on the phone with Bill, Bain took up a position in the shadow of the storage shed next to the stable. He had just finished checking the outbuildings, and he noticed that there were lights on in the smaller house now. There hadn't been any previously.

In the one chance sighting of Emilia the night before, she had come out the main house's front door to take a walk, going so far as to check out the stable. Bain hoped she would do it again tonight. Then he would knock her out, throw her over his shoulder, and carry her back to the jeep. Taking up position in the shadow of one of the buildings, he had a perfect view of the main house and the smaller one.

Shortly after 11:00 p.m., Bill called Mike back. "I feel like a match-maker. I've been hiding out in the dark in the living room to see if Emi takes a walk. She just left and headed in the direction of the stable again. Go get her, son. She's a keeper."

Mike hung up the phone with a massive smile on his face and his heart hammering. He sure was going to try. He knew Emi was a keeper when he was seventeen years old. Unfortunately, life had gotten in the way.

CHAPTER 18

IT had been a long day, and Emilia was tired. She'd prepared all three meals for Bill, Peggy, and herself. Peggy wasn't eating much, so Emilia had asked Peggy what she thought she might be able to stomach. Then, Emilia worked around that to round out the meals.

That morning, after cleaning up the breakfast dishes, Emilia did some light housekeeping. Not regular nursing duties, but with room and board, an excellent salary, and the BMW sedan as a bonus, Emilia would never complain. She would do whatever it took to make Peggy's and Bill's last days comfortable.

Emilia began her day by assessing and charting Peggy's and Bill's conditions. Then she administered the physician's prescribed medications for both of them. While she was helping Peggy dress for the day, she assessed Peggy's skin to ensure there weren't any wounds that needed tending.

After breakfast, she spent time reading quietly to Peggy from a book of poetry that was one of Peggy's favorites. Bill spent that time in the study doing some paperwork for the ranch. After settling Peggy in for a nap, Emilia cleaned a couple of bathrooms. She dusted the furniture in the dining and living rooms, and she processed laundry at the same time.

Peggy and Bill told her stories about how they'd met and their early years of marriage while Emilia folded laundry after lunch. While Peggy rested, Bill took Emilia out to introduce her to a couple of the ranch hands and two young high school students. The students worked on the ranch during the summer months and weekends during the school year. The ranch hands were the same two men Emilia noticed and spoke to briefly on the way to the house on Friday morning, Sean Hannity and John Marshall.

Sean gave Emilia another one of his cheeky grins and said, "Well, hello again, beautiful. See, you found your way to the house. Settling in well enough?"

Bill gave Sean a look that told him he was out of line, so Sean's grin disappeared.

Emilia said, "Things are going very well, Sean, thank you." She shook John's hand and said, "Hello, John. It's nice to officially meet you since we didn't get the opportunity to speak to each other on Friday when I arrived."

John said, "It's a pleasure to meet you, ma'am. Welcome to the Circle R."

The high school students were introduced as Tom and Jake. Both sixteen, they were going into their junior year of high school. Jake, who reminded Emilia of Michael, would be a constant reminder of her lost love if she had to spend any time in his presence.

Finally, the day was over. With Peggy settled in bed for the night, Emilia went to her room to grab some clothing and then to take a shower. She shaved all the necessary body parts that desperately required a trim, as well. After donning her cotton nightie and a lightweight wrapper, Emilia tiptoed through the house to the front door. She didn't want to disturb Bill and Peggy, but she knew she wouldn't be able to sleep yet. Some fresh air would be nice, and she wanted another look at the horses in the stable. Iain and Bain didn't keep any, so this was her first experience with the enormous animals.

At about 11:00 p.m., Emilia stepped out onto the front porch and closed the door behind her. As she made her way to the stable, Bain, who watched from his hiding place, could see that Emilia was wearing a thin cotton nightie covered only by a loose wrap. Bain's cock hardened instantly at the sight of her. Her attire did little to hide the lovely shape of her tits and ass.

Bain waited for his chance to make his move. Just when he thought he'd given her enough time to settle in, the door opened to the smaller house. The light that spilled from the doorway outlined a tall guy wearing a cowboy hat. He looked to be about Bain's height, maybe a bit shorter. The door closed, cutting off the light, but Bain could see him making his way across the yard to the stable. Chance lost, Bain inched closer to see what would happen and to hear any conversation. He didn't want this guy anywhere near Emilia while she was indecently attired.

As Emilia made her way down the row of stalls in the stable, she stopped at each one to read the name plaque on the stall door. She was a little frightened by the horses. Did they bite? They had such big teeth. When one dun-colored horse stuck its head out, wiggled its lips, and snorted at her, Emilia startled and jumped back. Once again, she jolted when she heard a very male laugh that she assumed was at her expense.

Turning, Emilia eyed the very tall cowboy standing in the shadow of the doorway where she'd entered the building. She couldn't be sure, but he looked to be slightly taller than her late husband but definitely much taller than six feet. He had a solid muscular build with broad shoulders, narrow hips, and long legs. Wearing a Stetson hat, jeans, a plaid shirt, and boots, Emilia admired how he filled out his clothes. He didn't look familiar, so she knew he wasn't Sean or John.

Very aware of her skimpy attire, Emilia admonished herself for coming to the stable in her nightgown. What was she thinking? When the cowboy took a step closer, her eyes went wide, and she took a step back.

Moving forward into the light, the cowboy said, "Hello, Emi."

Surprised, Emilia gasped, "Michael? Is that really you?" Emi couldn't believe her eyes or her ears. It wasn't possible.

"Yes, sweetheart. It's really me. It's been a long time."

With that, Emilia sobbed, closed the gap between them, and launched herself into Michael's arms. Thankfully he caught her as she wound her legs around him and climbed him like a tree. Wrapping her arms around his neck, she proceeded to place feather-light kisses all over his forehead, cheeks, eyelids, nose, and corners of his mouth.

Stunned, Michael stood there, letting Emi have her way with him. When his brain cells started to fire again, Mike tightened his hold and backed her up against the wall. Taking control, he cupped her chin and tilted her face up. As Mike swiped his tongue over her bottom lip, he slid his hand along her jaw to cradle the back of her head. Then he deepened the kiss.

When Emi made a soft mewling sound in the back of her throat, Mike was lost and knew he needed more.

Carrying Emi to the door, he turned off the light and headed for the house. Getting a tighter hold, he dug his hands into the soft flesh of her bottom. A bottom that he noticed was very scantily clad. The hard-on Mike was now sporting twitched and rubbed painfully against the zipper of his jeans.

Two shadowed figures watched Mike's and Emi's progress across the barnyard. Mike caught sight of the one standing in the front entryway of the house. It was Bill, and he was giving Mike a thumbs up. Mike tipped his head in acknowledgment. Then Bill turned and slipped inside the house.

Mike was too busy focusing on the woman he loved and what she was saying to notice the second shadow.

"Michael, what are you doing? Oh, God, I'm so embarrassed at throwing myself at you like that. You're not married, are you? Your wife will kill me," Emi babbled. "I'm so ashamed. Please put me down. I was just so happy to see you that I couldn't contain myself."

"Shush, sweetheart. It's okay. When the woman I've loved for thirty-two years launches herself into my arms and kisses me silly, I'm doing what any red-blooded man would do. I'm taking that woman to bed, and no, I'm not married," Mike said with a wink.

"No, Michael, put me down. We can't do that. I work here. My employers are going to fire me, and it's only my third day. This isn't appropriate behavior," Emilia admonished as she squirmed to free herself from Mike's embrace.

"Darlin', hold still before I drop you. Bill and Peggy are going to be very pleased that we're together. Now hang on because I owe you millions of kisses and thousands of orgasms. I promised to bring you a lot of pleasure. I'm just keeping my promise. Besides, you promised to be my wife. You aren't going to renege on a promise, are you?"

With that, Mike opened the door of his small home, kicked it closed behind him, and carried the love of his life to his bed. Emi was too stunned at what she'd set into motion to say anything until Michael had her moaning beneath him. Then the only words she was capable of uttering were his name repeatedly as he brought her the pleasure he'd promised.

The shadow Mike missed while he was distracted belonged to a very furious Bain Andersen. Bain watched their progress with fisted hands and a murderous look on his face.

CHAPTER 19

BAIN had all he could do to suppress the rage coursing through him. He waited in the shadow of the outbuilding watching the house Emilia had been carried into by that damn cowboy. They'd been in there a long time. Then the lights went out.

It was now close to 4:00 a.m. After taking a good look around to be sure he wouldn't be detected, he made his way stealthily to the door of the house and turned the knob. Bain was in luck, or maybe just plain crazy for what he was about to do. The door was unlocked, so he eased it open. Taking a penlight from his pocket, he kept it cupped in his hand and turned it on just long enough to get a sense of the interior's layout. A hall led off an open area that included the living room, dining area, and kitchen. Slipping past the leather sofa to the hall, he made his way soundlessly to the open door on the right.

The sight of Emilia lying tangled in the sheets, one glorious breast and slim leg exposed to view boiled the blood in his veins. It was a good thing he was not a murderer, or the man that had dared to touch what belonged to Bain would be dead.

The chance he was taking was insane, but he moved to the bed and gazed down at Emilia's beautiful face. Reaching out, he cupped her bare breast lightly, then ran his fingers down her soft skin to touch her intimately. When Emilia sighed in her sleep, he yanked his hand back. Quickly making his way back out into the hall, he slipped into the shadows to watch undetected.

Emilia had fallen asleep wrapped in Michael's arms after making love for the third time, the last time in the shower. Since she was still attuned to waking at the slightest sounds that Iain had made towards the end of his illness, she was sensitive to noises. Emilia stirred and looked around. Something had woken her up. Lying there quietly, she tried to discern what had disturbed her sleep. She had this feeling that someone had touched her naked breast, then trailed those fingers along her torso to the juncture of her legs. It wasn't Michael. When she turned towards him, she could see that he was lying sprawled on his back with a well-muscled arm thrown over his head, dead to the world.

Emi couldn't hear anything, but she had this tingling, hair-raising sensation and felt like she was being watched. That happened quite often when Iain and Bain had invited their friends over. Finally, she convinced herself that she was only dreaming and was being ridiculous. So, Emilia pushed the feeling aside. She needed to get up and get dressed, anyway. She should be sleeping in her own room in the main house should Peggy need her during the night. That was her job.

Emilia slipped from the bed and hunted for her nightclothes. Bain watched from the darkness of the hall as Emilia searched for her panties. She was so beautiful, naked. Bain's cock swelled at the sight of her. As the man reached out for Emilia and grabbed her by the wrist, Bain heard Emilia's squeak of surprise. Undercover of their conversation, Bain eased his way back down the hall and out of the house. Moving into the shadows, he waited.

"If I was actually wearing my panties, you would have scared me out of them, Michael," Emilia said.

Mike chuckled, then asked, "Where are you going, sweetheart? Come back to bed. I think I'm good for another round." Then he tried to suppress a yawn.

"I'd love that, but I need to go do my job. I can't stay here all night. I have patients who may need me," Emilia responded.

"Okay, just let me get dressed. I'll walk you home. That way, I get to steal a kiss at the door before you turn and go into the house. It will be the end of our first date. Do you kiss on the first date, Emi?" Mike joked.

"You're silly, Michael. It seems I do a lot more than kiss on a first date. You're the only one I would do it with, however, and that's because I love you. Anyway, it really isn't necessary for you to walk me home. I don't think anyone or anything is going to attack me from here to Bill's front door," Emilia said as she tried not to giggle. "Go back to sleep. I'll see you in the morning."

Mike raised up on one elbow and grabbed Emi's arm before she could get away. "You still love me, Emi?"

Leaning down, Emilia captured Michael's lips in a searing kiss, then said, "Always, but there is something important I need to tell you. Then you're going to be very angry with me and probably will never speak to me again. So, I'm just going to leave now. We'll talk tomorrow night after Peggy and Bill go to bed. Okay?"

As he watched Emi leave the room, Mike had a bad feeling that he shouldn't let her go but ignored it and called out to her retreating back, "I'm going to hold you to that. I'm not happy about this."

Mike already knew what Emi planned to tell him, and none of that was her fault. When he heard the front door close, he slumped back down on the mattress and huffed out a deep sigh.

CHAPTER 20

BAIN couldn't believe his luck when Emilia opened the door and stepped out. Closing the door behind her, she turned and walked away. This was Bain's chance. Moving quickly, Bain slipped his arm around Emilia's neck and exerted pressure on her carotid arteries. With his elbow pointing outward and upward, he used his other arm to increase the pressure.

Emilia, distracted by her thoughts, wasn't paying any attention to her surroundings. She tried to scream when powerful arms dug into the delicate skin of her neck, but it was too late. In just a matter of seconds, she felt exhausted and dizzy, then the world swam away.

As Emilia slumped to the ground, Bain injected her with the needle from the kit he'd bought from the drug dealer. The injection would keep Emilia knocked out for about twenty minutes. The unexpected trip she'd get from it would probably keep her out of the way for a least a day. Maybe longer.

Lifting her quickly, Bain turned to head back to the jeep. Striding towards the shadows that lay between the stable and one of the storage sheds, Bain made the fatal mistake of pausing long enough to capture Emilia's lips in a kiss. Before he could safely make it back into the shadows, he caught sight of another cowboy rounding the corner of the stable. Damn place was overrun with cowboys all getting in the way of what his heart wanted. He just wanted to go home to his dairy farm in Pennsylvania with the woman he loved and leave fucking Montana behind.

Bain dropped Emilia to the ground and took off running. Just as he reached the end of the out-building, he heard the guy yell. Emilia had been discovered. Keeping to the shadows, Bain raced back to the jeep and burned rubber in his haste to escape. When he reached his rented room, he called the airline and booked a flight. After taking a two-hour nap, Bain washed up and ate the perishables he'd purchased at the grocery store. Grabbing his backpack, he locked the door to his room. Knocking on his landlord's door, he paused long enough to pay in advance for a few more weeks' stay. Then he started the jeep and headed for the airport.

Bain knew he should have stuck to the plan. He'd blown his chance, but he wasn't giving up. Going over his options, a new plan formed in his head. He didn't know who that cowboy was or why Emilia had sex with him after so short an acquaintance, but Bain intended to bring that man as much pain and misery as possible for touching her. He'd make him pay, and then Bain would take Emilia home.

It was a good thing the drug he'd injected Emilia with caused amnesia. When she woke up, she wouldn't be able to remember what happened. It was time to go home, regroup, and then he'd try again.

CHAPTER 21

JAKE was heading into the stable when he noticed movement out of the corner of his eye. Stopping, he turned his head and noticed something lying in a heap on the ground near the storage shed.

Making his way to what looked like a lumpy pile of sheets, he discovered Mrs. Andersen. When she didn't respond to being shaken, Jake placed his fingers to the side of her neck and noticed the erratic heartbeat. Scared, Jake rushed to Mike's front door.

Beating on the door, Jake yelled, "Mike, open up."

Jake continued to pound on the door when Mike didn't answer immediately. Finally, the door swung open, and Mike stood in the entryway wearing nothing but his jockey shorts. His hair was sleep-tossed, and he was having trouble focusing due to lack of sleep.

"What the heck is wrong with you, Jake? What's all the pounding and yelling about?" Mike yawned.

"Come quick, Mike. It's Mrs. Andersen. She's lying in a heap on the ground," Jake stuttered.

Shoving his feet into his boots, Mike yelled, "Go! Where is she?"

When they reached Emi, Mike knelt next to her prone body. "Is she just as you found her, Jake?"

"Yes, sir. I was headed in to start mucking out the stable when I thought I saw some movement. I found her just like this. She didn't respond when I shook her, and her pulse is erratic. That's when I came to get you. I didn't know if I should move her."

"Good job, Jake. I'm going to carry Emi into my house. Can you get the door for me?" Mike asked.

"Sure thing, Mike. What do you think happened?"

Lying Emi on the sofa in the living room, Mike hunkered down and patted her cheeks to try to rouse her. Then he checked her head to see if there were any signs of trauma, thinking she may have tripped and fallen. He studied her eyes and checked her airway for obstructions. Her eyes were dilated, but she didn't seem to be choking on anything. He couldn't find any signs of snakebite on her legs, either.

"I don't know, Jake. It doesn't look like she fell and knocked herself out. I don't feel any bumps on her head."

As Mike was checking Emi's arms and legs, she started to moan and shake uncontrollably. Lifting her, Mike sat and pulled Emi's body into his arms to hold her tight.

"Jake, get a few blankets from the closet in the hall, please. Let's cover her up," Mike requested.

CHAPTER 22

EMILIA floated through a fog of swirling grays and blacks interspersed with distant flashes of light. She felt like she was part of one of those classic black-and-white science fiction movies seen late at night on television. She had a terrible metallic taste in her mouth that made her want to gag, and a strange buzzing sound filled the void. Flashes of memories from her childhood rode the streaks of lightning that skated between the clouds.

An alien-like mist filled the air around her, and Emilia felt a twister of swirling emotions. Nauseous, she closed her eyes. As the debris of a lifetime of imperfect recollections accosted her, Emilia had the sensation of something large and heavy slamming into her body. She felt like she was flying through the air, then the pain of impact as she fell to earth. When she opened her eyes, she gasped at the sight of her body lying bruised and broken.

As tears slid down Emilia's cheeks, she woke with a start. Confused and agitated, she jerked her head around. Something was holding her tight, and she panicked. Emilia tried to speak, but only a wealth of incoherent dyslexic noises spewed from her mouth.

Closing her eyes again, Emilia let the waiting darkness steal her away into its comforting embrace. There wasn't any pain there. Only the hope that someday she'd be reunited with her child, who was the final memory Emilia had viewed.

Having heard the strange sounds Emilia was making as she convulsed in Mike's arms, Jake worriedly asked, "Do you think we should call an ambulance, Mike?"

"Yes, call 911 while I get dressed. Answer any questions they have and stay on the line," Mike told him as he laid Emi's body gently on the sofa.

Jake's eyes went wide when Mike leaned down, kissed Emi tenderly, and then told her that he loved her.

Mike saw the expression on Jake's face and said, "It's a long story, Jake. I'll tell you all about it someday. All you need to know for now is that I love this woman with all my heart and soul. I'm going to make her my wife. Watch over her for me, will you? I'll be right back."

Jake called 911 and talked to the dispatcher while Mike was in the bedroom getting dressed. He gave his location, then answered as many questions as he could, telling the dispatcher Emilia's name and current condition. When Mike came back into the room, he was able to supply Emi's age. Then began the wait for the ambulance to arrive. Emi didn't regain consciousness while they were waiting, and both Jake and Mike were worried sick.

As soon as the emergency medical technicians had Emi loaded into the ambulance, Mike told Jake to take care of the chores and dashed to the main house.

Bill and Peggy were still asleep, so Mike left a note on the kitchen table about what had happened. Stopping at Emilia's room, he found her purse. Mike grabbed it, knowing the hospital would need information that the purse or wallet might contain. Then he ran for his car. Mike had to get to the hospital. Parking in the emergency room lot, he was out of the vehicle as soon as he'd thrown the gear shift into park.

Thankfully, it was a quiet night, and Mike knew he was lucky. Usually, the emergency room was wall-to-wall people seeking help. When it was his turn, Mike told the woman staffing the front desk that he was the fiancé of Emilia Andersen and that the ambulance had just brought her in. Mike answered the questions he could, hunting through Emilia's purse when asked for her social security number. When asked about insurance, Mike gave the attendant the policy information for all Circle R employees. Then Mike was told to take a seat and wait. He would be allowed in as soon as Emilia had been evaluated.

CHAPTER 23

EMILIA could hear moaning that sounded like it came from a great distance. Someone was in distress, and as a nurse, she should try to help. It must be Iain, but her eyes were so heavy. Why couldn't she wake up? She needed to go to her husband. He was in so much pain from cancer ravaging his body. She called out his name and told him she was coming. He needed her, but she just wanted to fall back into the darkness and sleep. Finally, her eyelids fluttered, letting in a bright light that caused excruciating pain to tear through her head. Her stomach roiled, and she moaned loudly. Her mouth and throat felt like they were coated in dry desert sand but tasted like she'd been licking the bottom of a dirty litter box.

"Emi, its Mike. Can you open your eyes for me, honey? Come on, sweetheart. You need to wake up now. Here, take a drink for me."

Emilia felt a straw pressed to her mouth. Pursing her lips, she drew in the cool liquid. It felt like heaven as it dribbled down her parched throat.

"That's enough, honey. You don't want to drink too much at once. It will make you sick. Come on, darlin'. Open your eyes. Everyone's so worried about you."

Emilia scrunched her forehead. Why was anyone worried about her? Where was Iain? She had a feeling that she'd failed Iain terribly. Opening her eyes into mere slits to filter the harsh light, she could see shadowed figures bending over her. Voices whispered. When the shadows transformed into real people, she said, "Michael?"

"That's my girl. You need to wake up now."

"What happened? Where am I? Have I been sick?" Emilia asked.

"You're at the hospital, honey. It's okay. Bill, Peggy, and Jake are here with you, too. We've been worried sick. You've been out for about fourteen hours," Mike said as he squeezed Emilia's hand tight. Then he leaned over the bedrail and kissed Emilia softly on the brow.

Emilia moaned and tried to rise. "I think I'm going to be sick," she groaned. Mike grabbed the bedpan and propped her up as she emptied her stomach. Peggy went into the bathroom and came back with a cold washcloth. Tenderly brushing the hair away from Emi's sweaty brow, she proceeded to bath Emilia's lips and face.

When Peggy was finished, Mike gave Emilia another drink of water but told her to just rinse her mouth and spit it out. Then he wiped her mouth gently and kissed her on the lips.

"That's my good girl," he crooned.

Just as Emilia asked once again what had happened, a doctor entered the room. "Ah, Mrs. Andersen. You're awake. Good! How do you feel?" he asked as he took her wrist in his fingers to take her pulse? Without giving Emilia a chance to respond, he paused to listen to her heart and lungs, then asked her to track his finger as he moved it back and forth in front of her face. The motion turned Emilia's stomach.

When the urge to vomit had passed, Emilia said, "Please tell me what happened."

Satisfied, the doctor finally introduced himself. "I'm Dr. Johnson," he said as he took her hand in his. "Mrs. Andersen, it appears that someone has injected you with a date rape drug. You were found unconscious. Do you remember anything?"

Emilia tried to shake her head, no, but it hurt too much. "I don't understand. Was I on a date? I can't remember. I'm so tired, and my head hurts badly," she said.

"That's to be expected," the doctor told her. "You're very fortunate that you were brought to the hospital so soon after being injected. The drug that was used leaves the body within a few hours. It wouldn't have shown up, otherwise."

"What is the last thing you remember?" the doctor asked again.

"I was with Mike," Emilia said while blushing. "We fell asleep. Something woke me up, but I don't remember what. Then I got dressed and headed back to the main house. I don't remember anything after that."

"Alright, we're going to keep you a little longer for observation, and then you can go home. You'll need someone to watch you overnight. You should be back to normal in a day or so," the doctor responded before he left the room.

Mike put the bed rail down and sat on the side of the mattress. He took Emi's hand in his and kissed her fingertips. "Jake, can you take Bill and Peggy home, please?" he asked. "I'll bring Emi as soon as she's released. The police have already talked to both of us. I know they're waiting in the hall to talk to Emi. Please send them in when you leave, so she can get this over with."

"Okay, Mike. Is there anything I can get for you or Mrs. Andersen?" he asked worriedly.

When Mike told Jake that they'd be fine, Bill and Peggy both kissed Emilia on the cheek and told her they'd see her at home. Jake, looking embarrassed but determined, kissed Emilia as well. It seemed to Mike that Emi was capable of bewitching all the men who entered her vicinity. He was not surprised. Even mussed, she was beautiful to behold.

A few minutes after Jake, Bill, and Peggy departed, two police officers entered the room and introduced themselves to Emilia. Unfortunately, there was nothing further she could add to what Mike and Jake had already told them. It was their conjecture that it might have been someone passing through who'd found an easy target. Mike was told to beef up security around the ranch just in case. Then the officers left to write up their reports.

Emilia silently started to cry. She was overwhelmed by what had happened.

Mike pressed a kiss to Emi's forehead and said, "That's okay, honey. We'll talk more after you've rested."

Mike pulled an armchair close to the side of the bed, took Emi's hand in his, and kissed her palm. When his cell phone rang, Mike saw that it was Bill.

"This doesn't make sense," Mike told Bill. "She was fine when she left my place. I'll get her to agree to a checkup to be certain there aren't any long-term effects from that drug. Are you and Peggy going to be alright without Emi's help for a couple of days?"

"Don't worry about us. We'll manage. Let's just get our girl better. That's what matters at the moment. Talk to the ranch hands when you get home. They're acting like old mother hens hanging around waiting for word that Emi's alright," Bill responded.

Mike nodded, but when he realized Bill couldn't see him, he said, "I'll call and talk to Sean. He can tell the others. We'll need to take shifts patrolling the grounds for a while, I think."

"Okay, Mike, I'll see you when you get home," and Bill hung up.

When Sean answered his cell phone, Mike told him, "Mrs. Andersen woke up. She seemed groggy and disoriented. I gave her some water and told her to rest. She went right back to sleep."

"Does she know what happened?" Sean asked. "We're all worried about her."

"The doctor said she was injected with a date rape drug. Emilia doesn't remember anything. I'll keep you posted. In the meantime, the police said we need to beef up security. Work out a schedule for nighttime hours. Include me in the rotation, so we're not dragging our butts from lack of sleep. Anyway, thanks for being worried about her and taking care of all the chores for me. I really appreciate it. Why don't you all go eat and get some rest? I don't think we'll have any answers until tomorrow."

It amazed Mike, again, how quickly everyone on the ranch had come to care for Emi. He needed to have a talk with Sean, however. Mike didn't want to give the man false hope. Emi belonged to Mike.

Now to convince Peggy and Bill that he would be spending his nights in Emi's bed in one house or the other. Either bed worked for him.

When Emilia was finally released, Mike gingerly placed her in the car. After fastening her seat belt, he lowered the seat to allow her to rest comfortably on the drive home.

"Go to sleep, sweetheart. I love you." Mike told her as he placed a chaste kiss on her lips.

"I love you more," Emilia whispered as she closed her eyes. She was out in a matter of moments.

Mike carried the still dozing Emi into the house when they arrived back at the ranch. Bill heard the car pull up and was waiting with the door opened. Mike nodded his thanks as he passed. Placing Emilia on the bed in her room, he removed her shoes and covered her with the quilt. Mike turned the lamp on the nightstand to its lowest setting, kissed Emi once more, and went out to talk to Peggy and Bill. Mike found the couple in the living room waiting for him.

"What do you make of all this, Mike?" Bill asked.

"I've no idea. Let's give Emi a couple of days to rest. Then she is going to the doctor. Even if I have to hogtie her to the roof of my car to get her there. I'm going to stay in Emi's room. Does that bother either of you?"

"No, I think the two of you have been separated long enough," Peggy responded. "We'll see you in the morning."

CHAPTER 24

EMILIA was anchored to the bed. Something heavy lay across her middle, and something hairy that tickled lay across her legs. Something was also poking her in the back. Emilia remained very still because she felt disoriented. Opening her eyes, she tried to get her bearings. Running her hands gingerly over the anchor at her waist, she realized it was an arm. The weight across her thighs was a hairy leg, but the hair was oh so soft. Very carefully, she slipped out of bed and turned to discover that the owner of the arm and leg was Michael. Her heart swelled at the sight of him. She loved him so much. Walking on wobbly legs, she made it out of the bedroom to the hall. Thankfully, the bathroom was only a few steps away. She had to pee so very badly.

By the clock in the bathroom, Emilia could see that it was 6:30. Confused, she wondered how she'd ended up in her own bed. Why was Michael sharing it with her? The last thing she remembered was kissing Michael and leaving him in his bed. Emilia couldn't imagine what her employers would say when they discovered that she'd slept with him. She'd be out on the street with nowhere to go. Maybe she could sneak Michael out the back door before Peggy and Bill got up, and they'd never know.

Slipping back into the bedroom, Emilia shook Michael until he stirred.

"Michael, please. It would be best if you got up. I'm going to lose my job. It would help if you went home," Emilia implored him.

"Honey, you're awake. How do you feel?" Mike asked as he yawned.

"I'm feeling alright, but what are you doing in my bed?" she responded.

"Honey, what do you remember?"

"I don't understand. I left your bed and ended up in mine. I don't know how I got here, though. The last thing I remember is leaving your house."

"Emi, Jake found you passed out in the stable yard. You didn't make it to the house. That was yesterday morning. We had to call an ambulance to take you to the hospital. You don't remember any of that?"

Shaking her head, Emilia started to shake. "Yesterday morning? No. Michael. Why are you teasing me?"

As Emilia stared at him, clearly confused, Mike pulled her into his arms. Tucking her close to his body, he kissed her brow.

"Shhh, darlin'. Everything's going to be alright. Rest today. I'll help Peggy and Bill. Later, when you're feeling up to it, we'll all talk," Mike promised. Slipping from the bed, he placed a kiss on her forehead and tucked the blankets around her. "I'll make everyone some breakfast and come get you when it's ready."

After Michael left the room, Emilia worried her bottom lip with her teeth. She couldn't stay here, knowing the pain and disappointment she would cause Michael when they talked. There wasn't any hope that he would forgive her for never having the chance to get to know his daughter. Ashamed, Emilia burrowed her head into the pillow and started to sob. Life was so unfair. She'd finally found the man she'd loved for thirty-two years, and now she was going to lose him again.

Mike found Peggy and Bill sitting at the kitchen table having a cup of coffee. "I'm going to make us breakfast. Do you think you can handle some scrambled eggs and toast, Peggy?"

"That'll be fine, dear," Peggy responded. "Is Emi awake?"

"Yes, I left her tucked up in bed. She doesn't remember anything past leaving my house yesterday morning. I told her we'd all talk after we eat breakfast. It's time to tell her about Elli."

While Michael was cooking breakfast, Emilia concluded that it was time for her to leave. Rising, Emilia made her way to the closet to pull out the boxes of belongings she had yet to unpack and stacked them by the bedroom door. Emilia had a sense of déjà vu. She was running away again. After piling the boxes, Emilia chose an outfit to wear and made her way to the bathroom. She would pack the rest of her belongings as soon as she showered. Emilia sobbed while allowing the hot water to pound against her. When she felt like she'd been wrung dry, she washed quickly. While she was shampooing her hair, Mike slipped into the room. Undressing, he joined her in the shower and wrapped his arms around her waist. Startled, Emilia gasped as shampoo stung her eyes. Leaning out of the stall, Mike grabbed a dry towel and tenderly dried her eyes.

Staring down at her, he quizzically asked, "I saw the boxes. What are you doing, sweetheart?"

While tears slid silently down her cheeks, Emilia reached up and laid her hand along the curve of Michael's jawline. With a trembling voice, she said, "I don't want to hurt you or Bill and Peggy. I need to leave. I'm going to call a cab as soon as I get dressed. I hope all of you can forgive me."

Confusion clouded Mike's eyes. "Why on earth are you leaving? We've just found each other again. I love you, Emi. There's no way I'm letting you go. I meant it when I said we're getting married."

"You say that now but once I've confessed what I have to tell you, you're going to hate me. I'm a coward. I can't live, knowing that you can't stand the sight of me. Please, just let me go," Emilia plead. Then she covered her eyes and started to sob again. She was positive she didn't have any tears left to shed, but she was wrong.

Mike pulled her close and pressed her head against his chest. Then he leaned down and kissed her. Lifting her, Mike wrapped her legs around his waist and pushed Emi back against the tile wall. Sliding his fingers between her folds, he found her center and nudged the tip of his cock inside. Emilia hid her face against Mike's neck and moaned as he pushed inside her to the hilt.

"You're not going anywhere," Mike told her. "Say it, Emi. Say you belong to me."

"I belong to you, Michael. I always have," Emilia agreed. Then Michael kissed Emi as he drove into her repeatedly until they both came together.

Stepping out onto the mat, Mike wrapped a towel around his waist. After drying Emi's skin and hair, he wrapped her in the towel, lifted her, and carried her to her bed. Laying her down, he covered her body, nudged inside again, and slowly began to pleasure her.

"I can't get enough of you," Mike whispered against Emilia's ear. "You're just as beautiful now as you were when we cracked heads in the library the first time we met. Your sweet pussy still fits me like a glove made just for my cock. I'm going to spend the rest of my life worshipping your tight body, Emi. I'm the last man that is ever going to touch you like this. You'll have to accept that because it's the truth."

When they were satiated, Mike pulled Emi tight against him and covered them with the quilt. "Take a nap, honey, and then we'll get dressed so we can spend time with Bill and Peggy."

Curving her naked body to fit the curve of Michael's, Emilia fell into a deep sleep. When a nightmare gripped her, she began to struggle. Someone had her in a chokehold, and she couldn't breathe.

"Emi, wake up." Mike shook her worriedly.

"Someone was choking me," Emilia said.

"It's okay. It was just a bad dream. You're safe now," Mike told her. "Let's get dressed. It's time for that talk, and you still haven't eaten anything."

Finished dressing first, Mike told Emi that he would meet her in the kitchen.

Emilia paused to grab the photo album and documents she had taken from her mother's safety deposit box three years ago. It was time to tell Michael the truth. He's been a father for thirty-one years.

CHAPTER 25

TYLER was working in the office when he heard the knock on the front door. Baby Lianne was lying in the cradle next to Tyler's desk. He paused to adjust the blanket around his sleeping daughter, then went to answer the door.

Stunned at the sight of the man standing on the front porch surrounded by luggage, Tyler pulled his father, Alastair Caelan Thompson, known to everyone as Alex, in for a hard hug.

"Dad, what are you doing here? We weren't expecting you for another two months," Tyler said with a pleased smile. Grabbing the suitcases, he said, "Come in. Elli's in the kitchen with the kids. She's starting their homeschooling early. Come in the office. I'm babysitting Lianne."

Alex peeked at his sleeping granddaughter before taking a seat beside the cradle. "She's so beautiful. She looks a lot like your mother. She has her hair color, but that will probably change."

"Elli thinks Lianne looks like Mom, too. Do we have any photos of Mom as a baby? Elli wants to compare," Tyler asked.

"Your mother kept scrapbooks. I should have given them to you after you and Elli were married. Patti would have been so pleased with your choice of a wife. I remember when you were seventeen. I took you to dinner for your birthday, and we had that talk. You told me then that you were in love with Elli."

"I remember that talk, Dad. It was the father-son talk about the birds and the bees," Tyler laughed. "It was probably something we should have discussed several years earlier. It was soon enough, though. I wasn't sexually active at that point. I was hoping my first time would be with Elli."

"Well, you said you didn't plan to do anything about your feelings for Elli because of Rick. I remember I told you not to give up hope. I'm so proud of you and happy that it worked out. You knew what your heart wanted. How is everything between the two of you?" Alex asked.

"It couldn't be any better, Dad. I love that woman more every day. It's like she's the other half of my soul, and we get along so well. Knock-on-wood, we haven't had any quarrels yet. We made a promise to each other to always tell the truth and not to keep secrets. Elli's loving nature makes it so easy. The only thing that hurts is that it took Rick's death for Elli and me to be together. I still miss him, and I know that Elli does, too. She's been having strange dreams about him that have me worried."

"What kind of dreams?" Alex asked quizzically.

"He keeps telling her something is going to happen and that she's to rely on me for support. I'd die for that woman, Dad. I wouldn't let anything happen to her. I don't think I could live without her," Tyler grimaced.

"Well, they are just dreams. Just remember to love Elli the way she deserves. That's the only thing you can do," Alex responded. "Okay, I'm here early because I handed in my resignation. I've had enough. I want to spend time with my son, beautiful daughter-in-law, and six grandkids. Tell me, are there any plans to add to that number, or are you finished adding to your brood?" Alex asked with a chuckle.

Tyler smirked. "Well, I wouldn't be averse to adding to that number. Maybe a baseball team's worth?"

"Nine children? That's ambitious, but if anyone has enough love for nine children, it's you and Elli. What does she say about that? She is the one who does all the work, after all." Alex quirked his eyebrow at his son.

"I haven't told her yet," Tyler sighed. "We are having sex without protection, though, so she's smart enough to understand what can happen."

Alex laughed. "Well, good luck with that, son. Now, tell me what I need to do while you're on vacation in Montana."

Before Tyler could respond, the baby began to fuss. "Hey, there, sweetie pie. Guess it's time for a diaper change, and I bet you're hungry. Let's go find your mommy."

Alex said, "Let me," and lifted Lianne from the cradle. Placing the baby against his shoulder, he supported her head and back. As he placed a gentle kiss on her forehead, he breathed in the scent of her and sighed. "I love the smell of a baby. You're a lucky man, Tyler, because your mom and I were only blessed with one child. We would have loved to give you brothers and sisters."

"I know, Dad. I think that's why I found Rick. He was the brother you couldn't give me. Okay, let's take Lianne to her mommy, and you can spend time with the rest of your grandchildren. I hope you're ready. They haven't seen you since Lianne was born. They're going to be rowdy," Tyler said as he led his father to the kitchen.

Elli was working with the children at the kitchen table. She planned to homeschool Blair, Peggy, and Logan. They would be starting kindergarten in the fall since they'd turned five years old at the beginning of March. Billy, now four, was advanced for his age. So, Elli intended to teach him the same subjects. Jessica, their oldest at twelve years of age, would be starting ninth grade, having skipped three grades in elementary school. She was helping her mother with the younger siblings.

Elli looked up as Tyler and Alex entered the room. Surprised at the sight of her father-in-law, she leaned in and placed a gentle kiss on his cheek. "Dad, I'm so happy to see you."

After handing Lianne to Elli, Alex hugged his daughter-in-law and kissed her in return. Blair, Peggy, Logan, and Billy crowded around him, each vying for their grandfather's attention. Peggy clung to his leg as Alex leaned over to embrace Jessica. "Hi, honey. How's the most beautiful granddaughter in the world? You look more and more like your dad every day."

"Hi, Grandpa. Did you get me the information about veterinary schools? You promised you would put a list together for me? I've made up my mind that I want to be a veterinarian for large animals. I'm going to ask my great-grandpa if I can set up a clinic on the Circle R ranch after graduation. I love Montana." Jessica quizzed Alex as she embraced him.

"Jess, all of that can wait. Grandpa is here to stay," Tyler admonished. "Help the little ones clean up. All of you can spend time with Grandpa in the living room." Turning to Elli, he kissed her and the baby. Giving Elli a nudge towards the stairs, he said, "Go take care of our daughter while I make lunch."

While Tyler laid out makings for grilled cheese sandwiches and his homemade soup, he could hear hoots of laughter from the living room. His dad was entertaining the kids with stories of Rick's and Tyler's misdeeds when they were children. Rick came up with the most impressive practical jokes to play on people, and Tyler was stupid enough to go along with him. They spent a lot of time in detention after school. Tyler was surprised that they both managed to graduate. Hopefully, the kids weren't taking notes. So far, he and Elli had been lucky. Jess, Blair, Peggy, and Logan hadn't shown any signs of taking after their father in the practical joke department.

Mrs. Simon arrived, just as everyone was sitting down to eat. Alex jumped up from the table and went to say hello. Tyler and Elli looked at each other quizzically when Alex hugged Mrs. Simon and said, "Hi, Anna. It's good to see you again."

"Mr. Thompson. It's good to see you also," Mrs. Simon blushed as she responded.

"Now, none of that. You promised at Elli and Tyler's wedding that you would call me Alex."

"Yes. So, I did. It's good to see you, Alex. Are you here for the day, only?"

"No, I'm done with working on Wall Street. I placed my apartment on the market. I sold off all of the furnishings and the contents that I won't need through an auction house. A moving company will be delivering the items that I've decided to keep here next week. The realtor doesn't think it will take any time at all for the apartment to sell. I have the house here in Stillwater, but Tyler wants me to live on the farm. So, I guess I'll put that house on the market, too. Then I can spend quality time with my family before I miss more of the important things that make life worth living," Alex responded.

"Mrs. Simon, come sit down. I'll get you some lunch," Tyler said. As Tyler passed his father, he quirked his eyebrow at Alex and mouthed, "What the heck, Dad?"

Alex just winked at Tyler and went to pull out a chair at the table so that Anna could sit. Taking the seat next to her, he turned to his grandchildren. "Who's up for a game after lunch?" he asked.

The response to Alex's question was a resounding chorus of, "Me!"

CHAPTER 26

AFTER lunch, Alex convinced Annabelle Simon to play several games of *Go Fish* with him and his grandchildren. He hadn't enjoyed himself so much since Tyler was little. He remembered when he and Patti took their son to an amusement park for the Fourth of July. Tyler's favorite rides were the bumper cars and the Scrambler. The small family had a blast on the water rides and the Tilt-A-Whirl, too. Alex remembered how Tyler fell asleep on the way home that evening, all worn out from their day of laughter and fun. When Alex carried the young boy up to his bed and tucked him in, Tyler looked at his father with eyes full of hero-worship and said, "Thanks, Daddy, for the best day ever."

Alex was busy building his client base, and work hours were crazy after that. Alex spent less and less time with his wife and young son. Tyler started to get into trouble, most likely due to Alex's neglect. That's when Alex bought the house in Stillwater, New Jersey, to get Tyler away from the harmful influence of the boys he was hanging with in New York City. Tyler made friends with Rick Whrite on his first day of school at Stillwater Elementary. Although they got into mischief by playing practical jokes, it was all harmless fun. Rick became Tyler's best friend until Rick passed away.

When Patti was critically injured in an automobile accident by a stupid jerk texting on his cell phone while driving, the joy went out of Alex's life. Patti died, and Alex's heart died with her, but Tyler was the one who suffered the most. He lost his father, also, that day because Alex became withdraw.

Alex planned to spend the rest of his life showing his son Tyler, daughter-in-law Elli, and grandchildren how much they were loved. Maybe, he could convince Anna to be a part of that, too, and not only as the family's housekeeper. That's if Alex played his cards right. He was tired of being alone. He'd been celibate for the most part since Patti passed away, except for the monthly hook-up with women Alex hired from an escort service. Those hook-ups were only to scratch an itch, and he was sick of that. It was time to keep the promise made to his wife before she slipped into a coma, not to spend the rest of his life mourning her loss. He was in his late fifties, but he was still virile. Sex with the right woman, preferably a woman who would agree to marry him, would be ideal. Alex believed he'd found that woman in Annabelle Simon the day he attended Tyler's marriage to Elli.

When they were tired of playing *Go Fish*, Mrs. Simon bundled the children into the Mercedes Benz eight-seater SUV. She planned to spend the rest of the afternoon visiting her sister's family in Sussex. Tyler and Alex watched as the SUV pulled away and traveled down the gravel drive until it was out of sight.

"If you have those other three children, you're going to need a bus," Alex teased his son.

Both Tyler and Alex laughed as they climbed the stairs to the porch and went inside. Tyler ran up the stairs to the nursery where Elli was breastfeeding their daughter to convince Elli to rest while Lianne was down for her nap. Then Alex and Tyler walked over to the construction site for the new house Tyler was having built for his growing family.

"It's just about finished, Dad. All that is left is the flooring, tilework, and trim. The landscapers will be installing the shrubbery and lawn at the end of August. The children will have individual bedrooms at one end of the house. Elli and I have a suite at the other end, so we'll have plenty of privacy. The bottom floor opens up to the outdoors with a private entrance to a suite for Mrs. Simon. There is another at the other end for you."

"This is amazing, son. You designed it yourself?" Alex asked.

"Yes. As you can see, three of the children's rooms are big enough to be divided later if Elli is willing to have three more children. Are there any multiple births on your or Mom's side of the family?" Tyler asked with a grin. "Maybe, we can do this as a one-shot deal like Rick with the triplets. Rick was so looking forward to having a lot of kids. I'm glad he had the chance before he died. Rick was a very happy man, but I'm the one who reaped the benefits. I love those kids so much, and they're a constant reminder of my best friend."

"I never told you this, Dad, but I almost blew my chance with Elli," Tyler admitted.

Alex turned to his son with a concerned look and asked, "What do you mean, Tyler?"

"Do you remember the last time I disappeared to my cabin in Vermont? It was just before Elli and I were married," Tyler answered.

"Yes, I remember. You only called once to let me know where you were. I was worried sick, but you refused to tell me why you were staying there again. Especially after you spent eight months at the cabin after Elli and Rick were married," Alex responded.

"Just before I ran off, Elli tried to tell me that she'd loved me since tenth grade, but I misunderstood. I thought she was admitting that she was in love with her cousin, Tim." Tyler winced at the remembrance. "I'd just made love to Elli for the first time and was filled with remorse. I thought I'd taken advantage of her. She was in a terrible place emotionally. So, like a coward, I took off."

"I had been at the cabin for three months and still couldn't get Elli out of my heart. So, like an ass, I tried to push her out by picking up a woman at a barroom. It was the first and only time I'd ever brought a woman to my cabin. I had her naked in my bed, and I couldn't perform. My head was full of thoughts of Elli. I felt like I was cheating on her, and I was ashamed of myself," Tyler admitted.

"So, what happened?" Alex asked with concern. He could see that Tyler was in pain from the admission.

"The woman asked me who had my heart all tied up in knots. After we got dressed, we talked over coffee. I told her about Elli and the kids and Rick's death. I told her about having sex with Elli but that Elli was in love with Tim. That woman is the one who made me understand that it wasn't Tim that Elli loved. And she was right."

"I got home just in time. Elli was getting ready to pack up the kids and move home to Montana. She'd written me a letter thanking me for all of my support and about the baby she was carrying. My baby, Dad! But she was letting me off the hook and taking all of the blame for the baby's conception. If I hadn't gotten my head out of my ass and come home in time, she would have been gone. She would never have believed that I wanted her for herself. She would have thought I was only proposing because of Billy."

"Did you ever tell Elli about the near-miss with the woman in Vermont?" Alex questioned.

"It's funny that you should ask that, Dad. I told Elli on our honeymoon. We were talking about honesty and never hiding anything from each other. That's when I told her about that woman," Tyler admitted.

"What did Elli say, Tyler? Was she angry?" Alex asked worriedly.

Tyler shook his head, no. "Just the opposite. She asked me to try to find the woman. Elli wanted to meet her to thank her for convincing me that I needed to come home. That's the kind of woman Elli is. Her heart is so pure and loving. I can't believe how lucky I am to have her in my life."

"So, were you able to find the woman?" Alex questioned.

"Her name was Sandy Adams. Elli and I researched online, plus we went to the barroom where I met Sandy. We couldn't find anyone by that name, and no one at the barroom recognized my description of her. It was like she didn't exist. I'll always be thankful to her, though," Tyler said.

"Well, that certainly was a strange thing to be doing on your honeymoon. Looking for a woman that you almost had sex with so that your new wife could thank her. Elli is a special woman, and you're a good man, Tyler Thompson. I'm so proud to have you as a son," Alex said as he pulled his son in for a hug. "Now, let's make a list of what I'm supposed to oversee while you're away. I don't want to mess up."

Tyler took his father back to the house, and they sat at the desk in the office. Tyler created a list of contractors that still had work to do on the house. He also gave Alex a list of things that needed to be checked daily and weekly on the adjacent farm concerning the greenhouses, beef cattle, and the vineyard.

"I've given you access to my accounts, and here's the telephone numbers for Mr. Daniels, my attorney, the bank, the architect, and all of the contractors. Dennis Davenport and his family are the caretakers for the farm next door. These are Dennis' cell and house numbers. The number is on there for the Circle R ranch and the cell number for Mike Willis. Mrs. Simon said that she would feed the chickens and take care of the horses. You can help her with those chores if you want. Maybe she can teach you to ride. Let me know if you can think of anything else. Hopefully, we'll be leaving in a couple of weeks. Elli wants to surprise her grandparents. So, they don't know we're coming. Mrs. Simon will prepare your meals for you and take care of your laundry. She always takes Sunday and Monday off. She goes to visit her sister right after church on Sunday morning. So, you'll be on your own those days."

"If you want to go through your house here in Stillwater to pack up what you intend to keep, there's room for storage in our basement. Then you can put your house on the market. Your suite in the new house includes a living room and eat-in kitchen. So, you may want to keep some of the furniture or buy new, or maybe a little of each. If you want, I'll tell the contractors to concentrate on your suite first to get it finished so that you can move in permanently."

"Sounds good, Tyler. I'm looking forward to getting settled. Don't worry about me. I'll have plenty of things to keep me busy while you're gone," Alex said.

When they'd finished making a list, Tyler and his dad went into the kitchen to prep for dinner. Tyler was making a tender filet mignon wrapped in a buttery pastry recipe that he had created for the restaurant he owned before he married Elli. He was pairing it with a flavorful oven-roasted potato and vegetable dish made with new baby potatoes, bell peppers, zucchini, and mushrooms. It was one of his children's favorite dishes and ensured that they had vegetables in their diet.

Elli found the two most handsome men she had ever met with their heads bent together over the chopping block in the kitchen when she came downstairs from her nap. After hugging and kissing her father-in-law, she wrapped her arms around Tyler's waist and said, "Hey there, handsome man. Missed you. What can I do to help?"

"Well, sweet girl, you can park your beautiful butt on that chair and keep us company. I'm trying to impress my father with my culinary skills. There is just enough time to get the food ready before Mrs. Simon and the kids get back. You know how hungry the kids are after they've spent the day playing at Jeanette's farm," Tyler said as he grazed his wife's cheek and neck with his lips. Leaning close to Elli's ear, he whispered. I hope you're horny. I intend to make you moan later."

Elli blushed and nodded her head, yes, hoping that her father-in-law was too busy chopping mushrooms to notice.

Tyler winked at her, having noticed the blush creep up his wife's neck. Bedtime couldn't arrive soon enough as far as he was concerned.

CHAPTER 27

BAIN went straight to the barroom from the airport. He needed to establish an alibi. It was a slim possibility that Emilia might remember something after she woke up from her date rape hallucinations. So, Bain wasn't taking any chances.

He'd called Shawn from the airport and told him to meet him. Shawn was already waiting at the bar nursing a beer when Bain arrived.

"Hey, man. Welcome back! Did you find Emilia?" Shawn greeted him.

"No, not yet. Was a false lead. I came here directly from Bethlehem to regroup and get clean clothes. Can you do me a favor, Shawn? If anyone asks, I've been home all along. I don't want anyone knowing my business. I'll make it worth your while if you can do that for me. How are the cows?" Bain asked.

"We're good, Bain. I won't tell anyone that you're looking for Emilia. The tanker showed up for the milk just as I was finishing the afternoon chores. The bull can smell the heifers waiting to be bred. He's getting antsy. Otherwise, there haven't been any problems at the farm. You said I could stay in the house while you were gone, so I've been sleeping in your guestroom. Hope that's alright?" Shawn responded. "Are you leaving again, or are you giving up?"

"No, I'm not giving up. I'm going to stick around until I get a few major chores completed. You can help me with those. Hopefully, we can get the bull in with the girls and get them bred before I take off again. In the meantime, maybe we can pick up a woman to share tonight, two if we're lucky. What do you say? Are you game, Shawn?" Bain said with a wink.

Looking around, Shawn spotted two college-aged women seated in a corner booth. One was a redhead, and the other was a blond. They were dressed kind of sleazy in tiny tank tops and skirts that barely covered their asses. They were eyeing up the men sitting alone at the bar, probably hoping some poor schmuck would pay for their drinks in exchange for a hookup. Shawn nodded in their direction. "What about those two, Bain?" he asked.

"I'll take the redhead," Bain responded as he stood up. "She's bigger. I don't think my dick will fit in the little blond. Let's go introduce ourselves."

Bain wasn't interested in the slutty looking redhead, but he needed to make it look like he'd been home all along, in case anyone asked. If it looked like he was on the prowl, no one would suspect that he had been in Montana drugging and attempting to kidnap his sister-in-law.

Both men grabbed their drinks and headed to the booth occupied by the two women. Shawn paused next to the blond and said, "Hello, ladies. Mind if my friend and I buy you both a drink?"

The blond nodded her head enthusiastically and scooted over to make room. Shawn slid in beside her. The redhead looked Bain up and down and started to giggle. "Man, you're a big one, aren't you?"

Bain smirked, "About nine inches. Think you can handle it?"

The redhead blushed, "Holy shit! One night with you, Mister, and a woman would be ruined for any other man. She'd never want anyone else. I think I'll have to pass on that. You don't look like you're interested in anything other than a one-night-stand. I love sex too much to spend the rest of my life going without because I want someone I can't have all the time."

Bain laughed. "Your loss, then. How about you, blondie. Care to take a once-in-a-lifetime ride?"

The blonde nodded her head and said, "I'm game." So, Shawn stood back up and slid in next to the redhead.

"Well, that's settled. What are you drinking, ladies? The night's young, and I'm thirsty," Bain said as he slid in next to the busty blonde. After ordering a round of drinks, Bain slipped his hand under the woman's skirt and quirked his eyebrow at her when he discovered nothing but bare skin. Nudging her legs apart, Bain pushed his middle finger into her cunt, pumped a few times, and pulled it out. Giving his finger a sniff, he wiped it off on the blonde's skirt, grabbed some cash from his wallet to pay for the drinks, and got up to leave.

"Where are you going, Mister?" the blonde growled. "You promised me a thrill ride."

"I've changed my mind. It's been a long day. I'll see you back at the house, Shawn," Bain replied. Then he got the heck out of there.

He'd wait for Emilia. She was sweet, unlike the skanky blonde who smelled like curdled milk.

After he got home, Bain took a hot shower and jerked off to thoughts of Emilia in that tiny white nightie. Then he went downstairs to the kitchen and grabbed some hefty garbage bags. Taking the stairs two at a time, Bain stomped down the hall to the master bedroom. Yanking all of Iain's clothes out of the dresser and closet in frustration, he stuffed everything into the bags until they were full, then tied the tops. When he was finished, he flopped on the bed and sobbed for the loss of his little brother.

Shawn came home about two hours later with a six-pack of beer and a couple of pizzas. "Bain, you upstairs, man? I've got beer and pizza. Come eat."

Bain went into the master bath and washed his face with cold water. Grabbing the garbage bags full of his brother's clothing, he dragged them down the stairs and dumped them at the bottom. "You're the same size as my brother, right?" he asked.

"Yeah, we've shared clothes in the past," Shawn responded.

"Good, take what you want. I'd appreciate it if you would take the rest to the donation bins in the church parking lot. Please!" Bain hung his head as he passed Shawn. Bain pulled plates out of the kitchen cabinet, helped himself to the pizza and beer, and flopped on the sofa in the living room.

"You, okay, man?" Shawn asked, concerned because he had never heard Bain say the word please in his life.

"I've been better. I miss my brother. You didn't tap the blonde, did you? She was rank."

"Nope. A girl I've slept with before showed up right after you left. I nailed her on the front seat of my truck. The blonde and redhead were pissed off when you just got up and left," Shawn laughed.

"Yeah, I hope my finger doesn't rot off. That blonde's pussy has been around the block too many times. When I marry Emilia, I'm done hunting. She's going to be it for me. I've loved that woman for twenty-five years, Shawn. She has to come home," Bain said.

Then he threw his plate against the wall. The slice of pepperoni pizza slid down the wall, leaving a streak of grease behind. Thankfully, he'd used a paper plate.

Bain looked at the mess he'd made and yelled, "Fuck! Now I have to clean that shit up. Emilia will have my hide if she comes home to a filthy house. She took good care of Iain and me and our home all those years."

Then he went to get a bucket and rag so he could clean up the mucky mess he'd made.

CHAPTER 28

EMILIA knew that she was the topic of discussion when she entered the kitchen. All conversation ceased, and the three people sitting at the table all looked up at her expectantly. Bill and Michael were drinking coffee. Peggy, wrapped tight in a heavy sweater, was drinking tea. Michael jumped to his feet and pulled out a chair for Emilia to sit. She placed the items she was carrying beside the cup and silverware on the table in front of her. Mike went to the warming tray in the oven and pulled out a plate. It contained toasted crusty bread topped with avocado, scrambled eggs, and cherry tomatoes, tossed with shredded mozzarella cheese and fresh basil.

Stunned, all Emilia could say was, "Wow! I'm impressed, Michael."

"Well, being a bachelor all of my life, it was learn to cook or eat out all of the time. So, I learned to cook," he said with a wink.

Emilia was stunned, again, by Michael's admission.

"You've never been married?" she asked.

"Nope, the love of my life went missing about thirty-two years ago. I looked for her, but couldn't find her. No other woman has ever measured up. I got lucky, though, because I found her again. Now, I just have to convince her to give me a second chance," Mike said. "What would you like to drink, sweetheart?"

Emilia, who had bowed her head while gripping her hands tightly in her lap, reached out to pick up her fork. She was shocked that Michael had waited all those years for her. She was ashamed because she'd married the first man who had offered her any security. What a mistake that had proved to be. A mistake that she had paid dearly for making.

"Ummm...orange juice if you have any. Thank you," she responded.

Before she took her first bite, she looked at Peggy and Bill. "I need to apologize to both of you. I don't know what happened, but I know that I haven't made much of an impression. I'm supposed to be taking care of your needs. If you want me to leave, I'll understand. Mr. Goldstein, the man who brought me your offer of employment, said that you had other qualified applicants that you had considered. Hopefully, one of them is still available to accept your generous offer. I fully intend to repay both of you for any monies you've expended on my behalf. I am very sorry for the trouble I've caused you. You don't need this drama with everything else you have to contend with." By the time Emilia was finished speaking, her eyes were bright with unshed tears. She thought to herself, "God, I am so tired of crying."

Peggy, who was sitting directly opposite Emilia, reached out and took Emilia's hand in hers. "What exactly is it that you're apologizing for, dear? You were attacked and drugged on our property. It is we who should be apologizing to you. The police have no leads, but we've stepped up security. Mike will be staying with you in your room at night to keep you safe. Now, eat up. I believe that you told Mike you have something to tell us, and we have some things that we need to share with you. I'm going to lie down while you eat. Then we'll all meet in the living room for our discussion."

At that, Bill helped Peggy from her chair and led her from the room. Emilia had dropped her hands back into her lap and clenched them tight while Peggy was speaking. Mike pried her hands apart and brought them to his lips, where he kissed each of Emilia's fingers tenderly.

"Eat your food, Emi. You haven't eaten anything since Sunday night. And stop worrying," he told her. Then he kissed her and turned her to her plate. "Eat." Going to the refrigerator, he took out the carton of orange juice and poured her a glass.

"I want you to make a doctor's appointment, Emi. We need to be certain the date rape drug that you were injected with didn't do any damage," Mike told her.

"Can we wait a couple of weeks?" Emi asked. "I'm not particularly fond of doctor's visits."

"I'm surprised at you, Emi. You're a nurse and should know better. So, I don't like that idea. However, if you make the appointment today, I'll agree to an appointment a couple of weeks from today. Promise me?" Mike responded.

"Okay, I promise, but only if you haven't asked me to leave after we have our talk," Emi said. Then she took her first bite of the appealing breakfast that Michael had cooked for her.

"This is delicious, Michael. A woman would be fortunate to be married to you. I'm certain you'll find the right woman, and she'll make you very happy," Emilia said.

"I've already found the right woman. Her name is Emilia Addison Mackenzie Andersen. I'm going to change that last bit to Willis as soon as possible if she's agreeable. She may not want me, though. I am just a cowboy, after all," Mike teased her.

Emilia swallowed hard and started to cry again. "Oh, God! All I do anymore is cry. I've cried so much, I should look like a shriveled-up prune."

Mike grabbed a box of tissues off the kitchen counter, dabbed the tears from her eyes and cheeks, then handed her some clean ones. "Blow," he told her.

That reminded Emilia of when she'd met Iain for the first time in the grocery store. Iain had told her to blow her nose, too. Emilia started to cry harder. She was an emotional mess.

Mike, dismayed, pulled Emi into his lap and rocked her. Placing kisses to the top of her head, he crooned a lullaby his mother used to sing to him when he was upset as a child. Gradually, Emi's tears ceased. With a stuffed-up nose from all the crying, she said, "I think I'm done crying. At least for now, anyway."

That made Mike laugh outright, and he kissed her hard on the mouth. Placing her back in her chair, he asked, "Do you want something else to eat? That's probably cold."

"No, it's excellent. I intend to eat every bite." And she did.

When she was finished, Mike took Emi's dishes, rinsed them, and placed them in the dishwasher. Then he wiped up the table and the top of the counter and made a fresh pot of coffee. Taking a tray from the cabinet, he arranged cups, spoons, sugar, creamer, and tea bags on the tray and took them to the living room. Emilia followed, carrying two trivets, the freshly brewed coffee, and a pot of hot water for tea. Then she went back for the envelope she'd placed on the table. She took a seat on the sofa and waited nervously for Michael to fetch Bill and Peggy.

Michael was carrying a pile of file folders when he returned. "Bill and Peggy will be out in a few minutes," he told her.

After placing the folders on the end table beside the sofa, Mike sat down next to Emi and grabbed her hands to still their trembling. "Everything is going to work out. I promise. I know that my promise may not hold much weight. I promised to come back for you when I graduated from high school, and I promised you that we would get married, have children, and spend the rest of our lives loving each other. I did try to come back for you, Emi. I just couldn't find you. I hope you'll forgive me for taking so long to keep those promises. I intend to keep every single promise I've ever made to you." Then he squeezed her hands, pulled her slim body in tight against his where she fit just right, and wrapped his arm around her. Tipping her head up, he kissed Emi to seal those promises with his lips. That's how Peggy and Bill found them when they entered the room. The sight pleased the elderly couple.

CHAPTER 29

ONCE Mike finished pouring coffee for himself and Bill and tea for Peggy and Emi, he lowered himself next to Emi on the sofa. As he pulled her in tight, he could feel her trembling with nervousness. Her hands were ice cold, and her right leg was bouncing. Mike laid his hand on Emi's knee and leaned in to place a kiss on the corner of her mouth. Mike knew Emi was nervous because she feared that he would reject her when she was finished telling him about their daughter.

After taking a sip of her tea, which stuck in her throat, Emilia placed the cup back onto the coffee table. Glancing at Michael shyly, she bowed her head to stare at her hands which she gripped tightly in her lap. They were white-knuckled. She would concentrate on her hands to avoid the expressions on the faces of these three people whose opinions she valued. She didn't want to see their eyes fill with condemnation at what she had to tell them.

Clearing her throat several times, Emi asked them not to interrupt her until she had finished telling them what she needed to say. All three agreed to her demand.

"Michael knows a little bit about my childhood. How my mother would beat me and lock me in my room if I did anything to displease her. That was only part of my story, however. Some of it I didn't discover until my mother died in a car accident three years ago. She kept documents and a diary in a safety deposit box at the bank. That's how I learned the truth about myself."

"My father wasn't my mother's husband, Phillip Mackenzie. She tricked Phillip into marrying her when she got pregnant by the senior partner at the law firm where she worked at the time. My real father's name was Bryan McDonnell. So, in truth, I'm illegitimate."

"I met Michael when I was in tenth grade, and Michael was a junior. We were in the library, and I had dropped my belongings. We both bent down at the same time and cracked heads. I don't know if you believe in love at first sight, but Michael was it for me. When I looked into Michael's eyes, I was lost. We spent as much time as possible together that whole school year, and we became intimate."

Mike could see a blush steal its way up Emi's neck into her face but didn't say a word as she continued.

"At the end of the school year, Michael came to see me one last time. His dad was moving his family to Montana. We were both devastated and made promises to each other. Then Michael left. We haven't seen each other since. I tried to find him three years ago when I discovered what was in my mother's safety deposit box, but I was unsuccessful."

"What Michael doesn't know is that the last time we were together, we made a baby." At this admission, a single tear slid down Emilia's cheek. She impatiently brushed it away.

"When my mother found out I was pregnant, she moved us to western Pennsylvania. That's why Michael couldn't find me when he came back for me. I was locked in my bedroom for the duration of my pregnancy. My mother paid a midwife to deliver the baby. As soon as I gave birth, my mother took the baby and gave it away."

"Until three years ago, I didn't even know if the baby was a boy or a girl," Emi said as she reached for the envelope. She handed it to Michael.

"I'm sorry, Michael, that you've missed out on having a family because of me. There's an album in this envelope containing photographs of our daughter. One picture for each year of her life until she graduated from high school. There's also a letter. My mother gave our baby to a man named James Roberts and his wife, Lilianne. James is the half-brother I never knew I had. They named the baby Eloise Lianne Roberts and falsified a birth certificate naming themselves as her parents. I swear I didn't know any of this until three years ago. Then I tried to find them, our daughter, and you on the internet. I was unsuccessful in my search to locate any of you. I hope you can forgive me."

Sobbing, now, Emilia rushed from the room and out the front door. Running across the yard, she entered the stable and slumped down in a corner behind a pile of hay where she cried some of those tears, she was so sick of.

The minute Emi rushed from the room, Mike jumped up to go after her.

Peggy implored, "Wait, Mike. Give her some time to compose herself. Look through the album and whatever else is in the envelope."

Mike nodded and sat back down. Taking the contents from the envelope, he handed Peggy a letter to read, who then passed it over to Bill. Mike opened the album that contained pictures of his daughter, Elli, as a child. It was the first time he'd seen pictures of her at that age. Her face in the graduation picture looked like the young woman he'd met when she came to the ranch. No wonder he was confused when Elli stepped down from Tim's plane. She looked just like her mother, Emi when she was sixteen. Mike's eyes were glassy as he handed the album over to Peggy to share with Bill. Then he went out to find the woman he loved.

CHAPTER 30

MIKE was almost frantic when he couldn't find Emi immediately. He took a quick glance into the stable, first, then went over to his house to see if she had gone inside. She wasn't there. Worriedly, he searched around the outbuildings and finally went back and entered the stable for a thorough search. That's where he found Emi lying behind a pile of hay. She'd cried herself to sleep.

Lifting her quickly, Mike cradled Emi in his arms and sat down onto a hay bale with her in his lap. Brushing the hay from her hair, he kissed her forehead, eyelids, cheeks, and mouth. Then he nuzzled her neck and nipped her earlobe. Whispering near her ear, he implored her, "Wake up, darlin'." When her eyelids fluttered, he told her, "I love you, Emi. I'm so sorry you had to go through all of that by yourself. It's all my fault. I didn't use protection, and I got you pregnant. Can you forgive me?"

Emilia shook her head and vehemently said, "No, that's not right."

"Does that mean you can't forgive me?" Mike implored. "I'll never be able to make it up to you."

"That's not what I meant, Michael. I don't blame you. What you gave me was a precious gift. I lost our baby. I know you'll never be able to forgive me for that. That's why I asked you to let me go. Now, you'll hate me, and I can't bear that," Emi sobbed.

"No more tears, honey. The story isn't over yet. Let's go back so Peggy, Bill, and I can tell you the rest." With that, Mike carried Emi to the house. "Go wash your face and brush the rest of the hay out of your hair. I'll meet you in the kitchen. We'll eat lunch. The rest of the discussion can wait a little longer."

Emi did as she was told. She didn't understand what Peggy, Bill, or Michael could possibly have to say that would expand on her story about her daughter.

Mike went back into the living room.

"Is Emi alright?" Bill asked. "You were gone for a while, and we were getting worried."

"I had trouble finding her, actually," Mike admitted. I finally found her behind a pile of hay in the stable. She'd cried herself to sleep. She's washing up. I told her we'd have lunch and then tell her our side of the story. Why don't you take Peggy to your room so that she can rest? I'll come to get you when lunch is ready."

"Sounds like a good plan," Bill agreed.

As Bill led Peggy from the room, Mike loaded the dirty cups onto the tray and carried everything back to the kitchen. Then he went in search of Emi. He found her lying on her bed, hiding her head under a pillow.

"You're not crying, are you, babe?" he asked her. The pillow covering Emi's head moved from side to side. "Are you hiding, then?" Again, the pillow moved from side to side, paused, and then changed direction to an up and down movement.

Dropping down beside her, Mike raised Emi's top and pulled her left nipple into his mouth through her bra. That got Emi's attention, and she arched her back. Mike chuckled. His Emi was so responsive. Mike ran his palm over the other breast, squeezed, and then pinched the nipple as he bit the one, he was suckling.

Abandoning her breasts, Mike shifted and languidly pressed a trail of kisses across Emilia's stomach. When he reached her navel, he paused and dipped his tongue into the recess. As his hand slipped inside the waistband of her pants, he cupped her mound.

Emilia gripped Mike's shoulders and dug in her nails as she began to squirm. Rising up, Mike glanced at Emi and said, "Ah, there you are. I see that you're not hiding anymore," because she had removed the pillow from her head.

Emilia blushed and said, "No, I'm not. I was never able to hide from you."

Mike stared at Emi intently as his hands slid over the plains of her stomach. Then he gripped the waistband of her pants and gently pulled the fabric down her thighs. Removing them altogether, Mike tossed them on the floor. Without breaking eye contact, he lightly ran his fingers over her panties, noting the dampness with a grin, then slid them off.

"Let's take the rest of your clothes off, honey. I need to make love to you."

Emilia grabbed the hem of her top and yanked it over her head. It joined her pants and panties on the floor. Reaching behind her back, she undid the clasp of her bra. Mike pulled the straps down Emi's arms to the wrists, then used the bra to bind her to the headboard. Emilia's eyes widened, and she shifted restlessly.

"I think someone has entirely too many pieces of clothing on," she said.

Mike smirked. "Then I guess I'll have to rectify the situation." Standing up, he pulled his shirt off and gave it a toss. His pants and jockey briefs quickly followed, exposing his engorged shaft. Emilia licked her lips. She desperately wanted to touch Michael and told him so.

Mike raised his eyebrows in surprise, then knelt by Emi's head so that she could reach his aching member. Raising her head, she licked the pre-cum from the tip. Then she took him into her mouth as far as she could and sucked until Mike groaned and pulled away.

Lying down beside her, Mike kissed Emi hard. When she opened her mouth, his tongue slipped inside and danced with hers.

Spreading Emi's legs, he shifted over her, lined himself up, and thrust inside. Emi moaned and arched her upper body off the bed, pushing her breasts against his chest to increase their skin-to-skin contact. Then she rocked her hips, and they found a rhythm together.

"Ohhhh…I'm going to come, Michael," she said as her legs trembled.

"Come for me, baby. You feel so good," he responded.

As Emi's inner muscles bore down and squeezed him tight, Mike pumped harder and came with a groan. Emi continued to spasm, then she called out his name as her orgasm overtook her.

Nuzzling her neck, Mike said, "Wow! I don't know what to say other than we've gotten better with age. That was amazing."

Emilia squeezed his cock tight. "I think we need more practice," she giggled. "Maybe we can do that again later."

Mike kissed her, smacked her on the butt, and said, "I think we need to practice a lot."

CHAPTER 31

LIFTING Emi from the bed, he carried her into the bathroom and sat her on the sink top. Emilia let out a squeal, "Yikes, that's cold."

Mike chuckled. "That's because you just had hot sex, and your backside is still on fire," and reached into the shower. After adjusting the temperature of the water, he lifted Emi again and stepped inside the stall. Wrapping her legs around his waist and leaning her against the cold tile, Emi let out another squeal.

"Looks like I need to warm you up," he grinned as he leaned in to capture her lips in a searing kiss. Then he slid his fingers through her folds and began to fondle her. When he slipped a finger inside and hooked it to find her G spot, Emilia moaned into Mike's mouth.

Nipping his bottom lip, she said, "You're insatiable."

"Well, you said we needed more practice. I aim to please, My Lady," he joked. Lining himself up, he teased her with the tip of his cock until she started to squirm. Lowering her legs down, he put her back on her feet, turned her to the tile, and spread her legs wide. Entering her with a hard thrust, he rammed in and out until they both came together. Legs trembling, Mike pulled Emi back against him, kissed the side of her neck, and whispered, "Damn, I love you so much."

Emilia sighed, "I love you more."

When they were finished cleaning up, they got dressed and went to the kitchen to make lunch. Mike and Emilia found Peggy and Bill sitting at the table. Bill laughed and said, "Where's lunch? You're late."

Mike chuckled, gave Bill a wink, and replied, "Emi was upset. It took a lot to persuade her to calm down."

Emilia blushed prettily, opened the refrigerator door, and poked her head inside the cold interior to cool her cheeks and hide her embarrassment. With a muffled voice, she said, "We have some lean cuts of chicken that I think Peggy can tolerate. We could have some rice with it or some buttered pasta coated with parmesan cheese. Peggy can have some melon with that, and the rest of us can eat a salad. Does that sound good, everybody?"

While Mike made a fresh salad and set the table, Emi sautéed the chicken in olive oil and prepared the pasta. Conversation during the meal concerned the ranch. A couple from Kentucky would be dropping off a mare with good bloodlines the following week. Mike had purchased the horse as an investment. It would be bred by one of the Circle R quarter horses, Midnight Blue. They were also planning to replace the bulls to change up the genetics. Bill wanted Mike's opinion on several animals they were considering.

Finished eating, Peggy and Bill got up to leave the table. "We'll meet you back in the living room when you're done with the dishes," Bill told Mike and Emilia.

Mike was holding Emi's hand when they entered the living room about forty minutes later. Peggy looked at Bill with a pleased expression. Mike knew Emi was once again nervous, thus the hand holding. Pulling her in tight against him on the sofa, he gave her hand a squeeze and said, "Relax. Everything is going to be okay."

Emilia gave him a slight nod, then sat on her hands to keep them from shaking.

Turning to Bill, Mike asked, "Would you like to begin?"

"Yes, but I'll make the same request of Emi. No questions until I'm finished, please," Bill said.

Emilia nodded in agreement and once again stared at her lap.

"Well, where to begin. Hmmm. About twelve years ago in March, Peggy's nephew Tim Jones brought a nineteen-year-old girl to the ranch. You'll meet Tim and his wife Jeannie and her daughter Sophie this weekend, Emi. Tim owns a small aircraft charter service outside Kirk, Oregon, and we have a landing strip here on the ranch for his use," Bill told her. Then he continued.

"The girl was running away from her parents when she made her way to Tim in Kirk. She'd discovered that her parents planned to sell her unborn child when it was born. She was hoping that she would be able to fly to Montana to find a women's shelter in Billings that would take her in. When Tim called about the girl's plight, Peggy and I agreed for her to come here. We've fostered six children in addition to raising Tim over the years. The photographs of those children are the ones adorning the hall to your bedroom."

Emilia looked at Bill questioningly. What did this have to do with her? She wanted to ask, but she had promised not to interrupt until Bill had finished his story. So, she lowered her eyes back down.

"During a conversation Peggy and I had with the girl the day of her arrival, I made an astonishing discovery. She said her name was Eloise Lianne Roberts and that her parents were James and Lilianne Roberts. Now, I don't know if you've wondered at the coincidence that my last name is Roberts. It may not have seemed of any significance to you. There are lots of Roberts in the world, after all. The truth of the matter is that James Roberts was my son by my first marriage to Eloise Sanders. So, when Elli told us her story, I believed that this young girl was my granddaughter. Since I'd been estranged from my son since I divorced his mother, I was unaware of Elli's existence."

Shocked at the names and Bill's admission, Emilia gasped. With a startled look, she bit down on her bottom lip to keep from speaking.

"James and Lilianne lived in Fair Lawn, New Jersey when Elli was born. They moved to Stillwater, New Jersey when Elli was about three years old. Elli was verbally and physically abused by James as a child. He beat her and locked her in her bedroom as punishment for any imagined misdeeds. I doubt tremendously that Elli ever did anything to deserve his ire. She is the sweetest, gentlest woman I have ever met, other than my Peggy, and now you."

"When James found out that Elli was pregnant, he moved the family to northern California. Elli was confined to her bedroom for the duration of her pregnancy, just like you were, Emilia before you gave birth."

Bill continued, "Elli gave birth to her daughter, whom she named Jessica, the very next day after she arrived here. We brought her and the baby home to live with us, believing that she was our granddaughter and that Jessica was our great-granddaughter by blood. Shortly after Jessica was born, James and Lilianne were given permission to come for a brief visit. They were killed in an accident in Idaho while enroute to the ranch.

Having just given birth, Elli requested that I handle the details of her parents' estate. Tim flew me to his airport in Kirk and then accompanied me to California to meet with James' attorney. I was given access to James' safety deposit box and home. After examining the documents that I discovered, I figured out that Elli wasn't my granddaughter, after all. My ex-wife, Eloise, had given Elli to James and Lilianne when she was born. None of the documents, however, mentioned the name of Elli's birth mother."

"I've never told Elli that she's not really my granddaughter. She has always been treated as such, and that will never change. Shortly after discovering those documents, I hired a private detective agency in Pennsylvania to search for my ex-wife and Elli's birth parents. The head of that agency is Samuel Goldstein."

Emilia gasped again as tears slid down her cheeks, unheeded.

"It took time, but the trail eventually led him to Elli's real mother, Emilia Addison Mackenzie Andersen. The detective discovered that you, Emi, were in an abusive relationship but that your husband, Iain Andersen, was dying of cancer. So, Peggy and I decided that we would wait before approaching you. We didn't want to exacerbate your situation. About two weeks before Iain passed away,

Mr. Goldstein finally uncovered the name of Elli's real father, Roger Michael Willis."

Emilia looked at Michael, her cerulean blue eyes an ocean of raging emotions.

Mike grazed his fingers along the line of Emi's jaw and kissed her tenderly on the lips. "Elli doesn't know yet. We'll tell her together."

Emi sighed and nodded her head in agreement.

When Mike jumped up from the sofa and went into the study, Emilia looked at Peggy and Bill questioningly, but they just smiled at her. Mike was back a few minutes later bearing what looked like photo albums. "We have six grandchildren, Emi," Mike told her as he sat beside her and placed the albums on the coffee table. "Elli, her husband Tyler, and the children will be coming for a visit shortly."

"The albums are in chronological order, dear." Peggy reached out and tapped a leather-tooled album with embossed lettering. "This one starts with pictures that were taken of Elli at the hospital, just after giving birth to Jessica."

"What are the children's names? Where do Elli and her family live?" Emi questioned.

"They live in Stillwater, New Jersey, on a farm. Elli actually married the father of her first child. Jess is now twelve years old. The father's name was Richard Blair Whrite. Rick and Elli had triplets after they were married. The triplets are Richard Blair, Peggy Lynne, and Tyler Logan. They're now six years of age. A few months after the triplets were born, Rick was killed in a farming accident," Mike told her.

Emilia covered her mouth with her hand to prevent a sob from escaping. She'd lost a son-in-law she would never get to meet. "You said six children? You only mentioned the names of four."

"Yes, Elli married Rick's best friend, Tyler Logan Thompson, in a double wedding, here at the ranch on the Saturday after Thanksgiving. Tim and Jeannie were married at the same time. So, the couples share an anniversary. Their sixth anniversary is this fall. Tyler is the father of William Timothy and Lianne Susanna. Billy is five, and Lianne was born roughly seven weeks ago."

"Wow! Just, Wow! So, Bill. Was I hired because of what you discovered?" Emilia asked.

"Only partly. You were thoroughly investigated and cleared by Mr. Goldstein. We do need your nursing skills, plus I think Peggy and I were trying to play Cupid a little bit," Bill smirked. "We're very fond of Mike, you know. We want to see him happy. He's a good man, Emi, and I consider him my son. He deserves to be surrounded by the people he loves."

Emilia sighed and brushed the tears from her cheeks with the sides of her hands. Turning to gaze into Michael's eyes, she said, "I agree. Michael is a very good man. He deserves to be happy. I can't thank you both enough for bringing me here and for telling me about my daughter."

"Mike, give Emi the folders with Mr. Goldstein's reports when she's finished looking at the photo albums. They belong to you and Emi, now. Emi, I don't want you to take walks outside alone until we're certain the person who attacked you isn't coming back," Bill told her in a complete change of subject.

"Did Sean make up a roster for the hands to take turns standing watch at night, Mike?" Bill asked.

"Yes, I'm standing first watch beginning at 8:00 p.m. tonight. We'll each stand a two-hour shift. That way we'll all get enough sleep," Mike confirmed.

"Sounds good. Hopefully, the police were right, and it was just a drifter. Okay, time for Peggy's afternoon nap. Emi has been given a lot of information that she'll need to digest, and I think she should rest as well. At least until it's time to make dinner," Bill said with a wink. "We'll see you both later."

Once they were alone, Mike grabbed Emilia by the hand and said, "Come on, it's time for your first riding lesson. We'll finish looking at the photos later." Then he led her to the stable.

CHAPTER 32

"NOW, you're not actually going to ride today," Mike told Emi as he led Cinnamon from her stall. We need to get you comfortable around the animals first and teach you about the proper riding attire. Did your husband own horses?"

"No, it's a dairy farm. The brothers also kept chickens for eggs and meat and a pig for butchering each year. No horses," Emilia responded.

Mike looked at Emi perplexedly, wondering what she might be unwilling to share concerning her marriage. He'd read Sam Goldstein's reports to the point where he could probably quote them word for word. What Mike didn't understand was why no children were produced from the union. Michael fought to ignore the consuming jealousy he felt because another man had intimate knowledge of Emi's body. The jealousy was misplaced after all. The man died a little more than a week ago.

As he attached the horse's lead to hooks on either side of the center aisle, Emilia could see that Michael wanted to ask her something but was afraid to do so. He kept stealing worried glances at her. Finally, he worked up his courage. "Emi, tell me to mind my business if I ask you anything out of line or that makes you uncomfortable."

"What would you like to know?" Emilia asked in a subdued voice.

Mike stared at her worriedly, "Why is Elli your only child? Did something happen when Elli was born that prevented you from having more?"

Emilia looked at the floor and searched her brain to find just the right words. Finally, she decided that telling the truth was the best course of action because she didn't like to lie anyway. With a tremulous voice, she responded, "I broached the subject of children with Iain about one year after we were married. He said he didn't want smelly, messy, expensive brats. I was to focus on his needs." Emilia could feel herself blush as she admitted, "He was always careful not to touch me without sheathing himself with a condom first. He told me that I wasn't to be trusted regarding protection because I would probably try to trick him. I wanted more children, but truthfully, you were the one I always dreamed of having those children with. In the end, I was thankful that Iain used those condoms every time we were intimate."

"Why is that, honey?" Mike questioned.

"I never had an inkling," Emi whispered so softly that Mike had to lean down to hear her words. "Iain cheated on me for the entire twenty-five years of our marriage. Bain told me last Monday after the repast that he, Iain, and their friends picked up women at barrooms and shared them. If Iain hadn't used those condoms, he might have given me a disease. What fool is married for a quarter of a century and never suspects that her husband is a cheat?"

At a loss for words, Mike pulled Emi tight against his chest. She clung to him desperately as she wept over the loss of her husband, never having more children to love and the fact that she never knew the real Iain at all. She was devastated and humiliated beyond words.

It was an ugly cry full of gut-wrenching sobs. When Emi's cries of grief slowed to whimpers and finally ceased, Mike's shirt front was soaked. As she pulled away, Mike yanked his shirt over his head and said, "Here, blow your nose."

Emi stared at him with a watery smile and grinned, "Gee, thanks!"

After wiping her face, Mike threw the shirt on a bench near the stable door. Taking a brush from the shelf, Mike placed Emi's hand through the strap. Guiding her hand, he showed her how to brush the horse's coat. "It's actually very therapeutic. It calms your mind and brings you peace," he told her.

It was hard to focus on Michael's directions regarding proper horse grooming with his muscular chest and arms on display. Emilia licked her lips repeatedly while dirty thoughts raced through her head. Thoughts about licking every inch of the rugged plains of his chest and sucking on his nipples. She wanted to hear Michael moan the way she did when he pleasured her. By the time she was finished brushing the animal, however, she did feel much better emotionally. Unfortunately, she was now so horny, she squeezed her legs together and rubbed to give herself a smidgen of relief.

"See. Told you so," Mike said. "How did you like that?"

Concerned that Michael had guessed at her naughty thoughts because the evidence must be plastered all over her face, Emilia blinked furiously. Then she smiled prettily, fought to control the blush she could feel creeping into her cheeks, and said, "She's so beautiful, and I'm not as frightened as I was."

Mike winked at her. "Okay, first lesson. The most important aspect of riding is what you should be wearing. You need an approved riding helmet while you're learning. I need to take you into town to get you a pair of boots with at least a two-inch heel and comfortable pants."

"Next. What does the horse wear?" to which Emi giggled, picturing the horse wearing pants, a shirt, and a cowboy hat and boots in her mind.

"Hey, no giggling," Mike teased as he grabbed her and tickled her sides until she was breathless. "This is serious business we're conducting," he laughed. As Mike stared down into Emi's luminous eyes, he said, "Ah, fuck. I want you again. Can we continue our lesson later?"

Emi gave him a sly grin, reached out to run her hand over the bulge in Michael's jeans, and said, "Behave yourself, cowboy. This is serious business we're conducting." Then, she ran as fast as she could and hid behind the hay bales.

Mike let out a whoop of joy, closed and barred both stable doors, and called, "Emi, where are you?" He heard a snort of laughter in return. Stealthily, he made his way around to the other end of the bales. When he peeked, he found Emi with her back to him. She was expecting him to come from the other direction. As he snuck up and grabbed her from behind, Emi let out a squeal and wiggled to evade his grasp.

"Oh, no, you don't. You've been a filthy girl. Grabbing a man's package and leaving him in need. Now, I'm going to have to punish you for that." After pulling down her pants, Mike dropped down onto a bale and placed Emi across his knees with her legs slightly spread. When he smacked one of the lovely cheeks of her ass, Emi went, "Ow, that." Before she could finish, Mike dipped a finger into her moist center, then quickly added a second and slid them in and out. Emilia had meant to say, "Ow, that hurt," but the hurt was quickly forgotten as she moaned and her muscles squeezed Mike's

274

fingers tight. Mike groaned in response. She was already so wet for him.

Withdrawing his fingers, he repeated the process until he had Emi making gibberish noises. She might have even made up a few new words. He could feel that she was getting close. Shifting her so that she was lying face-first over the bale, he stood, dropped his jeans, then coated his cock with her juices and plunged into her center. While he was punishing her with hard fast strokes, he remembered what Emi had told him. Her husband always provided protection because Iain didn't trust Emilia. Mike hadn't even given protection a thought. She'd felt so amazing bareback. He hadn't had unprotected sex with a woman since he made love to Emi before moving to Montana. Could Emi already be carrying his child again? He would welcome the chance to watch Emi grow round with a baby they'd made together. Should he say something about protection, or should he wait to see if Emilia brought it up? Maybe she'd already gone through menopause?

As Mike was having this internal debate, Emi's orgasm hit like an express train that made Mike forget everything he was thinking.

Her orgasm triggered his. Mike could feel his seed spill into Emi in

hot spurts that felt like they would never end.

CHAPTER 33

EMILIA was overcome by the power of her unexpected orgasm. She screamed out Michael's name as he slammed into her. She could feel the heat of his cum as he emptied himself into her, and she was struck dumb at her own stupidity. Since Iain had always provided protection against her getting pregnant, it never occurred to her to say anything. She was a nurse, for heaven's sake, so it should have been first and foremost in her subconscious. She'd neglected to take precautions and hadn't noticed that Michael wasn't using a condom each time they'd had sex in the last few days, either. And, oh, those encounters were so numerous, Emilia had lost count. She'd been so overwhelmed with stress by the loss of her husband and Bain's demands. Then her incredible but well-timed new job and the trip to Montana. Meeting her new employers and taking care of their health needs had consumed her upon arrival. Being reunited with the man who owned her heart and soul was just the icing on the cake. This was all her fault for not paying attention.

Her mind went blank. When was her last period? It had never been regular, and she'd been dealing with so much stress, especially during the previous two years due to Iain's cancer. Until Michael, she hadn't had sex in over a year. She could remember the last time she had an orgasm, though. That was thirty-two years ago when she got pregnant with Elli.

Michael slumped onto her body momentarily when he was spent. When he stood up, he quickly pulled his briefs and jeans into place and helped her stand. Emilia could feel the seminal fluid leaking down her thighs, she was itchy from the hay bale, and her hair must be a fright, she thought. As she gathered her thong and pants, Michael steadied her while she slipped her feet through the openings and pulled them up.

Emilia didn't understand the look on Michael's face as he studied her while she dressed. It almost looked like he was angry with her for some reason. Did Michael think she was trying to trick him by having unprotected sex so that she would get pregnant? Michael confirmed her worst fears when he backed away from her.

"Go take a shower. You smell like sex," Mike said dismissively. "I'll put Cinnamon back in her stall. Then I need to go to my house. I'll be back to help you make dinner for Peggy and Bill. After, I'll need to stand my watch from 8:00 until 10:00 p.m. You should get some rest."

Confused and hurt by Michael's strange attitude, Emilia nodded and walked away. When she reached the stable door, she paused and glanced back. Michael was now all business, dealing with the animal. Placing a fist to her mouth to hold in the sob that was desperate to escape, she turned and ran as quickly as possible. She rounded the house and went to the rear entrance to let herself inside, praying that the owners weren't in the vicinity of the hall near her bedroom.

Peeking inside, Emilia was relieved that the coast was clear. Grabbing some clean clothes from the dresser in her room, she headed to the bathroom for a shower and a good cry. More tears. Would they never end?

After a good scrub, Emilia gathered her dirty clothing and headed for the laundry room. After a quick look to see what laundry Peggy and Bill needed to be washed, as well, she started the washing machine.

It was time to get back to work. Emilia had signed a contract and was responsible for Peggy's and Bill's healthcare in the coming months.

If Michael thought she was trying to trick him for some reason, he could just get over himself. She didn't know she would see him again, especially here on the ranch where she was now an employee. She would talk to Peggy and Bill also about finding a replacement. It would be wrong to expose them to the drama of her life, given what they were already dealing with. Apparently, she had been right all along. Michael was angry at her for losing their daughter. And if he was angry, how was Elli going to feel? Emilia cringed at the thought.

"Well, I guess I never realized just how much of a coward I am." She was talking to herself out loud, now. Never a good sign. "Maybe I should have stayed in Pennsylvania. At least Bain had made his intentions clear."

CHAPTER 34

THE force of Mike's orgasm was unbelievable. He'd never experienced another like it. But even as he spent himself in the tight embrace of Emi's sweet pussy, he couldn't help worrying that he had taken an unfair advantage. He realized that not once had Emilia initiated their sexual encounters. It was all on him. She was used to her husband providing protection against the possibility of an unwanted pregnancy. Mike had failed miserably at that, as well.

How was Emi going to feel if Mike had gotten her pregnant? She was forty-eight years old. It would be a high-risk pregnancy. Mike was so angry with himself for his stupidity that he'd unwittingly spoken gruffly to Emi once she was dressed. He cringed at the remembrance of how dismissive he'd sounded, telling her to go take a shower because she smelled like sex. Of course, she smelled like sex. It was the best sex of Mike's life. He'd have her over that bale of hay again in a heartbeat if she was still standing here.

He'd seen the look of pain in her eyes when she'd turned back. Damn it, he'd hurt her. He'd also heard the sob she'd tried to stifle as she took off running, too. "Fuck!"

After placing the horse in her stall, Mike walked towards his house, head hanging so low, it was a wonder he wasn't dragging it in the dirt he was scuffing up with his boots. He could only imagine what was going through Emi's mind after the way he'd treated her. He owed her an explanation and a major apology. Maybe some flowers? Perhaps he should do what Tyler did with Elli.

Tyler had confided about how he'd almost lost Elli by running off to his cabin in Vermont for three months, leaving Elli pregnant and believing Tyler didn't like her. When Tyler finally got his head on straight, he came home to the woman he wanted, got down on one knee, and proposed. He had a beautiful ring in his pocket, just waiting for her answer so that he could slip it on her finger.

Mike had already made his intentions clear to Emi. He wanted to marry her. Maybe he should match action to words and place a ring on the proper finger of her left hand before he royally fucked it up and lost her forever.

Time to go shopping!

CHAPTER 35

PEGGY wasn't feeling well enough to eat, so she declined dinner. When Emilia helped Peggy to prepare for bed, she gave her a hug and a light kiss on the cheek. It didn't surprise Emilia how quickly Peggy's condition had deteriorated, but it hurt to watch it happening. Emilia had come to love Peggy very quickly. If Emilia had been given the right to choose her own mother, Peggy would have been a strong candidate.

Bill asked Emi to wait for him in the kitchen and make them each a bowl of soup. He wanted to sit with Peggy for a while. Then he'd be out to eat. It was just as well that a big meal wasn't necessary. Michael never did show up to assist her with the meal's preparation.

It was nearly 9:00 p.m. when Bill came into the kitchen. Emilia was reading the reports compiled by Samuel Goldstein over the years. She was embarrassed by the intimate details of her life that were portrayed in those files. It was right there in black and white about how her husband had treated her. It was humiliating to read about the number of women he'd had sex with on the seat of his pickup truck or in cheap motel rooms. Once, he'd even had sex in the alleyway between the barroom and the adjacent building. Knowing that he came home to Emilia and demanded sex again before going to sleep made Emilia feel dirty. She wanted to scrub her skin raw to wash away the stain of betrayal.

Bill slumped down onto the kitchen chair and motioned to the files. "Not pleasant reading material to go to bed on. I can't imagine those reports will inspire pleasant dreams."

"No. I don't imagine that they will. It's embarrassing to have such a bright light shone on the travesty of your life," Emilia sighed. "It was difficult living a life devoid of the normal things a woman would expect from a marriage such as children to nurture and love. But to have my face rubbed in the dirt of my husband's infidelity is very degrading. I'm thankful that I didn't know anything about that while it was happening. It would have destroyed me."

"I'm very sorry for what you were forced to endure, my dear, both from Eloise and Iain. You didn't deserve any of that. At least you have Michael again," Bill told Emi.

Emilia winced and turned away to hide the emotions playing across her face. Bill looked at her with concern. "You and Michael aren't together again?" he asked.

"No, I'm afraid not. Michael made it clear today how he really feels. In fact, I was hoping to have a private conversation with you," she responded.

Bill quirked his eyebrow to indicate that he was waiting to hear what she had to say.

"I think I should leave as soon as possible. I've come to care for and admire both you and your wife very much. I don't want to bring my drama into your home during this critical time in your lives. I'm going back to Pennsylvania, where I belong."

"Are you certain that is what you truly want, Emi? I think you should give it some time, plus your daughter and her family will be here soon. You need to stay to meet them," Bill demanded.

"Michael hates me for what's happened. I don't think I would be able to live with my daughter's hatred, as well. Better that she never know, I think. You've kept the secret this long. Why not continue to keep it to spare her the upheaval in her life, or maybe just tell her that Michael is her real father, but you weren't able to find me? Michael deserves to have his daughter's love," Emilia said.

"What does Mike say about this? I can't imagine that he would be agreeable to you leaving. You should have seen him when he found out you were coming. Then, when you didn't wake up in the hospital, and how confused and disoriented you were when you did. He was beside himself. I don't know what happened between the two of you today or what was said, but I think you may have misunderstood. Please, give it a couple of weeks. Please. I'll talk to Mike for you if you want to see where his head is at," Bill offered

"No, please don't do that. I couldn't bear to see the look of pity on Michael's face that I resorted to asking you to intercede on my behalf. I know that pride goes before a fall, but it's the only thing I have left. I'll stay until you've contacted a replacement and they arrive to continue your care. In the meantime, I'll do my best to be civil to Michael so that Peggy isn't affected. I won't let on that anything has

287

changed. Maybe I'll receive an Oscar nomination for my acting ability." Emilia tried to smile through her pain.

"Thank you, my dear. I'm going to bed now. You should, too. Please sleep on your decision."

Emilia nodded and watched Bill go. Then she gathered up the bowls and spoons and took them to the sink. More tears flowed as Emilia washed and dried the dishes by hand, then put them away. After gathering up the files, she turned off the lights and went to her room. She knew she wasn't going to sleep that night. It didn't matter anymore what her heart had wanted for so many years. She knew that she was never going to attain it. Her heart and soul were irretrievably broken because of it.

CHAPTER 36

IKE took a quick shower and donned a clean outfit after his intense sexual encounter with Emi in the stable. While he started a load of laundry, his mind raced with thoughts of the type of engagement ring that she might like. That made him think about what size to purchase. He could always have the ring sized if it didn't fit, but he would be so proud to be able to slip it onto her ring finger and have it fit perfectly.

Then Mike had a light bulb idea. Grabbing his cell phone, Mike dialed Tyler's number.

"Hey, Mike. What's up? Is everything alright?" Tyler answered.

"Hi, Tyler. I'm good. Just wanted to touch base and ask a question," Mike responded. "How are all of you? Any idea when you'll be coming for a visit?"

"Elli had her doctor's appointment about a week ago. She and the baby are doing great. The rest of the kids are good, too. Jessica informed us that she wants to become a veterinarian for large animals. I think she'll make a good one. My dad arrived unexpectedly. He finally quit his job and just found out this morning that his apartment in New York City sold for more than he was asking. Apparently, there was a bidding war. So, he's pleased about that. I'm taking care of some last-minute details about the wedding venue business and our new home's construction. As I already mentioned, Dad's going to keep an eye on things for us while we're visiting you in Montana. Dad will have a suite in the new house. I'm working with the contractors to finish that portion first, so he can move in. He's going to sell his house in Stillwater, as well. That pretty much sums up everything going on with us. We'll be coming for a visit as soon as I iron out the rest of the details."

"So, what's your question?" Tyler asked.

"Do you remember what size ring Elli wears?" was Mike's response.

Tyler chuckled and said, "Wow, that's an odd question. Wouldn't have seen that one coming. Do I dare ask why?"

"Well, promise not to say anything. I'm going to ask a woman to marry me, and she's built like Elli. So, I'm hoping that the ring will fit if I get the same size Elli wears," Mike admitted.

"Holy Cow. I didn't even know you were dating anyone. I'm so surprised, I'm speechless. Is it too soon to say congratulations?" Tyler asked excitedly. "Elli's going to be so happy for you when she finds out, but I promise to keep your secret. I bought a size five for her. She's so tiny."

"Thanks, Tyler. Give everyone my love. I'm going to run now. Have some jewelry shopping to do. Let me know when you're coming to the ranch. I'm going to wait to propose until the whole family is present. When I get down on my knee, I hope I don't make a fool of myself," Mike said.

Tyler laughed. "Good luck with finding just the right ring. I'll talk to you later." Then the line disconnected.

Mike made a quick call to the main house and told Bill he needed to run an errand. Then he shoved his feet into his boots, slapped his Stetson on his head, and raced out the door.

He knew of a good jeweler in Billings, where he'd purchased gifts for Elli and Jeannie as wedding presents. Hopefully, the store would have something appropriate. He wanted to buy something simple but elegant.

Mike was in the jewelry store so long, dinner had come and gone. Choosing a ring was hard work. Mike never would have guessed there were so many to pick from. He finally decided on a petite Magnolia engagement ring with a twisted band in 14-carat white gold. The diamonds' total weight was almost two carats. He also purchased the wedding ring to match. He'd have the rings engraved as soon as Emi made him the happiest man on the planet by agreeing to wear them.

By the time Mike returned to the ranch, it was nearly time for his shift to patrol the grounds around the houses, barn, stable, and outbuildings. Mike dropped the rings off at his home, placing them in the safe for protection. After grabbing a quick sandwich and bottle of water, he stopped by the bunkhouse to talk to Sean.

"Where'd you run off to in such a hurry earlier?" Sean asked.

"Needed to do some shopping. I just wanted to have a quick word with you, Sean," Mike said.

"Sure, what's up? Everything okay with Mrs. Andersen? That was some scare—her being attacked. I was talking to some of the guys from the neighboring ranches. No one's ever heard of anything like that happening around here," Sean mentioned.

"Mrs. Andersen is doing better. She resumed taking care of Peggy and Bill this afternoon. I actually wanted to talk to you about her, though. Bill mentioned that you might be interested in dating Emilia," Mike responded.

"Yeah, she's a special woman. I was considering asking her out to dinner. Do you think she'd be receptive?" Sean grinned. "I know she's a few years older than me, but I don't care about that."

"I'd appreciate it if you'd look elsewhere. I'm going to ask Emilia to marry me," Mike replied.

"Holy Fuck! You work fast, Mike. She's only been here a few days," Sean said with a wink.

"Yeah, well, Emilia and I share a history. That's all I'm going to say on that subject. I just didn't want any bad blood between us. I consider you a good friend," Mike emphasized.

"Okay, Mike. I'll back off, but if she says no to your proposal, then all bets are off."

"Never going to happen. Emi belongs to me. Now I just need to make her realize that."

Sean laughed as Mike walked away.

At 10:00 p.m., Tom took over patrol, and Mike went to the main house. He was beat. It had been a long emotional day. Emi was asleep when he entered the bedroom. The file folders from Sam Goldstein were spread across his side of the mattress. Gathering them into a pile, Mike placed them on the dresser. Then he stripped down to his briefs and climbed into bed. Tucking Emi in against him, he nuzzled the side of her neck, kissed her gently, sighed, and closed his eyes.

At 5:00 a.m., he slipped out of bed, dressed, stopped in the kitchen to turn on the coffee maker, and went out to clean the stable.

That set the tone for the next two weeks, never giving him any time to apologize to Emi or speak to her privately about anything. They'd fallen into a routine of sorts. He'd leave their bed at 5:00 a.m., share breakfast with Emi, Peggy, and Bill at 7:30, then go out to take care of chores. Emilia spent the day taking care of Peggy and Bill, the housework, laundry, and meals. At 8:00 p.m. every night, he patrolled the grounds. Emi was always asleep when he climbed into bed. Emilia spoke to him, but she seemed distant, and they hadn't made love again since their passionate encounter in the stable. They hadn't even shared a kiss since then. He'd caught Sean joking with her earlier that afternoon and making a pass. Emi never would have forgiven Mike if he'd gone all Neanderthal-like and punched Sean in the face. Mike wanted to act like a caveman, drag Emi by her hair to their bed, and fuck her brains out. Sleeping next to her each night without making love to her was giving him blue balls.

CHAPTER 37

EMILIA pretended to be asleep each night when Michael climbed into bed beside her. She wanted desperately to make love to him, but he'd never apologized for his dismissive behavior after the last time. It had been almost two weeks. She refused to be treated indifferently or disrespectfully, ever again. That type of disregard had formed the basis of all of her relationships in her life.

So, a routine was established. Michael left the house before she got up to begin her day. She pretended to be asleep when he came to bed each night after his two-hour stretch of patrolling the grounds to keep everyone safe.

Emilia had promised Bill that she would take the time to reevaluate her decision regarding going home to Pennsylvania. She didn't know what to do. It didn't seem like Michael had any intention of apologizing. So, she didn't think they could have a future together. Maybe he didn't feel he had anything to apologize for.

The only thing Emilia was positive about was that this pretending that everything was okay between them couldn't go on much longer. Tomorrow would be Saturday. If Michael didn't say anything today, then Emilia would give Bill her decision after breakfast in the morning. Bill had already found a replacement for her, and the woman could start first thing Monday morning. Emilia would pack enough garments in the small case she would carry on the plane, and the balance could be donated to charity. She would call Bain to find out if he still wanted her in his life. If he was no longer interested in a relationship, Emilia would contact her previous place of employment and find somewhere to live on her own. She needed to learn to be self-reliant. Enough depending on others to make her feel worthwhile. She could be a strong independent woman. If others could do it, so could she. Then the only one letting her down would be herself.

CHAPTER 38

TYLER had avoided telling Mike that he, Elli, and the children were already preparing for their flight to Montana. Elli insisted they keep it a surprise. Flying anywhere with a family of eight was a logistical nightmare. Tyler couldn't imagine what it would be like if the kids weren't so well-behaved. Maybe it was time to think about buying his own private plane and getting his pilot's license.

While they were waiting for their flight at the Allentown airport, the family watched as a couple tried to appease one small boy about seven years old. They looked like they were ready to pull their hair out. At one point, the child let out a scream, flopped on the floor, and started to flail about. His ear-piercing demands for a candy bar were attracting the gazes of all the other passengers in the departure lounge. Tyler gave the boy's father a look of sympathy. It was 6:00

a.m., and the kid wanted candy. The mother handed the unruly son the candy he was demanding. The resulting silence was a blessing.

Tyler gazed down at Blair, Peggy, Logan, and Billy. Their eyes were huge, having witnessed the boy's performance. He almost laughed out loud when Peggy turned to her brothers and, in her sweet five-year-old voice, told them, "If you ever act like that, I'll punch you so hard that you'll never ask Mommy or Daddy for candy again."

The boys just nodded solemnly at her, blinked, and turned away. Billy quipped, "I'd never want candy that badly. That was embarrassing."

Tyler looked at Elli and mouthed, "We have the best kids ever!" Elli grinned at her husband and mouthed back, "Love you, handsome man!"

Her love for him was evident in the look Elli gave him. Tyler wondered how soon he could get her pregnant again. She looked so beautiful when her abdomen was rounded, his baby growing safely inside her womb. Maybe Tyler should wait, though. Their youngest, Lianne, was only two months old, after all.

They'd been looking forward to this trip for months. They usually spent the entire summer at the Circle R, but this year they had to put off going because of the baby's birth in June. Then Elli didn't bounce back to her usual energetic self. They'd finally resumed sexual relations two weeks ago, and Tyler couldn't get enough of her. Elli was still as beautiful as the sixteen-year-old girl he'd fallen in love with in tenth grade when he'd kissed her in the hospitality shop at the hospital.

The only flight Tyler was able to book for their large family was one with two layovers. The first stop was in Pittsburgh. With no direct flights to Billings from Pittsburgh, they had one more stop to make. It was going to be a long day. It would have been a nightmare for most people with six children in tow, but Elli and Tyler's six children were a blessing.

After the hour layover in Pittsburgh, Tyler's family was finally settled into their seats. Elli was in the row behind him with baby Lianne and Blair. Jessica sat across from Elli and was entertaining her brother, Logan. He had the aisle seat with Billy and Peggy tucked in beside him. Peggy, of course, insisted on sitting next to the window. There was a huge man directly across the aisle from Tyler. The guy had to weigh two hundred and twenty pounds, and it was all muscle. He looked like he lifted car engines three times a day.

Shortly before the guy dozed off, Tyler engaged him in a pleasant conversation. The man told him about his dairy farm near Pittsburgh. He said he was on his way to Montana to meet up with his future bride. They intended to get married as soon as they returned to Pennsylvania. Tyler wished the man luck.

Tyler saw the man headed toward the airport exit when they'd finally reached Billings while he went in the direction of the luggage carousel with a concierge pushing a luggage cart. Tyler gave the man a one-handed salute. The guy nodded his head in return.

It was late evening, the children were cranky from sitting so long, and everyone was hungry. Expecting something like this to occur, Tyler and Elli had decided to wait until Saturday evening to complete their journey to the ranch. They had a surprise for the children the next day.

Tyler had booked a large suite at a luxury hotel near the airport. Elli waited for him with the children while he went to sign for the Mercedes he'd rented for their use. It was similar to the vehicle he'd purchased for Rick and Elli as a gift when Elli gave birth to the triplets. That vehicle seated eight, and they still owned it. Because of Lianne's birth, they had filled the Mercedes to capacity. Tyler would need to purchase that bus his dad was teasing him about as soon as he could knock up his wife again. That thought made Tyler laugh to himself.

After everyone finished eating the meal that had been delivered by room service, Tyler bathed the boys. Then he bundled them into bed and told them their favorite story. They loved to hear about how he'd met their mother, the beautiful princess, and how he and the princess had fallen in love. Tucked in, Tyler kissed each child and turned out the light. Entering the adjacent room, he paused to check on Jessica and Peggy, who were sharing a bed. Jess had given Peggy her bath and listened as Peggy recited her favorite book by heart. Tyler kissed both of them as well.

Elli was propped against the headboard of the bed when he entered their room. She had just finished nursing Lianne, and the baby had fallen asleep at her breast. Crossing to the bed, he knelt down beside Elli and caressed the silky hair on his infant's head. Taking

Lianne from her mother's arms, he told Elli, "Don't move. Stay just like that."

Placing Lianne in her cradle, he covered her with a blanket. Moving back to Elli's side of the bed, he knelt and took her right breast into his mouth. Elli's milk was sweet, and he'd steal a little from his daughter. After suckling greedily, he captured Elli's mouth with a hard kiss and slipped his tongue inside her mouth to give her a taste of her own sweetness.

Elli moaned and reached for the buttons on Tyler's shirt. Inpatient, Tyler grabbed the hem, yanked the shirt over his head, and tossed it on the floor. As he leaned in to capture her swollen lips in another kiss, he slipped his fingers beneath the hem of Elli's nightgown to finger her clit. She dropped her legs open to give Tyler better access and reached for the button on his pants. After pulling down the zipper, she palmed the bulge. The head of his engorged shaft peeked out the top of his boxer briefs, and a bead of pre-cum leaked from the crease. Lowering his boxer briefs, she wrapped her hand around his cock, giving it a playful tug, then licked the salty moisture from the tip. Tyler groaned and pressed his cock against her mouth. "That feels good, sweet girl."

Elli grinned mischievously, said, "I bet I can make it feel even better," and took him into her mouth as far as she could without gagging. Tyler was sure his eyes rolled back into his head while his wife pleasured him. When he could feel his impending orgasm, he pulled Elli beneath him, lined himself up, and forged inside with one powerful stroke. Grabbing her leg, he placed it over his shoulder to deepen the angle of penetration. Elli's eyes widened, and she moved her fingers to her clit to heighten the pleasure. Tyler enjoyed watching her pleasure herself. The force of the orgasm that tore through Elli brought Tyler to the brink, and he pounded into her mercilessly until they both collapsed in a sweaty pile of tangled limbs.

"Wow!" Elli exclaimed when she could catch her breath. "Miss me much?" she chuckled.

"More than you could ever believe," Tyler told her. "Give me a few minutes. I think I might be able to summon the energy to do that again. Maybe we should see if I can improve upon that performance."

Elli smiled and said, "If you get any better, the hotel staff will need a mop and bucket to clean the carpet. I'll have melted into a pile of goo on the floor."

That made Tyler laugh.

"Shhh, you'll wake the baby," Elli admonished, then kissed Tyler to hush him up.

CHAPTER 39

BAIN slept during the flight to Billings, Montana, on Friday morning because he was exhausted. The flight was packed, and there was a large family with six children seated in first-class near him. Bain struck up a conversation during the flight with the husband, just before taking his nap. The man's wife was seated in the row behind him, so he never really got a good look at her. She was focused on her children. He learned that they were from New Jersey and that their flight had to layover in Pittsburgh, where Bain had boarded the plane. The children ranged in age from twelve years to a baby that was two months old. Bain was impressed. The children were very well behaved. Bain hoped that he and Emilia would have two children just like that. They would probably both be boys. That's what ran in his family tree. The only girl produced in generations was his baby sister, who'd died at birth.

Bain had pushed himself and Shawn to complete everything he'd wanted to accomplish for the next couple of weeks. He'd use that freed-up time to put his plan into motion to bring Emilia home where she belonged and then spend time with her.

He and Shawn had moved the new bull into a pen with the heifers. They'd culled a few of the older cows and trailered them to an auction house to be sold to a slaughterhouse for meat. The milk cows were moved out into a paddock between morning and evening milking. During that time, they'd pressure-washed the entire interior of the barn. When everything was dried, they'd whitewashed the walls and limed the drops. The milk room was pressure-washed next, and everything was sterilized.

Bain missed Emilia. He hadn't realized just how much he'd come to depend upon her for even the most minor things like replacing the empty toilet paper roll in the bathroom. She'd always hummed softly while she cleaned or cooked, so the house was too quiet without her. She may be a petite woman, but her absence left a massive hole in his life.

Before catching his flight, he'd gone back to the drug dealer's house. He paid cash for several doses of a sedative that would be effective in knocking Emilia out. He would be able to keep her that way for a couple of days without any ill effects. This time Bain had a plan to ensure that none of the ranch hands were around to interfere.

When the plane finally landed in Billings, it was late evening. Bain passed the man he'd spoken to on the plane when he was on his way to the exit. The guy was headed to the luggage carousel. Bain only had a backpack that he'd placed in the overhead. No need to check or claim any luggage. Bain could just imagine how much baggage would be needed to take a family of eight on vacation. The guy gave him a one-handed salute. Bain nodded at him in return.

Bain rented a four-wheel-drive vehicle with tinted windows. Then he drove back to the house where he was renting a room to drop off his bag. The landlord waved at him through the window as he was getting back into the jeep to go scout out the Circle R Ranch. If everything went according to plan, Bain could be on his way home with Emilia within the next two days. He intended to keep her sedated. Bain would stop once at a cheap motor court during the twenty-two-hour drive home to catch some sleep. He'd already found just the right one on the internet. The place took cash and wouldn't bother to ask questions. He could carry Emilia into the room, get some sack time, clean up and get back on the road.

The only hitch in his plan was how he would convince Emilia to stay when he got her home. Maybe he'd have to remove any clothing from the house to keep her naked until he could get her pregnant. He'd worry about the details later.

Bain found a small access road a mile past the main entrance to the ranch. There was a locked gate, but the lock was easily picked. Following the dirt trail, Bain discovered that it dead-ended at a small cabin that stood on a low hill above a pristine pond. The place wasn't locked, so Bain went inside to check it out. The contents included a couple of bunks, a small table with two chairs, and shelves containing canned goods and some plates, silverware, and some chipped mugs. A small shed next to the cabin held a composting toilet and fencing supplies and tools. Bain assumed the place was used by the ranch hands when mending fences or herding cattle. A mile was a long way to carry what would essentially be dead weight. Still, if he left the jeep here, he was strong enough to carry Emilia's unconscious body to the cabin. Then he could rest before hitting the road for the trip home. He wouldn't bother to return the key to the room he was renting. He'd paid in cash for more days than he intended to use it. The landlord could have a new key made if necessary.

Driving back past the ranch entrance, Bain discovered at least a hundred head of cattle grazing near the fence line bordering the neighboring property. Bain grinned. That would provide his diversion. Toward dark on Saturday, he'd create a break in the fence. The grass on the other side of the fence was higher because it hadn't been grazed. So, it should be easy to drive a few of the cattle through the opening. The rest of the herd would be quick to follow. Then, he'd place an anonymous call to the Circle R to let them know their cattle were out. When the ranch hands rode off, he'd enter the main house, if necessary, grab Emilia, and get the heck out of there before anyone knew she was missing.

Driving back to the pull-off where Bain had parked the jeep two weekends earlier, he abandoned the vehicle and went on foot to check out the ranch buildings. It was now full dark. As he approached the back of the storage building next to the stable, he heard two of the cowboys talking. Slipping into the shadows, he crouched down to eavesdrop on the conversation.

"How much longer do you think we need to patrol the property, Mike?" the one man addressed the other. "There hasn't been any sign of anyone since the night Mrs. Andersen was knocked out."

As Bain crept closer to get a better look at the men, the other man shifted into the light from the stable. Bain recognized him as the cowboy who'd seduced Emilia. Bain ground his teeth in anger and balled his hands into fists.

"I spoke with the police today. It's been two weeks since Emilia's attack. They haven't found any leads, and no one else has reported attacks on unsuspecting females. The cops still think it was a transient, so consider it an opportunistic attack. We can probably go back to normal after tonight."

"Has Mrs. Andersen recovered fully?"

The one named Mike responded, "She's been extremely uncommunicative for the past two weeks, so I haven't really had the chance to talk to her much. Peggy's health is declining rapidly, so that has kept Emilia really busy, too."

"How much time do you think Peggy has left? She'll be missed, but it's hard to watch her suffer."

"I don't think she has much time left, Sean. The doctor gave her three months at most. That prognosis was more than three months ago. I guess that means she's living on borrowed time. I hope Elli, Tyler, and the kids arrive soon to be with her and have the chance to say goodbye. Tim, Jeannie, and Sophie will be flying in on Sunday, but only for the day. Tim has to be back in Kirk on Monday. I'm worried about Bill. He won't have much reason to live when Peggy is gone. The doctor gave him a year, but I think her death will destroy him," Mike admitted.

"Bill told us that he's leaving the ranch to you," Sean replied. "We were surprised that it isn't going to Elli."

"Yeah, well, it's a long story. I'll fill all of you in when the time comes. I'm going in now to get some sleep. I'll see you in the morning." The one called Mike turned and headed toward the corner of the main house, probably to enter the house through the kitchen or rear entrance. The one named Sean moved off towards the barn.

Bain made his way back to the jeep, then returned to his rented room. He'd learned a lot, so he would be able to get a good night's sleep. Bain would rest all day tomorrow as well. Then he would put

his plan into action.

CHAPTER 40

JOLTED awake from a terrible nightmare, Emilia raced from the room and made it to the bathroom just in time to wretch. Thankfully, she'd given the bathroom a thorough cleaning the previous day. There was nothing like praying to a dirty porcelain god. Hopefully, she wasn't catching anything. A virus would be certain to kill Peggy if she contracted one now. Emilia didn't really think it was a virus, however. It was too soon to be having morning sickness for most women, but she remembered what it was like when she'd been pregnant with Elli. She'd experienced nausea almost from the beginning.

After grabbing a quick shower, Emilia brushed her teeth twice. She gargled to rid her mouth of the terrible taste of vomit. Emilia felt much better, and as she looked in the mirror, she noted a little more color in her complexion. She didn't look quite so green anymore.

Grabbing a brush, she ran it through the length of her hair, then pulled it up into a high ponytail. It was time to get to work. She planned to run to the drugstore once she had Peggy and Bill settled in the living room after breakfast.

Making her way to her employers' bedroom, she knocked lightly on the door. There was a muffled request to enter. Poking her head inside, she realized that Bill was already up and dressed. Peggy was lying under multiple blankets with a painfully thin arm thrown over her eyes.

"Not so good today, Peggy?" Emilia asked softly as she noted the increased jaundiced look to Peggy's skin.

"No, I think most of my good days are now behind me. I don't have any energy, and my stomach hurts quite a bit," Peggy murmured. "I think I'm going to stay right here in bed today."

"Well, then let's go through our routine, except for the part about getting dressed for the day, and I'll get your medicine for you," Emilia responded.

"Alright, dear, but feed Bill first," Peggy demanded. "I'm not going anywhere. Everything else can wait."

Emilia looked at Bill questioningly. His face was pinched with concern, but he just nodded his head, kissed Peggy on the cheek, and turned to leave the room.

Emilia straightened the blankets around Peggy's thin shoulders, then quietly closed the bedroom door behind her. Finding Bill at the kitchen table, Emilia wasn't surprised to see that he had been crying.

Bill's hands were clasped on the table in front of him. Emilia dropped into the chair beside him. Then she closed her hands around his in a show of sympathy and support. Resting her head against his shoulder, she sighed and said, "It is times like these that make me aware of how fragile life is. I believe that you and Peggy have made good lives for yourselves and have always appreciated any bestowed gifts. You can be proud of everything you've accomplished. You've both come to mean so much to me in the short time I've known you. I wish there was more I could do for you."

Bill moved his hands to clasp Emilia's instead and turned to gaze at her thoughtfully. He started to speak, then hesitated when he noticed Mike standing in the doorway. Knowing Emilia wasn't aware of Mike's presence he gave his words careful consideration. "Did you mean what you said about wishing you could do more?"

"Certainly, is there something you have in mind?" Emilia asked questioningly. "I'll do whatever is in my power to help."

"Make an old man happy, then, and stay," Bill replied. "You've become very important to the people on this ranch. Everyone here either loves you or is very fond of you, so please stay."

Emilia searched Bill's face. He seemed so sincere. She wanted desperately to say yes to his request, but Bill wasn't the one she was worried about or running away from. Emilia opened her mouth to respond when she heard the sound of a throat being cleared. The sound came from close behind her. Turning, she found the most beautiful blue eyes attached to a very handsome face gazing at her intently.

"Please don't leave us, Emi. Don't leave me. I was angry at myself and was insensitive. I've hurt you so many times. You're probably sick of hearing me say I'm sorry. So, I'd understand if you decide you need to go," Mike said as his lips trembled. "Can you forgive me, Emi? I love you so damn much."

Emilia turned back to Bill and stared at him with a questioning look. She was looking for guidance. Bill nodded his head in understanding because he knew what her heart wanted. Emilia's head was the problem. It was trying to be the voice of reason. Emilia needed to lead with her heart. "Listen to what your heart wants, Emi, not your head," Bill told her.

Turning back to face Michael, Emilia swallowed convulsively. Michael had apologized. He said he wasn't angry with her, only with himself. "Why were you angry, Michael?" she finally asked him. She needed to clear the air before making her decision.

Bill stood up. "I'll just go check on Peggy. I think the two of you need to talk." Then he left the room.

Mike grabbed Emi and pulled her into an embrace. Then he lifted her and carried her to the room they'd shared for the last few weeks. Laying her on the bed, Mike dropped down beside her. Searching her face, he confessed. "I've pushed you to have sex repeatedly. I never even considered taking any precautions against getting you pregnant. The last time we made love, I remembered what you'd said about your husband always wearing a condom. That's when I realized we'd been having unprotected sex. I blamed and was angry with myself for being selfish. You felt so damn good skin-on-skin. Can you forgive me? I don't even know if you can or would want to have another child with me."

"Do you want to have another child, Michael? We're not exactly spring chickens, you know," Emilia grinned. "We'd be almost seventy by the time the child graduated from high school."

"Honey, I'd love the chance to see your belly grow round with a child we'd made together. But I know it wouldn't be safe for you. Don't they consider it risky to get pregnant at your age?" Mike asked.

"Hey, enough with pointing out that I'm an old grandma," Elli joked. "Besides, it might be a moot point, anyway."

Confused, Mike searched Emi's face. "What are you saying, darlin'?"

"Well, I wasn't going to say anything, yet, or maybe never if we didn't reconcile, and I decided to leave," she admitted.

Mike jumped off the bed, grabbed Emi up, and plunked down with her in his lap. "What are you saying, Emi? Are you pregnant?"

"Maybe?" she said, uncertainly. "I was going to the drug store after breakfast to buy a pregnancy test?"

"Were those questions?" Mike laughed. "Either you are pregnant, or you aren't, and you were going to the drug store, or you weren't. One of us is confused. Grinning, he told her, "I'll go, right now. I'm not going to be worth a damn until I know for certain."

Emilia laughed as Michael ran out the door. In his haste, he forgot to kiss her goodbye.

Returning to the kitchen, she found Bill with his head in the refrigerator. "What's it take to get a meal around here," he said with a laugh.

Emilia grinned. "Would you like a ham and cheese omelet this morning?"

"That sounds really good. I took some tea in for Peggy. She sipped at it a little bit. She said she doesn't think she can eat."

Emilia pressed a hand to Bill's arm in sympathy.

To change the subject, Bill said, "So, you've forgiven Mike? Does this mean you'll stay with us? Where did he go, anyway?"

"Well, the answer is yes to the first two questions. I'd rather not say to the last," Emilia said with a grin. "Michael will answer that one later if there's anything to report."

"Well, that's certainly cryptic," Bill responded.

Then Emilia created two beautiful omelets. Bill made them both toast. And they sat down to eat. Emilia was partway through her meal when she turned green and rushed from the room. Bill chuckled as he finished his breakfast because he already had the answer to that last question. Bill was going to be another honorary grandpa. Life never ceased to amaze him.

When Emilia came back into the kitchen, Bill was scraping the dishes. Emilia said, "Here, let me get those. Then I'll check on Peggy."

"Alright, my dear," Bill replied. I have some bills to pay. I'll be in my office."

As soon as Emilia was finished cleaning up, she threw a laundry load into the washing machine and then went in to give Peggy her medication. Her doctor had prescribed palliative remedies to help relieve some of Peggy's symptoms.

"Do you think you would like to take a shower, or should I give you a sponge bath?" Emi asked her. "Then I'll help you into a fresh nightgown if you're not up to getting dressed and coming to the living room.

"The sponge bath will do," Peggy admitted. "I'm not up to much of anything else."

"Would you like me to read to you after? I can read some more poetry to you."

"I think I'd like to tell you about Elli and Jessica after they came to live with us," Peggy replied.

"I think I'd like that. Thank you, Peggy," Emilia admitted.

When Peggy grew tired, Emilia fluffed Peggy's pillow, tucked the quilt around her, and told her to rest.

After moving the laundry from the washing machine to the dryer, she stopped at her bedroom to make the bed. There, lying on the dresser, was a pregnancy kit and a note from Michael. It read, "Love you, sweetheart. Have my fingers crossed that it's a plus sign."

With a smile, Emilia picked up the box and made her way to the bathroom.

CHAPTER 41

AFTER breakfast, Tyler and Elli surprised their children with a trip to *Zoo Montana*. It was a seventy-acre wildlife park including more than one hundred animals. Nearly fifty-eight species, including wolves, grizzly bears, red pandas, bald eagles, pygmy goats, Belgian draft horses, and scores of other animals, were all living in areas designed to mimic their natural habitats. The trip was the perfect opportunity for their home-schooled children to expend some of their boundless energy while experiencing the world in a safe environment.

Elli nudged Tyler's shoulder and nodded toward the youngest children. They had stopped to visit the miniature donkeys. Blair, Peggy, Logan, and Billy were holding hands as they studied the animals intently. The triplets looked out for each other and were very protective of their little brother, who was only fourteen months younger. All four talked at once and pointed excitedly at the animals' large heads and long ears. Jessica, as the oldest, watched out for all of them and was a font of information. She explained that the male was called a "jack," and the female was known as a "jennet." She was growing into a beautiful young woman. Lianne rested snug against her mommy's chest in a pouch designed for privacy so that Elli could nurse her unobtrusively. No one could see that the baby was getting a snack. Tyler kept his arm around Elli's waist, then held her hand to help her around an obstacle.

By midafternoon, the children were showing signs of tiring. So, they were holstered into their child safety seats in the Mercedes, and Elli changed her daughter's diaper and clothing before placing her in the rear-facing car seat.

Tyler climbed behind the wheel and turned to his children. "Who wants to go to Grandma and Grandpa's house?"

He was met with a chorus of, "Me!"

Tyler smiled at his wife, leaned over to give her a kiss, and then started the car. After the first fifteen minutes of their two-hour trip, Tyler was the only one still awake. He would tease his beautiful wife later about the cute noises she made while she slept, likening the sounds to those of loud growling animal snorts. Watching her lips purse as she blew out those gentle puffing snores gave him erotic ideas about Elli's plump lips wrapped around his engorged shaft. Time to think of other things like sweaty jockstraps, stinky sneakers, or curdled milk. Anything to ease his aching cock, which now pressed painfully against the zipper of his pants.

They stopped for dinner at a family-style restaurant, perfect for the family of eight. Two waitresses moved tables together. All of the restaurant's available booster seats were rounded up to accommodate the growing children. Blair, Peggy, Logan, and Billy demanded macaroni and cheese. Tyler said only if they each ate two helpings of vegetables to go with the macaroni.

When they were back in the car, the kids whispered amongst themselves, arguing over which animals were the best at the zoo. They were whispering because their mommy had fallen asleep again.

It was nearly 7:00 p.m. when Tyler turned into the drive and stopped under the Circle R Cattle sign that arched overhead.

"Hey, honey. We're here," Tyler said as he gently shook Elli's shoulder.

Elli woke with a start and looked around, confused. Finally, she glanced over at her husband and smirked, "Guess I fell asleep again. Sorry! I promise that you weren't boring me." Then she grinned at him sheepishly.

Tyler leaned over the center console, cupped her face in his hand, and whispered, "I'll make you pay for it later." Then winked. "Oh, by the way. You snore."

Elli blushed, then said in a resentful tone, "No, I don't. Hmmm…Do I?"

Tyler laughed so hard, he woke the baby.

"Now see what you did," Elli winked. Leaning in, she whispered, "I'll make you pay for it later. Oh, by the way. It's your turn to change her diaper."

Just then, a chorus of five yelled, "Lianne pooped! Phew, she stinks!"

Tyler shook his head, said, "Figures," restarted the car, opened the windows, and continued down the gravel drive to the main house. The house was dark, so he pulled around back, parked by the rear door, and popped the hatch to get at the luggage. Jessica helped him to unfasten the harnesses to the booster seats. While he was working on Billy's, which seemed to be stuck, he told the children to enter the house quietly and go to their rooms. Each room held some of the children's favorite toys given to them by their great-grandparents. "Play quietly until it's time for your bath. After you're dressed for bed, I'll read you a book," he told them.

"What about saying Good Night to Meemom and Peepop?" Peggy asked. That's what she called Peggy and Bill.

"You've all had a long day. You can see them in the morning at breakfast," Elli replied.

She was met with a bunch of sighs and, "That's not fair!"

Releasing her tiny daughter from the car seat, Elli handed the baby to Tyler. Then she told her children knowingly, "You'll find that not everything in life is fair or what you think you deserve. Sometimes you get stuck with poop."

Tyler mouthed, "Ha, Ha, you're hilarious."

Elli gave him a cheeky grin, then stuck her tongue out at him.

Tyler winked and said, "You can unload the luggage while I bathe Leanne."

Elli winced. She knew when she'd been outmaneuvered.

When the little ones were tucked up in bed, Elli and Tyler paused by the door to the room Jess was sharing with Peggy. Elli asked, "Do you want to come and talk to Grandma and Grandpa before you go to sleep?"

"No, I think I'm kind of tired, too. I'll just read for a little bit and keep an ear tuned to the brats. Oh, I mean the little angels," Jess replied with an impish grin. "That will give you and Dad some much-needed time to relax."

Tyler said, "Love you, sweet baby girl. See you in the morning." He pulled the door so that it was open just a crack. That way, Jess could hear the other children. Then he took Elli by the hand and entered the large bedroom at the end of the hall. It was the same one Elli stayed in when she first came to Montana and discovered her grandparents.

Going into the attached bath, he stripped naked, then went back into the bedroom. Elli had her back to him, bending over the cradle containing their sleeping daughter.

"I still think Lianne looks like your mom," she told Tyler.

Tyler pulled his wife tight against his body and slipped his hand inside her pants. "Time to get wet, Mrs. Thompson."

Elli giggled and said, "I think I already am."

"Well, we'll have to do something about that, then won't we," he replied as he lifted her. Carrying Elli into the bathroom, he set her on her feet and closed the door. It was a small room. Tyler was not a small man, but he'd make it work. Elli removed her feet from her pants and thong after Tyler slid them down her legs. He kicked the clothing to the side, turned his wife around, and placed her hands on the countertop to support her weight. Spreading her legs, he lined himself up and slipped between her folds to claim her. "Hmmm. You were right. You were already wet." As he paced himself with fast and slow strokes, he reached into the shower and turned on the water to drown out the moans issuing from his wife. When he could tell that Elli was close, he moved her hand to her clit. Hands joined together, they teased the tight bundle of nerves until her orgasm tore through her. The spasms of Elli's inner muscles milked his cock until Tyler felt like he would be turned inside out.

Elli moaned low and throaty. "That performance was an improvement. Where's the hotel staff with the mop and bucket. All that's left of your wife is a pile of goo."

Tyler chuckled and kissed Elli between the shoulder blades. "Bet I can do better next time, sweet girl."

"Mr. Thompson, are you trying to seduce me?" Elli asked him with an arched brow. "Or just get me pregnant again? Don't think I haven't noticed that you've been enjoying a lot of bareback sex. Just exactly how many children do you want, Tyler Logan Thompson?"

"Uh, oh!" Tyler winced. "Well. Hmmm. Would you consider nine? If I work very hard at it, maybe we can pop out a set of twins. Then you'd only need to get pregnant two more times."

Stunned, Elli looked at her husband and squeaked, "Nine?"

Unabashed, Tyler nodded and told her, "Just a suggestion."

Elli said, "We'll discuss it later while you're giving me multiple orgasms.

Tyler smiled. "I can do that."

CHAPTER 42

ELLI and Tyler peeked into their children's bedrooms as they passed on the way to find Bill and Peggy. Even Jessica was sound asleep. The visit to the zoo had worn them all out. Usually, Elli and Tyler would have announced their arrival immediately so that the children could spend time with their great-grandparents. Also, this would be the first time that Bill and Peggy would meet the newest member of the family, Lianne. The house had been quiet, however, when they arrived. No one had been in the living room or kitchen when they checked. Thinking that Bill and Peggy must have gone out for the evening, they were concerned. It was now after 8:00 p.m., and the elderly couple believed in early to bed, early to rise. So, they should be home.

The kitchen was dark, so Elli and Tyler made their way to the living room to wait there. They found Bill sitting in the twilit room, the only light filtering in through the windows. It wasn't dark outside yet, being summer, but the sight of Bill sitting alone in the corner of the sofa was unexpected. Startled, Elli went to him and said, "Grandpa? What's going on? Why are you sitting here all alone? Where's Grandma?"

When Bill's faraway look finally focused on them, he took one of her hands in his and said, "Elli, Tyler, you've come in time. Thank you!"

"Grandpa, you're scaring me. What's happened?" Elli plead as she sank onto the cushion and angled herself towards Bill.

"Where are the children? Did you bring them with you?" Bill asked hopefully.

Tyler dropped down onto the coffee table in front of Bill, concerned by the elderly man's confusion. "Bill, we thought you weren't home. We just arrived about an hour ago. So, we put the children to bed. They were disappointed that they weren't going to see you tonight. We told them they'd be able to at breakfast."

Bill glanced at Elli and told her, "It's just as well. It will give us a chance to talk. I have a lot to tell you. Do you know how proud we are of you, Elli? Having you come into our lives when you did gave us great deal of joy. Don't ever doubt how much we love you, Tyler, and the children."

"Now, you're really frightening me." Elli studied her grandfather carefully and didn't like was she saw. He looked like he'd aged years in the few short months since their visit in February. He had lost weight, too. "Has Grandma already gone to bed? Please tell us what's going on."

"I have a lot to tell you, so I'll ask you both to hold any questioned until I've finished explaining." Then Bill began the story that would destroy Elli's life as she knew it. He told her of the documents he'd found in his son's safety deposit box and wall safe when he'd handled the estate. Documents that proved that James and Lilianne were not Elli's birth parents. That meant that he was not her grandfather.

Elli's eyes widened in astonishment, and she reached across to grip Tyler's hand tightly.

Bill continued with the twisted tale of lies and betrayal that led to Elli's birth mother's discovery a few years earlier and her father just a few short weeks before. A man whom Elli already knew and loved as a friend. Then he wrecked her by telling her that Peggy only had weeks, maybe days, to live and that he had also been given a death sentence with only months remaining.

It took time to give Elli and Tyler all of the details, so it had grown dark outside. Elli had gotten to her feet by the time Bill had finished explaining. While slowly backing away, tears streamed unheeded down her cheeks. She shook her head from side to side, negating what she was hearing. When she started to make a keening noise, Tyler jumped to his feet and wrapped his distraught wife in a tight embrace. She looked at Tyler with unfocused eyes and mumbled, "When I told my father that I was pregnant with Jessica, he said it seemed that the fruit hadn't fallen far from the tree. Now I understand what he meant. He was comparing me to my birth mother. All I was to him was an illegitimate monthly meal ticket that he could belittle and abuse. The man never loved me at all."

As Tyler rocked Elli in his arms to soothe her, she pressed her face against his chest and told him, "My whole life has been a lie. I don't even know who I am supposed to be now. I want to go home. Could you take me home, Tyler? Take me home, please."

At her words, Tyler looked over at Bill, who was crying as hard as Elli. He knew that they couldn't just leave. Elli needed to deal with her new reality. If Peggy and Bill were both dying and she turned her back on them, she would never forgive herself. Grandparents or not, she still loved them very much.

Bill reached out an imploring hand toward the woman he'd come to love as his granddaughter. "Please stay, Elli, so that we can work this out together. Peggy and I love you very much. You're our granddaughter. Nothing that we've discovered changes that fact. Please don't go."

As Elli stared at the man she had trusted implicitly, the front door slammed open, and Mike raced into the room.

As three pairs of stunned eyes turned towards him, Mike pulled up short. Taking in the room's strained atmosphere, he looked at Bill questioningly, then turned to Tyler. "I don't know what I've interrupted, but I could use your help, Tyler. I got a call. About one hundred head of cattle got out through a break in the north fence. I'm the only one on the ranch because Sean and John went into the city. I have to get the cows back in before they wander onto the highway and cause an accident."

Tyler nodded in agreement, then turned back to his wife. "Elli, I have to go. Stay here and talk to Bill." Leaning in, he whispered in her ear, "You need to work this out. He and Peggy are sick. You'll never forgive yourself if you don't." As Elli acknowledged that she understood, Tyler continued in a normal voice, "I'll be back as soon as possible." After kissing her gently, he followed Mike from the room. When they reached the foyer, Mike paused to kiss a woman who was entering the house. Tyler stared in shock. The woman was the spitting image of his wife, Elli.

Mike said, "Let's go," and jolted Tyler into action. Tyler only had time to nod at the woman as he pressed past her to get out the door. He had a terrible feeling in the pit of his stomach that he shouldn't leave, but the more pressing issue of the cattle needed to be addressed first.

CHAPTER 43

BAIN had waited until full dark to scout the buildings at the Circle R. He wasn't surprised to find the bunkhouse deserted. He'd seen the ranch hands go by when he was sitting in the jeep waiting for night to fall. They were probably on their way to a barroom to get drunk. There was a light on in the living room of the tiny house. A quick look in the window had shown Emilia and the damned cowboy named Mike sitting together on the sofa. The big house was dark for the most part. The only light was in one bedroom at the rear of the building. Having located Emilia, Bain made his way back along the fence line to where the cattle were grazing. He'd purchased a pair of metal snips and sturdy work gloves along with some other miscellaneous items at a local hardware store. The added items were so that the purchase of the snips and work gloves wouldn't stand out if anyone asked.

The fence line was eight-strand high-tensile topped by barbed wire. The breaks would be easily mended with the proper tools. So, Bain wasn't doing too much property damage. After cutting the fence near the highest concentration of animals, Bain circled around the ones closest to the fence. Slapping his gloves sharply against his thigh, the noise startled the cattle. Bain waved his arms and yelled to get the cows moving in the right direction. Straight through the opening. Then he stood back as most of the other animals followed the leaders.

After making his way back to the jeep hidden in a turn-off, he made the call to the Circle R to report that the cattle were out. Bain slouched down in the driver's seat, waiting for the cowboy to show up with any available men. When they did, Emilia would be unprotected.

At 10:13 p.m., two men on horseback rode up to the break in the fence. Bain recognized the one named Mike and was astonished to see the man he'd talked to on the plane the previous morning. He was the man with six kids. They'd brought a couple of the dogs to assist in herding the cattle back onto the Circle R property. Then it would take the cowboys a while to mend the fence. Bain smiled, started the jeep, and took off. He needed to drop the jeep off at the line cabin, make his way to the ranch house, and grab Emilia before they returned. Bain knew he was driving way too fast, in a hurry because he didn't have much time. He wasn't concerned about his speed, though, because he hadn't seen a single vehicle go by in the past hour.

CHAPTER 44

EMILIA had spent the balance of the day taking care of household chores and reading to Peggy. She had wanted to share her good news with Peggy and Bill but needed to speak with Michael first. After all, he was the expectant father. In just a few short weeks, her life had changed dramatically. She had hoped and prayed that she would find Michael again but never truly believed it would happen. Now, here she was. Michael was part of her life, and she was expecting his child again. She would need to make a doctor's appointment as quickly as possible. Emilia was forty-eight years old, so considered high-risk. She would do anything necessary to protect the precious gift she was carrying in her womb. This time her mother wouldn't be around to steal the baby and give it away, either.

Emilia was worried about Bill. His condition had seemed to worsen over the last few days. He looked drawn and tired. She wondered how much of her drama had caused Peggy's and Bill's deterioration. She had prayed each night for guidance and strength to help the couple through their ordeal. Emilia had come to care for them so very quickly. If only she'd been privileged to have such wonderful people as parents.

When Peggy was settled for the night, Emilia sat with Bill for a while in the living room. He seemed despondent, but Emilia didn't know what to do to cheer him up. When Michael came in from doing chores, Bill told her he'd be fine on his own and that he'd be going to bed soon. So, Emilia went with Michael to his house. She'd make him something to eat while he got cleaned up.

As soon as Michael closed the door behind them, he swept her off her feet. As he carried her down the hall to the bedroom, he kissed her hungrily. After standing Emi on her feet, he worked the buttons on her blouse and undid the clasp on her bra. Emilia let the items fall away so that she was exposed to his questing hands, lips, and tongue.

As Michael pulled her nipple into his mouth, Emilia released the buckle on his belt, unbuttoned his jeans, and lowered the zipper. As she rubbed her hand over the bulge in his briefs, Michael pushed his erection against her palm.

After kissing her deeply, Mike said, "Okay, the suspense is killing me. Did you take the test?"

Emilia searched Michael's face looking for a clue to his true feelings about what she was going to tell him. "You said you wanted the test to be positive. Is that really how you feel, Michael? I don't want you to think that I was trying to trick you into marrying me by getting pregnant."

"I told you we were getting married that first night before I took you into my bed, Emi. Don't you want to marry me? A baby would be a blessing. Are you pregnant, darlin'? If you're not, I'll be happy to keep working on it until you are," Mike replied with a grin.

Emi placed her hands on Michael's shoulders and raised up to nibble at his ear. Licking the outer edge, she paused to whisper, "You're going to be a daddy."

Mike looked at Emi incredulously, then let out a whoop. "I can't believe it. Holy, fuck!"

Stripping Emi naked, Mike tore off his shirt and briefs and carried her into the shower, where he pleasured her until she was shaking with desire.

"Michael, stop teasing me, please. I need to come so very badly," she moaned.

"I won't hurt the baby, will I," he asked her worriedly.

"No, silly. We can have sex." Emilia laughed.

Mike didn't need to be told twice. He lifted Emi. "Wrap your legs around me, darlin'." Then he pressed inside slowly.

"Oh, for fuck's sake, Michael," Emi moaned. I need you to push harder.

His sweet girl swearing turned Mike on. "You dirty girl, you. I'm going to have to punish you for using naughty language."

Setting Emi down, Mike stepped from the shower and wrapped a towel around his waist. Emi stared at him, surprised that he wasn't going to finish what he'd started. When he grabbed her up, she let out a squeak.

Carrying her to the bedroom Mike dropped down onto the bed. Draping Emi over his knees, he gave her a light smack on her butt. Emi squealed, but she knew how this played out, and she was game.

Mike rubbed the cheek he had smacked, then dipped his fingers between her folds. Emilia was so close, she bore down as he pumped his fingers in and out. Unlike the last time they'd played this game, when Mike withdrew his fingers, he rubbed her swollen clit. Emilia groaned. When Mike slapped her again, she came hard, and her vision was reduced to shooting fireworks in the black canvas of a nighttime sky. Before the last tremors left her, Michael's cock replaced his fingers, ramming into her until she came again on a loud moan. Then they both collapsed in a sweaty pile of body parts.

When their breathing had returned to normal, they showered together, got dressed, and went into the kitchen to make something to eat. Mike had worked up quite an appetite. They sat at the kitchen table to eat the omelets, sausage, and toast they'd cooked, then did the dishes together.

When they were finished, they moved to the sofa and snuggled while talking about Bill and Peggy, the ranch, and possible names for their baby.

At 9:37 p.m., the house phone began to ring. Emilia saw the look of concern on Michael's face as he listened to what the person on the other end was saying. When he hung up, he said, "Gotta go, sweetheart. There are cows out, and it's just me. The guys went out to a barroom to try to get lucky. They won't be home until late."

Grabbing his boots and hat, Mike ran outside. Emilia followed after turning out the lights and closing the door behind her.

By the time she made it to the main house's front door, Michael was already on his way back out. A handsome young man followed close on Michael's heels. Emilia had never met the man before, but he looked very familiar. As he passed her in the entry, he nodded his head but didn't say a word. Emilia stared at his retreating back. Then she realized why she recognized him. She'd seen dozens of photographs of him. He was her son-in-law, Tyler.

Closing the door, Emilia turned towards the living room where Bill was talking to a young woman. The air in the room was charged with a lightning storm's worth of tension. Emilia could almost see the flashes of charged energy zigzagging between the two people engaged in a rather heated discussion. As Emilia stood in the archway, uncertain if she should interrupt, the woman glanced up. Emilia took a step back as the look of anger on the woman's face turned to disgust.

Rising from her seated position on the coffee table, the woman stepped forward into the light, and Emilia gasped. It was like looking into a mirror that contained a reflection of her younger self—a more youthful self who looked furious. The woman raised her arm and pointed at Emilia. As she started to sob, she said, "You've ruined my life. I don't know if I can ever forgive you."

Emilia, recognizing her daughter, Elli, turned and fled the house. As she ran down the gravel lane toward the road, she sobbed out her anguish. Her daughter hated her, just as Emilia had feared she would. They would never have a relationship now, so Emilia needed to go. She was the interloper here. She didn't belong, and she never would.

Desperate and blinded by her tears, Emilia took no notice of the vehicle barreling toward her as she darted out onto the main road. The driver, thinking it was a deer, swerved at the last minute but was too late to avoid her. The front bumper clipped Emilia, and her body soared through the air. The last thing she remembered before she made an impact with the road was the hallucination she'd had after she'd been injected with the date rape drug.

Yanking the wheel to the left, Bain slammed on the brakes. "Fuck!" Just what he needed. "Damn deer." He'd just clipped it with his bumper. Maybe the damage would be minimal. Climbing from the jeep, he went to check on the damage. The fender had a tiny crimp. Being a jeep, it was built like a tank. So, the damage wasn't bad. After giving the vehicle a thorough inspection, Bain turned to glance toward the deer. It wouldn't do to leave it lying in the road for some other unsuspecting driver to hit. The body had flown about fifteen feet just out of view of the headlights. Bain got back into the jeep and angled it to get a better look. What he found turned his heart to ice. The body lying crumpled in the road was Emilia.

Grabbing his cell phone from his pocket, he started to dial 911, then thought better of it. Lifting Emilia, he placed her in the back of the jeep. The sight of her twisted arm and damaged leg turned his stomach. Doing a search on his cell phone, he got directions to the closest hospital. Jamming the jeep into gear, he tore down the highway, desperate to get Emilia to someone who could save her.

After pulling into the emergency room parking lot, Bain gathered her broken body into his arms. "Please don't die on me, Emilia. I love you, honey, so much. I'm so sorry. I didn't mean to hurt you."

Carrying Emilia's body as if she were made of spun glass, Bain entered through the sliding doors. He kept his head turned down to make it difficult for any cameras to get a good look at his face. As he yelled, "Please somebody, she needs help," the attendant took one look at what he was carrying and ran for assistance. Bain was quickly relieved of his burden. As Emilia disappeared through a set of double doors on a gurney, Bain turned and fled the way he'd come in. As he climbed into the jeep, a police car, sirens blaring, raced into the parking lot. Two officers dashed across the pavement as Bain backed out and slowly drove away.

CHAPTER 45

IKE and Tyler discovered a hysterical Elli when they returned from herding the cattle back onto the Circle R property and mending the broken fence. A fence that Mike was positive had been deliberately cut. By then, it was almost midnight. Rushing to Elli, Tyler gathered her into his arms and rocked her to try to calm her enough to understand what she was saying.

Elli was alone in the living room when they arrived, and Bill was nowhere to be found. Mike searched the house, even checking on the children. They were all snug in their beds, hopefully with sweet dreams dancing through their heads. Mike got his first look at his newest granddaughter. At two months of age, Lianne was a perfect baby, already sleeping through the night. Mike placed a tender kiss on the child's forehead and adjusted her blanket. Then he tiptoed from the room so as not to disturb her and continued his search.

Emi was not in the bedroom she shared with Mike, and Bill was not in the master bedroom with Peggy. Mike only poked his head through the door to check. He didn't go all the way inside because he could see that the entrance to the master bath was open and the light was off. Peggy was in bed alone, lying on her side. She seemed to be sound asleep, probably due to the pain medication she was taking. Mike didn't want to disturb her, either.

When Mike returned to the living room, Elli's sobs had slowed to whimpers. Tyler was crooning a soft lullaby to her. One he sang to his children when they woke up from a bad dream. Mike hunkered down in front of Elli and gathered her into his arms. Elli turned her face into his shoulder and started to sob again.

"Oh, Daddy, I'm so sorry!" she cried. "I didn't mean to hurt her. I was so furious, and I took it out on her."

Stunned, it took Mike several minutes to be able to form a coherent thought. Elli had called him daddy. "It is okay, baby. I'm right here, and I love you so much. Can you tell me what happened?"

Elli buried her head further into his chest to hide her face. Mike looked at Tyler, whose face wore the same stunned expression.

Finally, Elli started to hiccup through her sobs. Both Mike and Tyler had to lean in to understand her. "I yelled at Momma and told her I didn't think I could ever forgive her. She ran out the door. When she didn't come back, Grandpa got worried and went to find her. I'm so sorry, Daddy. I didn't mean it. You have to find her so I can apologize."

Mike placed Elli back in Tyler's arms, then kissed her forehead. Searching her face, he looked directly into her eyes so that she would know he was speaking the truth. Eyes that were swimming pools of pain and anguish. "Everything will be okay. Your momma loves you just as much as I do. She's just hurting right now because she's waited so very long to find you. We'll find her and Bill. Now, Tyler's going to put you to bed. You need to rest and take care of your children. Dig deep and find that inner strength that has bolstered you through all the hurt and sadness you've been dealt with. I know that it has been a considerable amount, much more than anyone ever deserves in one lifetime. Especially, not you, my sweet girl. Find that strength Elli and harness it. Tyler and I will go out and look for Bill and Emi."

As Tyler stood to carry Elli to their bedroom, Mike told him, "I'll check the outbuildings and my house. If I don't find them, I'll meet you in the stable. I'll saddle the horses, so we can search along the drive and road."

Tyler nodded in understanding, then carried Elli from the room.

Laying Elli on their bed, Tyler removed her slippers and tucked the comforter around her. "Rest, sweet girl. I'll be back as quick as I can."

Elli pressed her fist against her mouth to stifle the sob that threatened to escape. She didn't want to wake her daughter. "No one has ever loved me. The people I thought were my parents never showed me the slightest bit of affection. All the kids at school laughed at me behind my back. Even Blair overlooked me. I was just an easy first fuck before marrying Carly, who truly held his heart. Then his willing broodmare so he could have the family he wanted. You left me twice. Why did you come back?"

Full of remorse, Tyler smoothed Elli's hair with a trembling hand. He had played a huge part in Elli's misperception of her own self-worth. "Sweet girl, Rick loved you from the first moment he met you. Carly never held his heart. It always belonged to you. I know that you're overwhelmed by your emotions right now. Too much has happened all at once. You'll see things more clearly when you've had time to process. I want you to sleep and dream of me. The man who loves you more than life itself. I always have, and I always will." Then he kissed her like it was their first time. "Sleep. You're going to need your strength. I guess I haven't been expressing myself very well. My heart and soul have always belonged to you, Elli. Love you, sweet girl."

Mike wasn't in the living room when Tyler returned from putting his distraught wife to bed. Grabbing a pair of boots kept in the entryway closet, he went out the front door and headed to the stable. He found Mike placing the saddle on the chestnut mare. "No signs of Bill or Emilia?" Tyler asked.

"No, and I checked every building and my house thoroughly," Mike responded.

Tyler stared at the man and cleared his throat, "So, you're really Elli's father?"

Mike nodded. "It's funny. Rick told me that he thought Elli looked like me. He jokingly asked if I'd had an affair with Elli's mother, Lilianne. My heart has loved Elli like a daughter, almost since the moment she stepped foot on Circle R soil. Guess my heart figured it out way before my head. Bill just told me that I was really Elli's father a couple of weeks ago. He has a whole file compiled by a private investigator named Samuel Goldstein from Pennsylvania, who uncovered the whole story. Bill brought Emilia here as a home health care nurse on the pretext of taking care of Peggy and himself. Truthfully, it was to bring Emi and me and Elli together as a family."

"I don't know what to say. Bill didn't even hint at any of this when he called in June to find out when we could come for a visit. He should have told me that he and Peggy were ill. Elli and I just thought we were coming for a happy family vacation."

"Well, right now, it's anything but happy. Let's ride. I have a sick feeling in my gut," Mike admitted. They both mounted up and headed down the drive toward the main entrance.

CHAPTER 46

THEY say that bad things come in sets of three. The *Circle R Cattle Company* ranch was struck by that set of three on a warm Sunday morning in August. It was nearing 1:00 a.m. when the first indication of the pain and heartache that would befall the Circle R residents was discovered.

On horseback, Mike and Tyler searched the ground along the drive with powerful flashlights. The bright lights shone across the fields, reflecting off the cattle who were calmly sleeping or chewing their cuds. It was Tyler who found the first of that set of three. With a shout of pain, he stumbled from his saddle. He almost fell in his haste to get to the fallen body lying in the middle of the driveway. Alerted by Tyler's cry, Mike saw where Tyler was headed and followed suit.

Both men dropped to their knees beside Bill's body. Mike took Bill's wrist, and Tyler placed his fingers to the side of Bill's neck. Both men felt for a pulse. Neither finding any, both men glanced up. Their gazes reflected their shared pain as glassy eyes stared back, one to the other. Tyler yanked his cell phone from his pocket and quickly dialed 911. When the dispatcher answered, Tyler's voice cracked before he could give the person on the other end of the line the details of their emergency. As Tyler waited for the ambulance, Mike rode back to the ranch house. His heart was heavy. He dreaded the job that had been assigned to him. He would be the one to tell Peggy that her beloved husband was gone.

Entering the master bedroom, Mike found Peggy lying exactly as she had been when he was searching for Bill. The knot in his stomach tightened as he placed his fingers on Peggy's emaciated wrist. He instinctively knew what he would find. Peggy's skin was cool to his touch. The beat of life beneath her thin skin nonexistent.

Mike gulped back a sob that he barely managed to suppress. Leaving the room, Mike went to sit at the kitchen table. It took a few minutes to compose himself before making the 911 call, requesting additional assistance at the Circle R. A second person had passed away.

Then Mike mounted Cheyenne and rode back down the drive. The ambulance and a police car, bright lights whirring, greeted his arrival. Tyler was standing next to his horse, valiantly trying to answer the questions he was being bombarded with. A blanket-covered gurney was being loaded into the back of the ambulance. Mike knew the emergency lights wouldn't be needed for the return trip. It would be making a delivery to the morgue of a funeral home.

Mike went to Tyler and the police officer. Tyler asked the question that begged to be asked. Was Peggy aware of what had happened? Mike hung his head. Tyler could see the additional pain in Mike's return gaze when he looked back up, but Tyler wasn't prepared for what Mike would say. Both beloved owners of the Circle R were gone. Elli would be devastated. Tyler's mind flashed back to the months after Rick's death. Elli had barely survived his loss. Would this loss destroy the woman he loved?

As the first ambulance pulled away, a second arrived. That one paused to get direction before continuing its journey to the house. The police car followed close behind. A few minutes later, Sean and John pulled into the yard, drawn by the emergency vehicle's lights. Thankfully, neither was drunk. Their assistance in the search for Emi would be needed.

All four men waited in the living room with the police as the EMTs did their jobs of assessing Peggy's condition. Her lifeless body was taken out through the kitchen door and loaded into the back of the waiting vehicle. It would follow in the first ambulance's wake.

Tyler had checked on his children and wife when he entered the house. Thankfully, all were sleeping peacefully.

As Mike and Tyler answered the additional questions thrown at them about what had prompted their search for Bill, the third and final alarming discovery was revealed. Mike was desperate to continue the search for Emi and was trying to enlist the officers' assistance. When he was giving Emi's description, both officers got stunned looks on their faces.

"Mr. Willis, a Jane Doe was brought into the Emergency Department at the Trauma Center. It appeared that she had been struck by a vehicle. The man who carried her in disappeared as soon as the woman was loaded onto a gurney. So, he left before he could be questioned. We have an APB out trying to find that individual."

Shell shocked, Mike asked, "What does that have to do with us?"

"Mr. Willis, it may just be a coincidence, but the Jane Doe matches the description of the woman you are searching for. If it is indeed her, I'm certain the hospital would appreciate any information you can supply. The last we heard, she was in surgery."

Panicked, Mike charged towards the front door. It took Tyler, John, and Sean to restrain him.

"Let me go." Mike fought against the hands that had latched onto his arms and pulled him to the floor. "You don't understand. Emi's pregnant. I have to get to her, now."

Stunned, the restraining hands were removed. Tyler reached out, gripped Mike's hand, and helped him to his feet.

The officer placed a hand on Mike's shoulder. "Sir, please calm down. It may not even be her. May I suggest that your men continue to look for her, and my partner and I will take you to the hospital? If the Jane Doe isn't Emilia Andersen, we'll bring you back and help in the search."

Mike stared at the men around him, took in their concerned faces, and nodded his head at the policeman. "I've been trying to reach Emi on her cell phone. It keeps going to voicemail. Tyler, please stay here with Elli and the kids. They're your number one priority. Call me if Emi comes back. Sean, you and John take the horses and check towards the line cabin. Maybe she made her way there. Also, check the neighbors in both directions in case they've seen her. She's on foot. She can't have gone too far. I don't think she'd hitch a ride with anyone."

Sean and John left immediately, patting Mike on the back as they passed. Sean turned and said, "We'll find her, Mike," as he walked out the door to begin the search.

Tyler shook the hands of the two officers and thanked them for their assistance. Then he grabbed Mike in a hug and whispered, "It's going to be okay, Dad. I have every faith." As Mike turned away, Tyler could see the unshed tears in his father-in-law's eyes.

CHAPTER 47

MIKE was thankful for the policemen's assistance. They used their lights and siren when necessary to get him to the hospital in record time. Their presence also facilitated cooperation in getting him past administration to see the people in charge of the Jane Doe case that had been brought in.

Mike and the officers were advised that the woman was now out of surgery. The patient had been taken to the intensive care unit. The doctor would be notified that they were waiting to speak to him. So, they went into the waiting room. Mike paced the floor, impatient to be on his way back to the ranch if he didn't need to be here.

When the doctor came into the room, Mike was asked to take a seat, and the doctor began. "We were presented with an unconscious female, age approximately mid-to-late forties, lab work revealing positive, so precautions were taken to protect the fetus. The patient sustained multiple abrasions to the skin, commonly known as road rash; a concussion was caused by impact with the road surface; a fracture of the left arm's ulna and wrist. An orthopedic implant was used to repair the fracture to the ulna. A displaced patellar fracture of the left knee required surgery to put the pieces of bone back together. There was also a fracture of the tibia. Both arm and leg were placed in casts, and the left leg has been immobilized. Surgeries were successful, but the patient is in a coma due to the concussion. The doctor sounded so impersonal, he could easily have passed for a robot.

Swallowing past the lump that had formed in Mike's throat, he asked the doctor if he could see the patient, and the three men were shown to the woman's room. Despite the swelling and discoloration, casts to arm and leg, all the wires and needles, and bandages, Mike had no problem making an identification. This was the woman who owned his heart and soul and was carrying his unborn child.

Mike turned as white as a sheet, so he was guided to a chair beside the bed. A nurse came into the room with a request for information regarding their unconscious patient. Mike told her that

Emi had just been in the hospital a few weeks prior due to an attack by an unknown assailant. The nurse said she would pull the necessary information from those records, thanked him, and left the room. The officers, however, said they were suspicious that the incidents might in some way be connected. They now had a name for their Jane Doe case. They intended to continue to look for the man who had dropped Emilia off in the emergency room and search for a connection to the attempted date rape attack.

Finally given some privacy, Mike took Emi's one undamaged hand in his, buried his face in the sheets beside her body to muffle the noise, and started to sob. When his cell phone rang, he quickly grabbed it and swiped to answer the call.

"Mike. It's Sean. We found Mrs. Andersen's cell phone. It was lying on the side of the road near the entrance to the main drive. There is a fresh set of skid marks that begin about fifteen feet before the entrance. No sign of Emilia, but there is what looks like small blood stains on the road near where the phone was lying."

Mike gripped the phone tight to tamp down the rage flowing through his body. "Sean, I'm sorry. I was just getting ready to call.

The Jane Doe accident victim is Emilia, so you can call off the search. She's currently in a coma, but I'll give you the rest of the particulars later. I need you to take the lead on managing the ranch for a while. The family will be going through hell, what with Emi's condition and Bill's and Peggy's deaths. There'll be funeral arrangements to make, too. Oh, Damn! I forgot. Tim is due this morning with his family. I'll need Tom to drive out to the landing strip to pick them up. Tell him to keep his mouth shut about what's happened. I'll come home quick to handle all the explanations and for a change of clothes. I'll be staying here at the hospital for the most part until Emi's out of the woods."

Sean's response was, "Fuck! I'm sorry. Don't worry about the ranch or the animals. I'm on it. Just take care of that beautiful lady. She's in my prayers, man. I'll let you go. Talk to you later." Then the call disconnected.

Mike then called Tyler, who answered, "Dad, what did you find out?"

Mike was so thankful for the man who could now legitimately be called son-in-law. Mike explained the details of Emilia's condition and everything else that they would be facing in the coming days.

Tyler's main concern was what Mike needed him to do to help. Mike requested that Tyler take good care of his wife and children.

"My daughter is going to need our love and support. We'll need to prevent her from descending into the pit of despair that almost destroyed her after Rick's death," Mike told Tyler. "Now that she knows that I'm her father, I want the chance to build a relationship. Maybe you should wait until I come home so we can tell her about Emi together. She'll be dealing with enough trauma when she wakes up and finds out that both Peggy and Bill passed away during the night. You know she's going to blame herself for what's happened to Emi, and it's not her fault. Oh, and Tyler, it makes me very happy that you're calling me Dad."

CHAPTER 48

IKE returned to the ranch just as Tim's plane circled the airspace over the main house. It was Tim's signal that he had arrived and someone should drive to the landing strip to pick up his family. It was 7:06 a.m.

Tyler had grabbed a few hours of sleep after speaking to Mike. The fussy baby was what woke him up. Elli blinked, then stretched. When she looked at her husband's face, she smiled tentatively and whispered, "Did you find Grandpa and Momma?"

Trying to keep a neutral expression, Tyler gave Elli a quick kiss and said, "Yes." Then to avoid any further discussion on the subject, he asked, "Do you want me to change Lianne for you? You can grab a quick shower and then nurse her while I take mine."

Elli looked at Tyler, confused by his abbreviated response to her question, but decided it was probably because he was tired. The previous day had been long and emotion-packed, after all. So, she pushed her husband onto his back and kissed him silly. Then she jumped off the bed and ran to the bathroom, having noticed that a specific part of his anatomy had risen to attention. She gave him a coy grin as she turned and closed the door behind her.

Tyler checked the baby, who was sucking her finger. Satisfied that he had a few minutes, he quietly opened the bathroom door. Elli was in the shower washing her face and hadn't heard him enter the room. Stepping in behind her, Tyler lifted her up before she could lodge a protest and quickly impaled her against the shower wall. "Thought you could get me all worked up and get away, did you? This is going to be fast, so hold on tight." Setting a new record for bringing his wife and himself to orgasm, he kissed her and said, "Thank you, sweet girl. I needed that." Then he wrapped a towel around his waist and went out to change the baby.

When Tyler entered the kitchen to begin preparing breakfast, he found his father-in-law seated at the table. Mike was drinking a cup of coffee. "Hospital vending machines have the worst coffee on the planet," he remarked. "Tim, Jeannie, and Sophie just flew in. They should be here momentarily. It's a good thing there are six bedrooms. The house is filling up fast."

Tyler pulled ingredients out of the refrigerator and began putting together a casserole consisting of bacon, potatoes, and eggs. The adults might not be in the mood to eat when everyone was advised of the current situation, but at least the kids would be well fed.

Mike rose from the table and went to help.

"Any improvement in Mom's condition," Tyler asked.

"She's holding her own. The doctor is mainly concerned about swelling of the brain. They are keeping a close eye on her. As soon as everyone has been updated, I'm going back to the hospital. I'd appreciate it if you and Tim would help me with the funeral arrangements. It's going to be a massive affair. Peggy and Bill were well-loved. They wanted to be cremated, and their ashes spread over the ranch from Tim's plane. So, there will only be viewings. Nothing at the cemetery."

"No problem. Just let me know if you want to hold the repast here at the ranch. I can contact local restaurants to assist with the food, plus make numerous dishes myself. The weather is expected to be good for the next several days. I can call a rental agency that will set up a tent and provide tables and chairs. That will reduce the foot traffic through the house."

"I think that will work. Let's do that," Mike agreed.

They could hear a lot of laughter and talk in the hallway, so the Whrite-Thompson brood had discovered Sophie, Tim, and Jeannie, who must have entered the house through the back door. Mike said, "Well, here goes. I'll direct the adults to the living room and the kids to you. Please feed the children while I upset everyone else. I've asked the ranch hands to come to the house. I want to do this in one shot."

Elli came into the kitchen with a bemused look on her face. "Daddy said you're going to feed the kids. He wants to talk to the adults. I assume you already know what he has to tell us since you're stuck in the kitchen?"

Tyler kissed her and said, "Go on now. Come back to me when you're done. I need a hug and kiss from my best girl," and he gave her a nudge in the right direction. Elli looked like she wanted to question him, but she finally turned and did as she was asked.

It was standing room only when Elli entered the living room, but they had saved a seat for her. Mike was standing in front of the fireplace, while the ranch hands Sean and John sat in the armchairs. Tom and Jake stood off to the side, and Tim and Jeannie were sitting on the sofa. Elli sat down beside them.

Mike dreaded what he had to say to the assembled group. He was dead tired, and he needed to get back to the hospital. He didn't want Emi to wake up alone. Sean and John were already aware of what Mike had to say. He could count on them to stay cool-headed and lend moral support while he told the others. So, he cleared his throat and began, "Early this morning, we lost two people whom we all love dearly. I just received confirmation that Bill passed away due to a massive stroke."

There were several gasps, and the women present began to cry. John was ready with a box of tissues that he started to hand out.

Mike continued. "Shortly before Tyler and I discovered Bill's body, Peggy passed peacefully in her sleep, for which I'll be eternally grateful. I found her when I went to tell her about Bill."

Tim was now crying and clinging to his wife, Jeannie. Jake went to Elli's side, crouched down, and wrapped her in a hug.

"Tyler is handling the majority of the preparations for the viewings. I'm hoping that Tim can assist him with that. Bill and Peggy wished to be cremated. They requested that their ashes be strewn over the ranch. They want Tim to fly over the property as their ashes are released."

Tim looked up long enough to nod his agreement.

Mike nodded at him in return and continued, "There's more. We believe that Emilia Andersen was struck by an unknown vehicle at the entrance to the ranch. An unidentified man delivered Emi to the hospital. He left as soon as she was taken away for treatment. That man is being sought for questioning by the police."

Elli jumped to her feet and ran to Mike for comfort. She wrapped her arms around his waist and turned her face up to meet his eyes. "Is Momma alright? Is she in her room?"

Mike looked down at his daughter and knew that he would have to hold on tight. "Your mother is in a coma, Elli. She suffered several fractures and a concussion. She's in intensive care."

Elli's face lost all of its color, her eyes rolled back in her head, and she started to slide to the floor. Mike was there to catch her.

Turning to the others, he said, "I'll be spending most of my time at the hospital until Emi's well enough to come home. She's going to be my wife. Sean is in charge of the ranch in the interim. John, Jake, and Tim, please follow his orders and keep things running smoothly for me. I appreciate everything you can do to help. I'll keep everyone updated. Thank you!"

He found Tyler serving the children breakfast when he carried Elli into the kitchen. Dropping the plate that he was about to fill, Tyler said, "Jess and Sophie, please finish feeding the little ones. After they've eaten, you can take them out to the stable to see the horses. Blair, Peggy, and Logan, please watch out for your little brother, and hold hands. Billy, you mind your siblings."

All of the children sat at the table, eyes as big as saucers. Peggy spoke up first. "Is Mommy sick?"

Tyler said, "No, sweet pea. She's just tired. She's going to lie down for a little bit."

Then, Tyler held out his arms for his wife, thanked Mike under his breath, and carried her to their room. Mike followed, stopping at the bathroom for some smelling salts.

It was just as Mike predicted. When Elli came too, her first words were, "This is all my fault. I'm a terrible, horrible person." Then she buried her face in the comforter.

Mike took Elli by the shoulders and turned her back to him. Then he forced her to listen. "Eloise Lianne Whrite-Thompson, I want you to listen to me, now. Nothing that has happened was ever your fault. It also wasn't my fault or your mother's, other than the fact that we were two young kids who loved each other very much. That love produced a beautiful baby. That baby was you. Circumstances and evil people prevented the three of us from becoming the loving family that we deserved. Still, we've been given a second chance. Now, I expect you to dry your eyes, wash your face and go into the kitchen. Tyler will make you some breakfast, which I expect you to eat. I know you're hurting, but you're going to be brave and help everyone else get through this because they are hurting too. Is that understood?"

Elli took in her father's sad countenance, blinked twice, turned to Tyler, and blinked again. Then she kissed Mike on the cheek and said, "Yes, Sir."

"Good girl. I'm going to grab some of that egg dish Tyler made, take a shower, and head back to the hospital. Call if there are any problems. I don't expect there to be any. Two of my most favorite loved ones have everything well in hand. Tyler, let me know when the viewings have been scheduled. I've asked Sean to spread the word amongst our friends and associates. I've already talked to the funeral home about the obituary notices for the newspapers. The funeral director said one of the Billings television stations is putting together a segment that will air on the seven o'clock news tonight. I've asked Jeannie to field any calls. Elli, you can help wherever possible when you aren't dealing with Lianne and the rest of my rambunctious grandchildren. Did I miss anything?" When Tyler and Elli shook their heads, no, Mike said, "Good. Let's get to it. I'm hungry."

CHAPTER 49

THE next few days passed in a blur of activity for everyone on the ranch. For Mike, the hours dragged by while he watched over Emi lying in her hospital bed. He spent the time telling her the details of his life before he'd met her and all of the years that he'd spent missing her since they'd parted company when they were still kids. He watched the monitors that measured the beats of her life, praying all the while that those beats would continue for decades to come. He prayed that she would come back to him because he missed her sweet and gentle nature, the beauty of her smile, and her sexy body. If she were awake, she would have laughed at that and told him he was just horny. He was thankful that the new life they'd created was firmly embedded in her womb. He suggested baby names, knowing she would probably reject them all if she were awake to hear them.

When he left her on the third day, he kissed her and told her he'd be right back. Then he drove home to the ranch to get ready for the viewing. Word had gotten out. The funeral home planned an additional hour because they were expecting that many people.

Mike stood before the room full of assembled mourners dressed in his best black suit with the satin piping, starched white shirt, silk tie, black Stetson, and shiny black boots. There wasn't a dry eye in the funeral parlor as Mike extolled the virtues of two of the people he loved most in the world. The same mourners laughed as Mike related how Bill hired a wet-behind-the-ears lad fresh from college and gave him a home. They laughed again when he told the story of the sweet lady who took care of him when he was tossed off a bronc and almost broke his fool neck.

After the final viewing, everyone was invited back to the ranch for the repast. Tyler exceeded Mike's expectations with the spread he'd created. The mourners filled their plates, then milled about while sharing stories about the Roberts and ranch life in general. When everyone's stomachs were filled to capacity, they all stared heavenward. A tiny Piper J-3 Cub circa 1947 flew over the ranch, as Peggy's and Bill's ashes blew away in the stream of air created by the prop. Peggy and Bill would forever be a part of the land they had come to love.

The hour was late when the last of the mourners drove away. Mike was running on empty, so he planned to spend the night in his own bed to get some much-needed sleep. He wouldn't be doing Emi any good if he became ill or had an accident himself and ended up in a hospital bed beside her.

CHAPTER 50

B AIN spent the days in hiding following the accident. How had everything gone so horribly wrong? Instead of taking Emilia home where she belonged, she was lying in a hospital bed fighting for her life. Bain was ashamed. He'd hit his beloved Emilia and then anonymously dropped her damaged body off at the emergency room.

He was thankful that the elderly couple who owned the rundown house where he was renting a room didn't have a working television, and seldom left their home. The couple's only source of news was an old radio that they tuned into in the evening. Since they were hard of hearing, they kept it turned up loud. Bain listened to the story about the woman who was a hit-and-run accident victim. It said the police were searching for information regarding the man who'd dropped her off and then fled. The description was vague, so there wasn't any possibility of the couple recognizing Bain as the person the police were seeking. He also heard the story about the deaths of the *Circle R Cattle Company* ranch owners. They were the couple Emilia had been taking care of as a home health care nurse.

Bain was able to catch the news on his phone as well. Thankful that newspaper people were so nosey, they kept him abreast of Emilia's injuries, surgeries, and the possibility of recovery. Bain learned that she was currently in a coma and being watched over by her fiancé. Bain bristled at that. Emilia was supposed to be his, but he knew that he had lost her. Bain also learned that Emilia was carrying a child. Bain just needed to see her one more time so that he could tell her how very sorry he was.

When the news report featured a segment about the details of the Roberts' funeral service and repast, Bain knew it would be his only opportunity.

Late on the night of the Roberts' repast, Bain slipped into the hospital and made his way to the ICU. Since it was late, the hospital was quiet except for the machines marking the passage of moments in people's lives. He hid behind the door of a room across from the nurse's station. One nurse was in charge of watching the monitors at that station, and Bain watched her. When she left to use the restroom, Bain slipped into the room occupied by Emilia.

Taking a seat beside her bed, he slipped her slim hand into his large one and kissed each of her fingers. Her hand was just about the only part of her beautiful body that hadn't been damaged when he hit her with the jeep. Resting his head beside her on the mattress, he begged her forgiveness. Then he talked about all of the years he had loved her, always wanting her for his own. As his mind wandered, the slim hand he clasped stirred. Shocked, he looked up and found the most beautiful cerulean blue eyes staring back at him.

CHAPTER 51

EMILIA felt like she had been run over by a steamroller. Every part of her body hurt, especially her head. She must have had too much to drink. She searched her mind. She remembered how Michael had given her such pleasure after she'd shared the news of the baby she was expecting. That thought confused her. Surely, she wasn't drinking alcohol, knowing that she was pregnant.

She needed to get up. Bill and Peggy depended on her to take care of them. So far, Emilia didn't believe she had earned her salary or their respect. She kept messing up, bringing more harm than good to their lives.

Opening her eyes hurt. The room was too bright. It took time for Emilia to focus. When the room's details resolved into monitors and fluid bags, wires and bandages, and what the heck, there were casts on her arm and leg, she became even more confused. Then she noticed the man holding her hand and her eyes opened wide in surprise.

"Bain? Where am I? What happened?" she asked the man she thought never to see again. Had it all been a dream? Was she still trapped in the life she'd made for herself in Pennsylvania? What of Iain? Was his death a dream as well?

Bain kissed the hand he held again. "Shhh, sweetheart. Don't upset yourself. You've been in an accident. You're in the hospital? You need to rest and get better, if not for anything other than the baby you carry inside you."

"I'm confused, Bain. What accident? I remember Iain's funeral, I think. You told me Iain gave me to you. Are you the father of my baby, Bain?"

"I truly wish I were, Emilia. I fell in love with the beautiful young woman that my brother brought into our home. Then I spent twenty-five years in purgatory, watching Iain mistreat you. I had to listen to him abuse your body every night while never giving you the children you deserved. I wanted to give you those children, knowing you had so much love trapped inside you that you needed to share. I came to bring you home with me so that I could give you those children. I was hoping you could learn to love me a little if I could give you that. Instead, because of me, you're lying in a hospital bed. Can you forgive me, Emilia? I never meant to hurt you."

When Bain started to cry, Emilia reached out, laid her hand along the curve of his jaw, and then tried to wipe away the tears coursing down his cheek. "I think I've always loved you a little, Bain. I've always known that you were the one who left bouquets of wildflowers for me when I was sad or feeling especially lonely. Unfortunately, I was also very intimated by you, and I heard the stories your friends told about your conquests and the sharing of women you'd picked up at barrooms. I wish I'd known that Iain shared the same proclivities. I might have worked up the courage to leave him."

Bain kissed Emilia's hand again. "You never deserved that. You were always the best wife a man could ever want, and Iain never appreciated it. I wish I could undo all the pain and heartache he caused you over the years and all the pain and heartache that I've caused you as well. I'm going to leave you in peace now. Will you call me if you ever need my help? I'll always love you and be there for you, sweetheart. I promise you that."

With that, Bain stood. Leaning over the rail of the hospital bed, he pressed a kiss to Emilia's lips. "Take care, Emilia. I'll miss you. I wish you the best of luck with your cowboy. He's one lucky son of a bitch."

Before Bain left the woman he loved behind, she gave him one piece of sage advice.

"Bain, instead of going to barrooms, maybe you should go shopping for a bride at the grocery store. It seemed to work for your brother." And even though it hurt, she winked at the look on Bain's face at her remark.

It was a long drive home to Pennsylvania. Bain had slept a lot during the last several days, so he planned to drive straight through. He hadn't gained the woman his heart wanted, but his heart was also buried deep in the soil of his birthright. Bain was going home to milk his cows, and maybe a trip to the grocery store was in order. He wondered what aisle they kept potential wives in.

CHAPTER 52

EMILIA drifted on a sea of gentle waves that brought her a profound sense of peace. She dreamt of her brother-in-law, Bain. He held her hand and told her all about his childhood growing up on the dairy farm he loved so much. Emilia wasn't afraid of Bain anymore, and maybe she shouldn't have been afraid of him in the first place. Just before the dream ended, Bain kissed her lips, told her that he would always love her, and then he set her free.

Her next conscious thought was that her body hurt everywhere, especially her head, but she needed to get up and go to work. Peggy and Bill relied on her, but she was tired, and her limbs felt like they were weighted down. She could feel Michael holding her hand, so the weight of his leg must be what she felt. Emilia loved that man so much. Maybe there was enough time for a quickie in the shower before she'd have to start her day.

Emilia squeezed the hand that held hers, then she opened her eyes with a plan in her head of seducing Michael into giving her a before breakfast orgasm.

The light in the room was so bright, it made Emilia's head thump. So, she scrunched her eyes. Ow, no more scrunching. Just that movement sent a mass panic of wild buffalo racing through her head. When the stampede slowed, and the herd of pain subsided, Emilia opened her eyes slowly. It wasn't Michael staring back at her or his hand holding hers. The cerulean blue eyes she beheld were swimming with tears of uncertainty and anguish. The hand that held hers trembled.

With a watery smile, the young woman Emilia was staring at opened her mouth. Then she spoke the best words Emilia had ever heard, "Hi, Momma."

Emilia had waited a lifetime to hear her daughter call her that. Emilia tried to shift to sit up but only managed to emit an, "Ow! That hurts!" And squeezed Elli's hand tight in reflex.

Elli said, "Lie still, I'll go get Daddy and a nurse. I'll be right back." Then she rushed from the room.

As Emilia took in the details of the room, she realized she was in a hospital. She took inventory of her aching parts, found her left arm and leg in casts, and boy, did she have a lump on her head. Now Emilia knew what was causing the stampeding herd through her skull. What had she been about that she'd fallen and hurt herself? Whatever it was, she had no plans to ever do it again.

A commotion outside the door to her room had her staring in that direction. When the door slammed back against the stop, the most handsome man she'd ever seen charged into the room with a nurse close on his heels.

"Mr. Willis, a little less noise, please. This is a hospital, you know," the nurse admonished.

Michael just gave the nurse a cheeky grin. Bending over the rail, he kissed Emilia soundly, then said, "Hey there, darlin'. I thought you were going to sleep right through the marriage ceremony and our honeymoon. It wouldn't be much fun going on a honeymoon by myself. What do you say? Let's get this show on the road and get you better. Then we can get you out of this place and back in my bed where you belong."

Emilia watched as the nurse blushed, then said, "Okay, out while I take care of my patient. You can come back in when I'm finished, but only if you behave. I have a feeling you'll cause my patient's blood pressure to spike, and we can't have that. At least until she's feeling better." Then she shoved Michael towards the door.

Mike winked and said, "I'll be right back."

Thus began a parade of hospital personnel in and out of her room. Thankfully, they had moved her to a private room so she would be able to have more than one visitor at a time.

After the nurse was finished with her vitals, Michael and Elli came in to sit with her. The nurse had raised the head of the bed a little so that Emilia could see them better. True to her nature, the first question Emilia asked was not about herself. It was unselfishly directed to the care of others. She asked, "Did you find someone to take care of Peggy and Bill? I'm anxious about them. Bill didn't seem right when I was speaking to him yesterday."

When Michael and Elli winced, Emilia asked, "What aren't you telling me?"

Mike spoke up first, "Emi, you've been in a coma. You didn't just speak to Bill yesterday."

Emilia blinked in confusion. "Okay, I guess the bump on my head was worse than I thought. Whatever I did, don't let me do it, ever again. So, who is taking care of Peggy and Bill?"

Elli burst into tears, and Michael moved to embrace her. As Emilia watched in concern, he whispered something in Elli's ear, which calmed her. She nodded her head, then grabbed some tissues from the box on the bedside table to dry her eyes.

When Elli had composed herself, Mike turned his attention back to Emilia. He leaned forward, lifted Emilia's hand, and placed a kiss on her opened palm. Then he cleared his throat. "Emi, honey, Bill and Peggy passed away several weeks ago."

In shock, Emilia struggled to get off the bed. "No, No, No! I don't believe you. I have to go. They need me."

Emilia's blood pressure spiked, and the commotion she was making as she struggled caused a nurse to come rushing in from the hall. As soon as she took in the situation, the nurse grabbed Emilia's shoulders and shook her a little to get her to focus. "Mrs. Andersen.

Emilia, you need to calm down now, or I'll have to sedate you, and your guests will have to leave. You don't want that. You need to think of your baby."

Emilia jerked at the reprimand, then collapsed against her pillow. "Please don't sedate me. I think I've missed too much while I was asleep. I promise to behave."

"Good. I'll hold you to that promise. Now, let's get you comfortable. The therapist will be coming in shortly to work with you. You need to start moving that leg and arm. He'll give you exercises to try, first. I'm sure."

After the nurse left, Michael and Elli took turns filling Emilia in about everything that had happened. They left out the part where Elli had said she could never forgive Emi. Michael and Elli had decided beforehand that it wasn't something that needed to be rehashed. If Emilia didn't remember that part, Elli and Emi could begin anew and build a solid relationship.

Emilia had lots of visitors throughout her hospital stay. At one point, Michael helped her to the windows because there was a surprise waiting for her. When she looked down, she noticed a large group of people gathered below her window, all staring up at her. Of course, she started to cry when she recognized who they were. Tyler stood proudly with his arm around Elli's waist, while she cradled her baby daughter, Lianne, in her arms. Four children, the towheaded triplets, Blair, Peggy, and Logan, and one dark-haired, Billy, all stood in a row holding hands. An older girl, Jessica, guarded them protectively. Behind them stood the ranch hands, Sean and John, and the teenagers, Tom and Jake. Emilia noticed that Jake was focused on Jessica. As everyone waved and smiled and pointed up at Emilia and Michael framed in the window, Emilia watched as Jake reached out tentatively to entwine his fingers with Jessica's. She looked up, gave him a shy smile, and then refocused on the siblings standing before her. But she never took back her hand.

Emilia grinned up at Michael and told him what she'd seen. Michael grinned back. "And, so it begins. I'll need to have a talk with that young man. Jess may be wise beyond her years, but she is only going on thirteen. However, if it's meant to be, they'll be the ones making that decision. We can only act as guides. Besides, if I remember correctly, her father told her she couldn't date until she turns thirty."

Emilia laughed so hard, she almost peed her pants.

The day the doctor signed the release for Emilia to go home was one of the happiest of her life. She couldn't wait to get out of there and sleep in her own bed again. Emilia followed her exercise routine religiously. The regimen included the active movement of her ankle, fingers, and toes, straight leg raises without assistance, knee press exercises, and non-weight bearing gait. Michael offered encouragement, held her, and wiped her eyes as she endured the pain. She never thought it would be so challenging to learn to walk with the help of crutches. As soon as the plaster was removed from her leg, careful knee movement exercises would begin to prevent the knee from becoming stiff and the thigh muscle from becoming weak. Emilia was not looking forward to that.

Mike carried Emi to the front door when they got home. Tyler was there with both doors open, so Emi wouldn't whack her bad leg going through the entry. Tyler bent to kiss her cheek as Michael carried her in and said, "Hi, Mom, welcome home!" and there went the waterworks again. Tyler was ready with a tissue.

The house seemed surprisingly quiet. Emilia was just about to ask where everyone was as Michael rounded the archway to the living room. When she was met with a resounding chorus of, "Surprise! Welcome home!" she almost jumped right out of Michael's arms.

Everyone she had come to love was there. Michael laid her carefully on the sofa, and her grandchildren gathered around. They were all very respectful of her injuries but full of questions. After a few minutes, Tyler came to herd them away, and Jess plopped down on the coffee table.

After giving her a kiss, she said, "Grandma, I started a family tree in February. Mom told me all about her life, and Dad helped fill in some of the blanks about my father's childhood. My father was Richard Blair Whrite. Tyler is my step-father, you know, but he may as well be my real father because I love and respect him that much. My father and Dad were best friends, but they had different personalities. My father was fun-loving, and Dad's a little more solemn and serious, but what I remember most is how they both looked at my mother with so much love in their eyes. I could tell both of them adored her. I hope I'm lucky to find that kind of love someday."

Emilia got a little misty-eyed at Jessica's admission. She was one lucky girl.

"Anyway," Jess continued, "my ancestry record has errors in it, now, since you're my real Grandma and Mike is my real Grandpa. I've already asked Grandpa to tell me everything he can remember about his life. Would you do the same?"

"I would like that very much, Jess, but I think it is going to be rather boring. I also think my childhood may sound a lot like your mother's. Anyway, I'd be happy to spend the time with you, and I hope you'll tell me all about yourself, too."

Jess gave Emilia a brilliant smile, kissed her again, and then ran off to spend time with Jake and Tom. Emilia saw the slight frown on Tyler's face when he noticed his daughter slip her hand into Jake's and smile up at him. Emilia expected the boy would be receiving more than one lecture on the subject of Jessica Blair Whrite-Thompson. But Emilia had come to admire the young man. He had a good head on his shoulders and knew what he wanted out of life. If one of the things Jake wanted was Jessica, he would have the patience to take things slowly. They'd get there if it was indeed what his heart wanted and what her heart wanted, too.

CHAPTER 53

ELLI took her mother for her first checkup with Dr. Kelly, the obstetrician. Emilia discovered her daughter had scheduled an appointment for herself, as well. After, they both went to lunch together. Not only were they becoming close as mother and daughter, but they were becoming good friends as well. Emi and Elli were both trying to make up for the years that they had been robbed of.

"So, I'm going to be someone's big sister. I've always wanted a sister or brother. It's kind of neat that Lianne will be able to play with her aunt or uncle because they'll be so close in age. However, the baby will have someone even closer in age than that," Elli said cryptically.

Emilia looked at her daughter quizzically. "Well, Lianne is much closer. She'll be less than a year old when I give birth."

Elli smiled and nodded. "Yes, that's true, but there'll be someone even closer. I want to share this with you first, even though it should be Tyler. I'm pregnant."

Emilia was so shocked, she almost fell off the bench she was resting her leg on to keep it elevated.

"That's just, wow! Was this planned? I had no idea you intended to have any more children," Emilia confessed.

Elli laughed. "If anyone planned this, it was Tyler. He's a very persuasive, handsome, sexy man. He told me he wants nine."

"Nine! Yikes! You're going to need a bus to haul the family around."

That made Elli laugh harder. "That's just what Tyler's dad said. Tyler's thinking about his own private plane, too. Taking the family on vacation using public transportation is a nightmare in logistics."

The thought of planes and her family made Emilia sad. Elli saw the change in her mother's expression. "Why the sad face, Momma?"

"Well, it's just that you will probably be going home to New Jersey soon. Jessica needs to go back to school. I know that you are homeschooling the little ones. And you have your new house to decorate and all your big plans for the wedding venue. It's just that I've just found you, and I'm going to miss you," Emilia sighed. "And now you're going to give me another grandchild."

Elli reached out and swiped the tear from Emilia's cheek. "Don't be sad, Momma. Things have a way of working themselves out. You'll see. Plus, we have a wedding to plan."

Emilia laughed, "There is that. I almost fainted when Michael got down on one knee at my Welcome Home party and proposed in front of everyone." Both women looked down at the beautiful engagement ring adorning the proper finger on Emilia's left hand. It was simple but stunning.

Emilia glanced at her daughter and got a mischievous look in her eyes. "We need to plan something special for when you tell Tyler that he's knocked you up again."

"Well, gee Momma. That was crass," Elli said with a grin.

Emilia just laughed.

Elli and Tyler got their special rendezvous. Michael and Emilia, with Jessica's help, took charge of the younger children one evening. Elli and Tyler left the house after Lianne had been nursed and put to bed. Emilia planned to read to her grandchildren, then Michael and Jess would tuck them in for the night. Jessica would spend time with her grandparents as they helped her add their stories to the family ancestry record that she was keeping.

Tyler had no idea what Elli had planned, so he was astonished when they were shown to the bridal suite in a fancy hotel in downtown Billings. A romantic table for two was already set, and their meal arrived soon after. One of the servers lit the candles and dimmed the room's lights before wishing them a good evening and taking his leave.

Tyler kissed his wife passionately before helping her to sit. "I must have done something right to deserve this."

"You always do everything right, Tyler. This is to say thank you," Elli beamed at him.

"I don't understand. Thank you for what?" Tyler asked.

"Just thank you for being you, for taking such good care of me, for the children we have," she said. "And," Then she paused.

"And, what?" Tyler asked with a confused look.

Elli grinned. "And for the one we are expecting in seven months."

"Holy shit," Tyler yelled. Then he grabbed his wife up and swung her around. "God, I love you, sweet girl!"

"Well, you did say you wanted nine, and you definitely have been working on accomplishing your mission. Now, put me down. The pregnant lady is hungry," she teased.

Tyler would always give Elli whatever she wanted. So, he set her on her feet, but not before stealing another kiss. Then he helped her back to the table and tried to hold her hand while they ate. Grinning all the while.

After a mostly sleepless night, where they pleasured each other multiple times, the couple had an excellent breakfast. Then they went home to their family. They had more than one bit of news to share with everyone.

CHAPTER 54

TYLER had called ahead, so the entire family was assembled in the living room when Elli and Tyler arrived. Tyler was sure he was grinning like a loon when he announced, "I'm going to be a father. We're pregnant."

Jessica laughed, "I think you already nailed that one a few times, Dad." That pronouncement had everyone laughing.

"Anyway," Elli turned to Mike and Emilia. "Our babies should arrive about the same time, so they'll have each other to grow up with, and Lianne to lord it over them."

Mike looked sad. "Yeah, well, at least they'll see each other on holidays and vacations. It's not quite the same, but it's better than nothing."

Elli took ahold of one of her father's hands and one of her mother's. Then she turned to her husband and said, "Tyler, I think we should tell them."

Tyler grinned, "Well, if you insist." Then he announced that the Whrite-Thompson family would be moving to the *Circle R Cattle Company* ranch in Montana, permanently.

Blair, Peggy, Logan, and Billy ran around the room, hooting and hollering until their sister Jess got them in line, told them to hold hands, and herded them from the room. On the way out, she turned to her parents and said, "Thank you for being the best parents a girl could ever hope to have. I've been praying every night that we'd come home to Montana." Then she took her younger siblings to the stable so she could share the news with Jake.

Mike and Emilia were full of questions, and the four adults started to make plans.

"Tyler, what about the wedding venue and your new house?" Mike asked.

"After Elli and I agreed that this is where we wanted to raise our huge family, we made some changes to our plans," Tyler began.

"Instead of continuing with the idea of a wedding venue, we're going to replace the dairy herd on Rick's farm. The caretaker's son and daughter-in-law on Elli's farm are expecting a baby. We're going to offer them the use of the house we're currently living in and the position of overseeing the dairy operation. The son has been assisting his father since he was a kid, so he knows the ropes. We'll still have the new house to vacation at so we can spend time with my father. I'm certain he'll be willing to manage both properties. Plus, he'll be able to visit us here."

"Elli's still going to homeschool the kids. Jessica will be transferred to the high school Jake and Tom attend. Having two handsome male juniors as friends will probably have the girls flocking in droves to get acquainted with her. I also think there's more than one reason Jess is so enthusiastic about living here. I've noticed a budding romance between her and Jake, plus they have a lot in common. Jake wants to be a vet, too. If Bill hadn't set up scholarships for Tom and Jake, I would have seen to it that they would have the chance to realize their dreams. Jake's family can't afford the tuition. Especially for the number of years of schooling that it takes to become a vet. He's a hard worker and focused, but you can bet I'll be keeping an eye on him concerning my daughter. Jess knows too much about how babies are made. Also, the pleasure derived from the act thanks to her mother." At that, Tyler gave Elli a stern look.

She said, "Who, me?" Then, stuck her tongue out at him and laughed.

"There's something else I'd like to discuss concerning my contribution here. It's true. I don't know anything about raising cattle. I'm certainly willing to learn, but I was hoping you'd consider offering a ranch experience to paying customers. We could set up a daily or weekly vlog on *Youtube* concerning ranch life, give riding lessons, and offer paying guests a ranch life experience including trail rides and overnight campouts. I would take responsibility for preparing meals for the guests. It would mean added income for the ranch and a boost to the local economy because we would need to hire additional employees. We would also need housing for the guests, so that would mean hiring local contractors."

"If you're agreeable, I also thought that we might ask Tim, Jeannie, and Sophie if they'd like to move here permanently. Bill left Tim the money to build a house near the landing strip. Tim might be interested in expanding the business to include flights from the ranch and give flying lessons. I'd be his first customer because I want to own my own plane. Taking my huge brood on vacation is a nightmare when we have to fly commercial. Tim could hire someone to manage the business he already owns in Oregon and travel there so that Jeannie and Sophie can spend time with relatives."

Mike looked at his son-in-law with amazement. "You've really thought this out. There's only one thing. I don't know if the ranch can swing all of that. That'll take a lot of capital."

Before Tyler could respond, Emilia spoke up, "Would I be allowed to invest? I have more than a million dollars just sitting in a low-interest savings account at the bank. If you let me, I'd really like to help make this happen."

Tyler responded, "I had intended to back the entire project, but I think Mom should be able to help, too, if that's okay with you, Dad?"

"You had me at Mom and Dad," Mike laughed. "Okay, let's do this. And let's make lunch. I'm hungry."

CHAPTER 55

O N the day of Elli and Tyler Thompson's and Tim and Jeannie Jones' joint fifth wedding anniversary, a very nervous bridegroom named Roger Michael Willis stood before a minister. The wedding was to take place in front of the same fireplace as the anniversary couples' nuptials, in the main house's living room on the *Circle R Cattle Company* ranch.

It had been a long time coming, but Mike was finally going to make Emilia Addison Mackenzie his bride. Mike slipped his finger under the wing collar of his white tuxedo shirt. Why did it seem so very tight? Was it hot in here? He was sweating bullets. Thank God for extra-strength deodorant.

Mike was wearing a black one-button western cowboy wedding tuxedo with a bowtie made of the same material as the bridesmaids' dresses. The shine on his hand-tooled black leather cowboy boots was enough to blind a man. Wait until Emi got a good look at his new ten-gallon hat. It was a humdinger. Tyler and Elli were lending the newlyweds the use of their cabin in Vermont for the honeymoon. Mike couldn't wait to get this show on the road so he could get his bride alone.

Tim Jones and his brother Alec Willis stood by his side, acting as Mike's groomsmen. They wore matching apparel, black jackets, white shirts, and black boots. Their ties matched the cerulean blue of the bridesmaids' and flower girl's dresses as well.

Mike's father, Malcomb, mom, Ailsa, and sister, Aileen, sat with the rest of his family, Alec's wife Patricia and children, Duncan, Dylan, and Dallas, and Aileen's husband David and twin sons, Doughall and Davis. None of the Ds, as Alec's and Aileen's children, were collectively known were married. Jessica was thrilled about the additional branches that she would be adding to her family tree. Malcolm and Ailsa were delighted with the granddaughter and great-grandchildren that they were adding to theirs. At least one of their grandchildren had managed to reproduce. Malcolm and Ailsa planned to visit the Circle R regularly now that they were retired. They wanted to spend time with their son Mike and new family members.

When the music for the processional began, Eloise Lianne and Jessica Blair Whrite-Thompson entered the room. Mother and daughter both wore cerulean blue gowns. Elli's was an elegant, off-the-shoulder maternity gown with a darted bust, cap sleeves, A-line floor-length silhouette, and soft waist pleats. Elli and Jess would be acting as bridesmaids.

Peggy Lynne and Richard Blair Whrite-Thomson followed as flower girl and ring bearer. Both Jessica and Peggy wore matching dresses. The gowns were designed with luxurious sequined embroidered bodices and lightweight skirts with a subtle shimmer. The dresses had a boat neckline and pretty cap sleeves. Blair wore an outfit that matched the groomsmen's attire. He looked so cute with his tiny cerulean blue bowtie and shiny cowboy boots.

The lovely bride, Emilia Addison Mackenzie Andersen, proceeded on the arm of her son-in-law, Tyler Logan Thompson, who would be giving her away. Emilia was radiant in an ivory maternity bridal gown that looked soft and sensuous. It had a delicate eyelash

407

lace overlay and three-quarter sleeves. The smooth drapes flattered and elongated her silhouette. At the same time, the gentle curve of the scoop neck showed off just enough of her glorious breasts. The figure-enhancing bodice with an empire line gave way to a full-length skirt. The gown was romantic and graceful. Emi had worked diligently at recovering her mobility. No longer burdened by casts and crutches, she walked gracefully toward her groom.

Both the beautiful bride, Emi, and bridesmaid, Elli, were proudly displaying their baby bumps.

Tyler was also attired in a black classic western cowboy tuxedo with satin lapels and matching pants. The white wing-neck tuxedo shirt was adorned with black onyx snap buttons. He'd opted for a bolo tie instead of a bowtie, and his shiny new belt buckle sported the Circle R logo.

The balance of the bride's family, which consisted of her grandchildren, Tyler Logan and William Timothy Whrite-Thompson, sat together. Both were well behaved, managing to only squirm a little. Annabelle Simon sat on one side of the boys, holding their baby sister, Lianne Susanna. Their grandfather, Alastair Caelan Thompson, sat on the other side. Being boxed in by adults might have contributed to the boys' good behavior. Grandpa Alex scooted down two seats to make room for Peggy and Blair when they had completed their duties as flower girl and ring bearer. The four siblings immediately joined hands. They were a united front against whatever the world might throw at them—all for one and one for all.

Tim's wife Jeannie and daughter Sophie, the ranch hands Sean, John, Tom, and Jake completed the list of invited guests.

The wedding wouldn't be complete without the people responsible for bringing these families together, William and Peggy Roberts and Richard Blair Whrite. Tyler had commissioned an oil painting of the Roberts, which now hung over the fireplace mantel. Another portrait of Blair stood on an easel in the corner. It would grace the space over the fireplace in the dining room after the ceremony. Everyone knew that Blair, Bill, and Peggy were there in spirit, watching over and smiling down on all of the people they loved.

The wedding reception/anniversary celebration was held in the dining room. When everyone had finished raising glasses numerous times in toasts to the bride and groom and the anniversary couples, Elli and Emi walked to the head of the table. They motioned for their husbands to join them. After clinking their glasses with their spoons to get everyone's attention, Emi and Elli each took their husband's hands. Together they announced to the room at large, "We're having twins!"

Mike and Tyler whooped so loud, they woke Lianne, who was sleeping in Jessica's arms. Tyler turned to Elli, winked, and said, "Well, sweet girl, that makes eight. One more to go." That made everyone laugh.

All of the plans Mike, Emi, Tyler, and Elli had discussed had been set into motion. On the day the Wright-Thompsons locked the door to the farmhouse in Stillwater, New Jersey, to begin their journey to Montana to live, the family gathered at the grave of Richard Blair Whrite. It was not to say goodbye. It was just to pay their respects and to let him know that he was loved and missed. All of them would be back to visit and definitely to celebrate the day of his birth. Elli and Tyler spent time at the gravesite, separately. Elli reminded Blair how much she loved him, thanked him again for the beautiful children he'd blessed her with, and for watching over her. Tyler thanked Rick for being the best friend any boy or man could ever hope to have. Before he turned to leave, he placed a kiss on the headstone and said, "Love you, Bro, so much!"

Tim, Jeannie, and Sophie would be moving to the Circle R as soon as their new house was finished. Sophie and Jessica, being best friends, were both thrilled and making plans for sleepovers and the new babies that would be arriving in April. The airplane runway was being extended, and Tyler had supplied the funds for constructing a hangar and office. Tyler was already looking into the purchase of a Cessna. He wasn't kidding about buying a plane to haul his family back and forth between Montana and New Jersey. Maybe he'd need to build a landing strip in Stillwater, too. It would be a good idea. He would need to return to Stillwater for business trips. He could fly Elli to their cabin in Vermont to get away from all of those children they were producing. Lianne had been conceived at the cabin. It might be the perfect place to love on each other and create number nine.

Tyler's father now owned half interest in the *Stillwater Farms, Vineyards, and Winery*. It would probably be five or more years before producing their first vintage wine, but it would be worth the wait. Alex had also set up a food pantry to distribute the food they were growing on the farms to the poor people residing in the surrounding counties.

Mrs. Simon had been enlisted to solicit other farms and businesses in the area in hopes of rounding out what types of food they would be able to offer. The Whrite-Thompsons were supplying the beef and fresh vegetables. Hopefully, others would contribute poultry, fruits, baked and boxed goods, and canned foods.

Tyler's and Elli's new home in Stillwater was now complete. When not homeschooling the children, Elli spent her spare moments pouring over catalogs and websites looking for antique furniture to fill the rooms. The number of children's bedrooms now numbered nine.

Elli intended to homeschool the younger children until they were old enough to enter junior high. She would be kept busy for years to come with so many young children living on the Circle R. Tim and Jeannie said they were trying. So hopefully, they would be adding to the number, as well.

Jessica would be fast-tracking through high school. She was hoping to enter college by the time she was sixteen. Jess secretly wanted to catch up to Jake, so they could enter college together. If she studied really hard, she might be in the same grade as Jake by the time

412

she turned eighteen. Jessica might only be thirteen, but she realized a good man when she saw one. Five years wasn't too long to wait for what her heart wanted. After all, her mom had waited twelve years for her father Richard Blair Whrite to realize that Elli Roberts was his heart and soul.

CHAPTER 56

THE flight from Montana to New Jersey had been long and exhausting. Tyler would be thankful when he'd completed his flight training and procured his license to pilot the Cessna he'd purchased. Then the family wouldn't need to use commercial transport anymore. Traveling with eight children was a logistical nightmare. Especially when three of them were under one year of age and still in diapers.

It was June. The Wright-Thompson family was coming home to Stillwater, New Jersey, to visit Grandpa Alex and Mrs. Simon with plans for a special celebration. Lianne would be turning one year old, and the family needed to pay their respects to the grave of Richard Blair Whrite, who would have turned thirty-two on the same day if he had lived.

Tyler watched his wife, Elli, sleep on the ride from the airport. She was making those cute little puffing noises again. Tyler planned to tease her. He loved how flustered she got. It made him love her all the more that she snored. After all, no one was perfect, but the woman his heart and soul belonged to was as close to perfection as one could get.

While he drove, Tyler reminisced about the birth of their twin sons in April. Elli had gone into labor two weeks early. In all the rushing around, Elli's mom, Emi, started to have contractions, too. Emi was due two weeks before Elli, so she should have given birth first.

Thankfully, Tim and his wife Jeannie were there to take charge of the rest of the children. It took Mike and Tyler almost a half hour to get the two pregnant women into the car for the trip to the hospital. Neither would leave without kissing Jessica, Sophie, Blair, Peggy, Logan, Billy, and Lianne goodbye. That was a lot of kisses.

The hospital staff was in an uproar when two pregnant women showed up at precisely the same time. Especially when they found out that the women were actually a mother and daughter who looked like twin sisters. What were the odds of that ever happening again?

It wasn't until much later that Mike and Tyler could take a breather and compare notes. Both men had been in separate delivery rooms with their wives. Tyler was getting to be an old hand at this, but it was Mike's first time. Mike looked a little green to Tyler when he found him pacing the hall near the waiting room after it was all over and both women had delivered without complication.

After comparing notes, they discovered that Mike and Emi now had a new son and daughter. Elli and Tyler had identical twin sons. That gave Tyler five sons and three daughters. Maybe he'd need to round that number out and make it an even ten. Identical twin daughters sounded good to him, but he'd better not mention it to Elli. At least not right away.

Elli and Emi were moved to a semi-private room so that the family would all be together. There, the men fussed over their newborn babies while their wives talked about names. Finally, it was decided that Mike and Emi would name their children Roger Michael Willis. Jr. and Addison Mackenzie Willis. Mackenzie was to honor the man who willingly gave Emilia legitimacy. Elli was so pleased that she was no longer an only child. She now had a sister and brother to love.

It seemed that Tyler and Elli were running out of loved ones to name their children after. So, after much deliberation, their twin sons were honored with Alastair Lachlan Whrite-Thompson and Caelan Angus Whrite-Thompson. They would be called Alex and Angus for short. The parents didn't know it at the time, but Addie, Alex, and Angus would become inseparable during their childhood and be known as the three A's. Roger, who was the oldest by twenty-seven minutes, would watch over them as a big brother/uncle should.

By the time Tyler pulled into the driveway in front of their new house in Stillwater, his entire family was fast asleep. So, as not to disturb them, Tyler got out of the car and shut the driver's door with a soft snick. Expecting to find his father in the new suite that had been designed for him, Tyler slid the door open and stepped into the living room. When he turned from pushing the slider shut, the bedroom door opened, and two semi-dressed individuals stepped out. Both people were clinging to each other and laughing over some shared joke. It was pretty obvious what they had been up to in the bedroom.

Annabelle Simon and Alastair Caelan Thompson both stopped laughing when they realized the frisky couple had been caught *in flagrante*. Mrs. Simon said, "Oh, Shit!" as she flushed beet red and hastily worked to button the front of her dress. Tyler's father quickly zipped up the fly on his pants.

To hide his embarrassment, Alex said, "Hi, Tyler. We weren't expecting you yet."

Shocked wasn't the proper word for what Tyler was feeling. He imagined his mouth was probably hanging open far enough to catch any flies buzzing about as he stared at them. The only thing he could think to say was, "What the heck, Dad?"

Mrs. Simon hastily donned her shoes and made her way to the door. Before she slid it open, she turned worried eyes towards Tyler. "I'm sorry," she told him. Then she slipped quietly away.

As Tyler and Alex continued to stare at each other, Alex finally broke the silence. "Where are Elli and the kids?"

"Thankfully, they're asleep in the car. I just came in to get you, hoping that you would help get the kids settled in their new rooms. I don't know what's going on, Dad, but I don't think I want to hear what you have to say right now. It's been a long day. I'll see you in the morning."

Alex said, "Tyler, I'm going to ask Anna to marry me. She's what my heart wants."

At that, Tyler nodded and left through the front door. Being a little bit upset, he slammed the door closed behind him. Well, maybe a little bit upset was too mild a term to use for what he was feeling at the moment.

CHAPTER 57

THANKFULLY, the older children were too tired to offer any objections when Elli and Tyler placed them in their new beds. After the twins and Lianne were fed and changed, they dozed off, as well.

When Elli slipped into bed beside her husband, she snuggled up against him. As she ran her fingers through the hair on his chest, she said, "Okay, what's wrong? You're upset about something. Did I do or say anything to make you angry, Tyler?"

Tyler shook his head vehemently. "Absolutely not. You're the best thing that's ever happened to me, Elli. I love you so damn much. Sometimes the feelings I have for you are so huge, I think my heart could burst."

"Then what's happened? You haven't been right since you woke me up in the car," Elli responded.

"It's what I discovered when we got here that has me upset. I'm not certain how I should feel."

"Okay, stop right there. I don't understand. What did you discover?" Elli asked.

"My dad and Mrs. Simon are having an affair. When I went into Dad's suite to ask him if he wanted to help with the kids, I caught them coming out of his bedroom." Tyler shook his head to try to get a handle on his emotions. "Dad said my mother was the love of his life. There hasn't been another woman in his life since she passed away."

"Are you angry or hurt that your Dad found someone else? Don't you think it's about time? You don't want him to spend the rest of his life all alone, do you? He's only in his late fifties."

"Well, when you put it that way, I guess I'm being selfish. Mom's been gone for sixteen years. She may have been the love of his life, but he shouldn't have to spend the rest of his life by himself. I guess I owe him an apology for how I reacted. I'll talk to him in the morning." Tyler sighed and pulled Elli in tight. "Can I make love to you, sweet girl?"

Elli gave him a swift kiss, winked, and slipped beneath the sheets. As she wrapped her lips around Tyler and marveled at how quickly his member jumped to attention, she heard Tyler let out a soft moan.

Tyler tried to pull Elli up when he could feel himself getting ready to come, but Elli refused to be deterred. With a groan, Tyler emptied himself, and his wife swallowed every drop. When he was finished, Elli reappeared from beneath the sheets.

"Stress all gone?" she joked.

"I'm certain that you are a witch," Tyler told her as he kissed her fiercely. "I love you, sweet girl. That was amazing." Then, Tyler left a trail of kisses down Elli's torso, settled his head between her thighs, and returned the favor. When Elli was close, Tyler was ready to be joined with her to share the joy of their lovemaking together.

"Okay, you did it again," Elli laughed when they were finished.

Tyler knew what Elli meant but pretended not to understand. "What did I do?"

"It's what you didn't do, Mr. Thompson. We have three babies. I don't think we are ready for another."

"Shit. Well, it's just that you feel so good when we don't use a condom. I can't help myself. Do you want to do it again? I promise to use one this time."

Elli laughed, shoved Tyler flat, and straddled him. Rubbing herself against him, she leaned down and captured his lips in a searing kiss. Then jumping off the bed, Elli ran to the bathroom. Maybe in the shower?" she giggled as she darted behind the door.

Shower sex. That was the best, Tyler thought, as he jumped off the bed to pursue his wife.

CHAPTER 58

WHILE Elli and Tyler were feeding Alex and Angus the next morning, there was a knock at the door. Tyler was feeding Angus a bottle while Elli was nursing Alex. Tyler went to answer the door after pressing a kiss to Elli's cheek and his infant son's forehead.

Tyler winced when he opened the door to find Mrs. Simon standing on the welcome mat before the entrance. Stepping to the side, he bade her enter, closed the door, and followed Mrs. Simon to the kitchen. Tyler asked her to sit. "I'll be right back," he told her.

Taking the baby back to the nursery, Tyler told Elli that Mrs. Simon was in the kitchen. Elli took the baby, then told him that he needed to go talk to Mrs. Simon alone. "Be honest with her, Tyler. She'll understand why you reacted the way you did."

When Tyler reentered the kitchen, he found Mrs. Simon standing by the counter. "Please sit," Tyler implored her.

"No, Tyler. I've only come to tender my resignation. I've cared for you since your parents moved you here to Stillwater. You and Rick were the next best thing to having my own children. I didn't mean to cause you any distress because I know how much you loved your mother. I would never presume to try to take her place. I never meant to fall in love with your father—my feelings for him just kind of snuck up on me. So, I've already packed. I just wanted to wish you all the joy life has to offer. Please tell your father, I'm sorry."

Before she could make her escape, Tyler grabbed her in a hug. "I'm the one who's sorry. I need to apologize for overreacting last night, and I want to thank you for making my father happy. At least I won't have to pretend that I care for the woman my father's chosen. You've been like a mother to me for the last sixteen years. You took such good care of Rick and me, and then Elli and all of the children. I don't know what we would do without you. Please don't go."

As Tyler was trying to convince Anna to stay, his father entered the room. Tyler saw that his father's eyes were shiny and wasn't surprised when Alex added his plea. "I second that, Annabelle Simon. Please don't go." As Anna turned toward Alex, he dropped to his knee in front of her and grabbed her hand.

"Anna, I thought I was going to spend the rest of my life alone. Patti made me promise that I wouldn't before she passed away, but I've never found anyone else that I thought I could love. Then I met you. Will you make me the happiest man in New Jersey and consent to be my wife?"

Tyler couldn't remember Mrs. Simon ever losing her composure in front of anyone, so he marveled at the tears that were coursing down her cheeks. With a soft sob, she said, "Alex Thompson, I love you very much, so I think I will have to say yes to your proposal."

After Alex slipped the engagement ring he'd fished out of his breast pocket onto Anna's finger, he let out a laugh, grabbed her up, and spun her around. Then, after kissing her soundly, he said, "I think we need some coffee so we can toast to second chances at love."

When Elli entered the room holding Lianne, she quizzically asked, "What did I miss?"

Tyler laughed. Grabbing his wife and daughter in a group hug, he said, "We just lost a housekeeper, but I have a new mom. We have to celebrate. I'll make breakfast."

Elli's mouth dropped open in an "o" of surprise.

EPILOGUE

O N the first day of Autumn, Tyler Logan Thompson stood beside his father in front of the fireplace in the house's living room on the *Circle R Cattle Company* ranch. All of the family was present to witness the joining of Alastair Caelan Thompson to Annabelle Simon in holy matrimony.

Tyler had flown in the bride's family and put them up at the *Riversage Inn* in Billings for the length of their stay. Guest cabins were currently under construction on the property. When completed, any family members who came to visit the ranch would have the use of those.

The bride's guests included her sister Jeanette and her husband, Charlie, plus their five children. The daughters' names were Charlene, Josephine, and Jasmine. Their sons included Charlie, Jr., and Jonathan. The youngest son, Jonathan, was one year older than Jessica.

Anna's younger sister, Brenda, and her husband, Kyle, were also present. Brenda and Kyle Miller didn't have any children of their own. Like Peggy and Bill Roberts, they had fostered several children over the years of their marriage.

The groom's guests included his son's family, wife Elli, and their eight children, Jessica, Blair, Peggy, Logan, Billy, Lianne, and twins Alex and Angus, Elli's parents, Mike and Emilia Willis and their twins, Roger and Addison, Tim and Jeannie Jones, their daughter Sophie, and of course, the ranch hands, Sean and John, and the teenagers, Tom and Jake.

Being older, the bride and groom opted for a semi-formal wedding with a barbeque to follow the ceremony.

The bride wore a champagne A-line silhouette, knee-length satin dress with cap sleeves. It featured a bateau neckline, lace-up corset back, and a full pleated skirt. The outer layer of material was a chiffon tulle lace decorated with appliqued flowers and sequins.

Anna's sister Jeanette acted as bridesmaid and Jessica served as flower girl. They both wore chiffon cap sleeve, knee-length dresses with lace embellishments in a shade of burnt orange. The dresses featured A-line silhouettes with scoop necklines and full pleated skirts.

The groom and best man wore chocolate brown, single-breasted suits. The groom's attire included a silk brown paisley vest and tie set, while the best man opted for a matching chocolate brown vest and burnt orange bow tie.

Toby, the Whrite-Thompson's golden retriever, played a unique role in the wedding ceremony. Jessica had trained Toby to act as ring bearer. Everyone laughed as Toby, wearing a silk paisley vest to match the groom's, pranced alongside Jessica as flower petals were strewn along the aisle between the seated guests. Bride's and groom's wedding bands dangled from the champagne-colored silk ribbons that were tied around his neck.

After the ceremony, the ranch hands manned the grill for the barbeque as the children played games of tag with Toby. It was a beautiful day full of bright sunshine and a cloudless sky. Everyone helped themselves to the delicious side dishes that Tyler had created for the feast. The wedding cake was along the lines of a romantic, countryside fête. It was a sweet cake with an elegant rustic style, combining smooth and textured buttercream frosting. It was decorated with champagne and burnt orange-colored roses, and wispy pampas grass. The cake topper was a pair of horse figurines before a split rail fence with a sign that read, "Git-N-Hitched." Several varieties of pies, donuts, cookies, and brownies surrounded the wedding cake centerpiece on log-like serving dishes to convey a country vibe.

After stuffing themselves, everyone laughed as they played games of croquette, lawn tic-tac-toe, barrel *Jenga*, and horseshoes with the kids.

When Anna was briefly seated by herself, Tyler took the opportunity to kiss his new stepmother. Anna cried when Tyler asked her if it would be alright if he called her Mom.

"I'm so proud of you, Tyler. You have grown into a fine man, and I'd be very pleased if you'd call me Mom. I love you, sweetheart as if you were my own."

Tyler got a little choked up and was grateful when his dad chose that moment to claim his bride.

When it was time for the newlyweds to leave for their honeymoon, Tyler handed his keys to the cabin in Vermont to his dad. "The fall foliage is going to be spectacular," he told Alex and Anna. Enjoy yourselves. When you get back, I'm going to put you both to work. There's a lot to be done around here."

Alex and Anna laughed, then got in the cab that was taking them to the airport.

When they were gone, Mike stepped up next to his son-in-law, Tyler, and asked, "What are you going to do with that huge house you built in Stillwater, since your dad and stepmom will be living here?"

"Yeah, didn't see that one coming when we decided to build a new home and fill it full of kids," Tyler admitted. "Who knew we'd be moving to a cattle ranch in Montana. Speaking of houses, you're going to need to add to yours since you only have two bedrooms. That will work for a while, but when Roger and Addie get bigger, they're going to want their own rooms. There are seven bedrooms in the main house. We have eight children so far. That works, too, until I talk Elli into adding the ninth. So, we may need to add on as well."

"Where are your parents going to sleep?" Mike asked.

"We gave them the master bedroom. Elli and I are comfortable staying in the room that Peggy and Bill gave her when they welcomed her into their home and their lives. They were good people with big hearts. I miss them a lot."

With that, Mike clapped Tyler on the back and told him, "That makes two of us. Let's go join our wives. I think my daughter has a bone to pick with you."

"Uh, oh! What did I do now?" Tyler asked.

Mike laughed as he guided his son-in-law to his waiting spouse. Really, man, I think after this one, you might want to think about using some protection."

Tyler's mouth dropped open in an "o" of surprise. Then he grabbed his wife in a hug and told her, "God, I love you, Eloise Lianne Whrite-Thompson, with all my heart and soul."

"Love you more!" was Elli's reply.

THE END

About the Author

B. E. Stalter grew up in Butler, a small town in Morris County, New Jersey. An obsessive bookworm, her formative years were spent with her nose in a book or walking to or from the Butler Public Library, where she exchanged those books for others. It didn't matter the genre. She read anything she could get her hands on, including the back of the cereal box at breakfast if no other reading materials were handy. In the rare moments when she wasn't reading, she was busy studying or doing housework for her mother. She was also drawn to the great outdoors, where she did yard chores for her father and participated in sports. Her younger brother was a constant companion for games, dunks in the pool, or long walks or bike rides to enjoy picnics in the woods. Now, when she can get her nose out of a book, she splits her time between caring for her husband and son, two cats, a herd of American Aberdeen Angus beef cattle, and a flock of chickens. *SECOND CHANCES – What His Heart Wants* is the 2nd Novel in the *WITH ALL the HEART and SOUL Series*.

Also by B. E. Stalter

Book 1 in the

A WITH ALL the HEART and SOUL Series

HEART OF GLASS

WHAT HER HEART WANTS

(Each Book in the Series is a standalone Novel)